QUICKIES

QUICKIES
Short Short Fiction on Gay Male Desire

Edited by
JAMES C. JOHNSTONE

ARSENAL PULP PRESS
Vancouver

QUICKIES
Stories copyright © 1998 by the authors
Introduction copyright © 1998 by the editor

ARSENAL PULP PRESS
103-1014 Homer Street
Vancouver, B.C. Canada
V6B 2W9

The publisher gratefully acknowledges the assistance of the Canada Council for the Arts for its publishing programme, as well as the assistance of the Book Publishers Industry Development Program, and the B.C. Arts Council.

Typeset by the Vancouver Desktop Publishing Centre
Author photo by Daniel Collins
Printed and bound in Canada

CANADIAN CATALOGUING IN PUBLICATION DATA:
Main entry under title:
Quickies

ISBN 1-55152-052-4

1. Gay men's writing. 2. Gay men—Fiction. I. Johnstone,
James C. (James Compton)
PN6120.92.G39Q52 1998 808.83'108353 C98-910080-4

Acknowledgements

I am grateful to Lawrence Schimel for the idea for this book, and for encouraging me to pursue this project.

Thank you, Brian Lam and Blaine Kyllo at Arsenal Pulp Press, for your ongoing support of the *Queer View Mirror* series and for giving me the chance to indulge in all these *Quickies*.

I am grateful to the many writers who have sent and who continue to send me stories over these past years. It is a pleasure to review your work, and an honour to be able to publish stories by such a diverse and talented group of men and women.

Val Speidel's exquisite rendering of Brent McTavish's evocative photo of models Loney Forde and David Meroniuk has given me a book cover beyond my wildest dreams. Thank you all!

Thank you, Keith Stuart, for your friendship and support, and for hearth, home, and a family which makes all things possible. Thank you, Karen X. Tulchinsky, for your continuing support and inspiration. Who would have believed ten years ago that these books and a partnership like ours could have emerged from all the shit we went through? Lastly, thank you Richard Rooney, for bringing so much love, laughs, sweetness, positive energy, and yes, all that great sex into my life. No one ever told me it got this good after forty. It's the best every time!

This book is dedicated to all the men, real and imagined, I have ever lusted after or longed for—and to Bob Tivey, Keith Stuart, Jim Balash, Gregory fitzGeorge-Watts, and my partner Richard Rooney.

Contents

Introduction

Less than a year after coming out, I read my first book of gay erotic fiction: John Preston's *I Once Had a Master*. What an eye-opener it was! Never having read SM fiction of any kind before, I recall I was both immensely excited and a little frightened by the book—and the writer.

It is ironic that, years later, the author of that book would be instrumental in getting me published for the first time. That first break encouraged me to write more and ultimately inspired me to co-edit my first anthology.

Since that first encounter years ago, I have read and continue to read and enjoy a broad spectrum of gay sexual writing. I am drawn to sexual writing, not so much because it helps me to get off—I respond more to visuals in this area—but because of the way it entertains, fascinates, and ultimately informs me. I am insatiably curious about sex, and all of its elements and nuances that combine to turn me and other gay men on. I am particularly fascinated by the power of sex: how sexual desire inspires, compels, and propels us all through life; the crazy things it makes us do, and the myriad barriers and boundaries —spatial, spiritual, mental, medical, racial, social, emotional, national, gender, and affectional—that our sexual desire and compulsion makes us challenge and sometimes cross. As a writer and a reader, and most importantly as a gay man facing many of those same challenges in my daily life, I am excited by the many different ways all this finds expression in stories written by and for gay men.

Quickies is a collection of sixty-nine of these stories—sixty-seven by gay men, and two by lesbian writers—from Australia, Canada, Germany, Ireland, South Africa, the United Kingdom, and the U.S.

Whether it's lust-filled loggers in a North American forest, or a jaded queen prowling Dublin tea-rooms, whether it's an encounter in a sauna in a Caribbean luxury liner, or a ride beside a sleeping sailor in the back of a bus, sex, desire, and obsession propel the characters in these stories. Fantasies and desires are sometimes fulfilled, sometimes frustrated. Sex, if attained, sometimes connects and uplifts, sometimes ends in an orgasmic crescendo. It also sometimes distances, ends in heartbreak and crushing invalidation. It sometimes even destroys.

Although some of these stories may coax a hard-on, many of the stories cannot be considered porn or even erotica in the strictest sense. Some of the stories, while erotic in content, came with a sharp pinch or a twist that left me gasping or giggling, and that's why I liked them.

The stories are all in the short short, sometimes called "flash," fiction format. Each story is 1,000 words or less and can be enjoyed from start to finish while on a coffee break, while riding on the subway or the bus, between cruising sessions at the park or the beach, or at bedtime before, um, sleep.

As with the *Queer View Mirror* books, *Quickies* combines the stories of well-known and multi-published authors with stories by emerging writers from a variety of backgrounds. Though one might expect that only gay men would send stories for *Quickies*, I was pleasantly surprised to receive, and happy to include, a number of stories written by women. I am particularly pleased to be able to include the work of a number of writers for whom this will be their first publication.

It has been exciting and great fun putting this book together. I hope you enjoy the read.

— James C. Johnstone
Vancouver, Canada
January, 1998

MICHAEL   THOMAS   FORD

The Burning
of Leaves

EVERY NOVEMBER, JUST BEFORE HE THOUGHT the snow
was coming, my father and I would gather up the leaves scattered
over the farm by the old maple trees. Very methodically, we went to
each tree, scooping the fallen leaves up in gloved hands. We stuffed
them into bags and carried them behind the barn, where we piled them
in the old stone fireplace.

My father would make a hollow in the pile of leaves, pushing them
into a bowl-like shape. Into this bowl he would put a large pine cone.
Then he would take a match out of his jacket pocket and, in that way
known to all farmers but kept a secret from the rest of the world, strike
it against his fingernail and bring it to life.

Once the match was lit, he cupped it in his hands and knelt by the
pile. Touching the match to the pine cone, he would blow softly,
encouraging the small fire to take hold. When the pine cone was
burning, he carefully placed leaves over it, until the hollow was once
again filled in, the pine cone slowly smouldering at its centre.

Because pine cones burn very slowly, it took a long time for the fire
to work its magic. I could see the smoke crawling out through the
spaces in between the leaves and rolling along the ground under the
colder air. But the flame itself was invisible.

Still, I knew it was there, slowly burning its way through the pile
from the inside, growing in intensity and fury. I waited for that
moment I knew would come when, unable to remain beneath its
paper-thin yellow and brown skin any longer, the fire would roar

upwards, sending a wave of heat flowing over my face, the remaining leaves collapsing at last into the fire's heart.

When this happened, I would stare into the very centre of the fire, not caring that the heat was burning my skin or that the smoke was stinging my eyes. I thought that if I looked hard enough I might see what the fire had revealed, the part of the leaves that couldn't be burned away, the thing that made them alive.

■ ■ ■

Many years later, the fall has come again, and the time for the burning of leaves.

When he touches me, I sense the match being struck against my skin, feel the flame spark up and take hold of the edges. As his hands move over me they burn gently, pulling at the first layer of what I have worked so hard to build up. I am surprised at how easily he can make the years fall away, at the strength of his fingers as they strip away the time I have spent avoiding this moment. Although I don't want to, I touch him, shivering when I realize that I am going to let him do this to me.

His mouth against mine is soft, and there is power behind it. Kissing me, he breathes heat beneath the quiet, cold flame that has been sleeping within me. Awakened, it stirs uneasily in its nest, stretching lazily as it grows stronger. Along with his breath, the fire slips inside my mind and I no longer remember how to get away from him, no longer want to.

Despite the mind-numbing veil of heat, I remember that I am playing with fire. Even as his arms encircle me and he pulls me in deeper, I hear my father's warnings about lighting matches, about the terrible consequences of being too careless. I wonder if this man knows what it is he is doing, or if he even cares. For a moment the fire is pushed back as I am surrounded by the fear that what is happening has not been created by the two of us, that it is, for him, nothing more than a continuation or remembrance of something he has begun in another place with another man. I hold him with my eyes closed, afraid that seeing his face will reveal that he is making love to someone else.

It takes some time to rid myself of this ghost, and it never does go away completely. Still, he is able to close my thoughts off enough to bring me back to where he is, enough to make me want what he is offering me to be the only thing that matters. I cannot see his eyes in the dark, but I listen to what his hands are saying, and I choose to believe them.

Unleashed once more, the flame reaches out, its strength increased by having been kept at bay. I can feel it gripping my heart. It throbs steadily and hungrily, filling me with heat that pushes at my skin from the inside, rolls over my bones in waves. I find myself wondering if he can feel it, too, where his body lies against mine.

I want to pull him down into my body, down through skin and bone and muscle, so that he can know what he has done, so that he can taste the burning ache that he has put there. I want to take his fire into me, feel it rage wildly through me and roar out through my skin, tearing away everything I have buried inside me in a blinding wave of heat and light. His breathing sounds in my head like wind howling through bare branches, blocking out whatever I am thinking. I try to match the rhythm of his heartbeat, try to feel the blood moving through his veins and become part of it.

As he enters me, the fire stirs restlessly. It has waited patiently for too long. The carefully-constructed walls that I have used to keep him out begin to tremble as their supports are burned away. For a moment I am terribly afraid, afraid that he will burn away everything I am and leave me with nothing, afraid that I have played a deadly game and lost.

Then the walls begin to collapse. They crash madly through one another, falling away and disappearing into the white-hot centre where the fire has been waiting patiently all this time to consume them. The last barrier gone, the flame rushes through what remains of my defenses, and I no longer care what it leaves in its wake because I know that it has cleansed me. It rises up through my skin in a final storm of heat, pouring out and washing the face of the little boy watching the leaves burn.

Through the flames I see him looking down into me, searching for what the burning has revealed.

Night Shift

THEY LAY AGAINST EACH OTHER, Geoffrey on the outside pillow, tapping a cigarette into the ashtray and sipping hot milk. The hollow in the mattress drew them together naturally. After the first uncertain moments, they settled close together, knowing an easy, warm intimacy, accepting the law of the three-foot bed, chatting about nothing.

Geoffrey's heart was beating unpleasantly, almost to a panic. He wanted to put his arm around the boy, but there was no pretext, no room for oblique reasons. Dale was smiling happily beside him, occasionally shifting his slender body against his in the intimate hollow they were relaxed into.

"Is it okay to put my arm around you?" Geoffrey whispered. The boy nodded as the arm moved up around his shoulders and gently drew him closer. They snuggled together and the boy lay his head on Geoffrey's shoulder. Geoffrey stroked his cheek and took deep whiffs of the boy's tousled hair. They lay like that for ages, content punctuated only by their breathing, the slow rhythm of it, and the occasional high-pitched laugh, half delight, half disbelief, when Geoffrey pressed his lips against a freckled cheek.

He wanted to stay awake to enjoy this quiet ecstasy, but he drifted into a half-world between sleep and wakefulness, conscious all the time of the quiet breathing next to him, not knowing if the boy were awake or asleep. He sensed a slight tension, as if they were waiting for each other to fall asleep.

Gently he eased his arm from under the boy and let it fall across his belly, spanning the gap between navel and the waistband of his shorts. The boy's breathing rhythm deepened as though asleep, and yet Geoffrey was aware of some alertness, almost as if sleep were listening out for sleep. Once, the boy's hand strayed, touched, and then withdrew again.

The room was no longer dark, but grey when sleep, or the game of sleep, ended. He became aware of the boy awake beside him. They looked at each other. Geoffrey's smile was rewarded by happy eyes and a shy grin that could have meant a dozen things.

"Did you sleep okay?" he asked.

Smiling, Dale nodded, got his elbow under himself and sat up. "What time is it?"

"Dunno," Geoffrey said, straining to see the digital clock next to the ashtray. "It's early. About six or so. Would you like to change places?"

Dale squirmed across him to the outside of the bed and Geoffrey simultaneously squirmed underneath him to the inside. They said nothing, just lay silently side by side, close as before, gazing into the grey dimness of the room. Outside, the birds were beginning to tune up, fruitily off-key, and the sparrows were rustling in the eaves of the thatch.

Geoffrey turned on his side toward the boy and was surprised that he'd fallen fast sleep. He snuggled close and drew the curve of the boy's back to him. The small, flat stomach rose and fell under his palm. Dale moved in his sleep and Geoffrey's hand came to rest at the living, dreaming softness below the elasticized waistband.

He felt a thrill of fear and ecstasy course through him. In a moment, he vowed, he would move his hand away; allowing it only for a moment to become a passive intruder. The moment grew. He lay there drowsing, so replete with happiness and love that it seeped from him and, with it, the will to stay awake.

Geoffrey's eyes closed for a moment. It seemed like that, but when he blinked awake, strong light dimmed a ten o'clock digital read-out, and the boy's eyes were brighter than before, alert and done with sleeping. Soon, the day would activate him, take him, and already Geoffrey felt the pangs of impending departure.

Lying next to the boy, he hoped against hope that time wasn't true, that the light was a lie. Dale raised himself onto his elbows and thoughts of elsewhere played across his face. Geoffrey hooked an arm around him and playfully drew him back onto his chest.

"What'll you do today?"

"I dunno. A lot of things."

The boy paused for a moment, then put an "R" in something and gargled it gleefully.

"I love when you do that," Geoffrey said, exploring his neck and jawline with lips and fingertips. He kissed the boy on the lips.

"What're you doing?" Dale's voice quickened a little and Geoffrey rummaged desperately in his mind for an answer.

"Hoovering your freckles," he said.

"Oh, you're wicked!" Dale laughed and arched his head back, letting Geoffrey kiss him tenderly around the lips, and seemed to give himself totally to that moment somewhere between sensuality and innocence.

Light played on the moist enamel of his smile. Geoffrey saw the gold cross-and-chain wink an imprimatur upon their moment. It had to end, their moment. But he felt the end was still a long way off when the boy left him to go to the bathroom, and was taken by surprise when Dale returned to the room and began to dress quickly, with an expression of matter-of-factness that seemed to say: This is what I do every morning, today is no different.

But the day was raw and different for Geoffrey, and no day would ever be quite the same again. He felt his world break and build around the boy and his love for him. Geoffrey sat on the edge of the bed, in socks and jeans, and deliberately fumbled with the clasp of his cross-and-chain. The boy smiled, perhaps indulgently, and leaned over to clinch it, neither resisting nor responding when Geoffrey's hands stole around his hips. Still smiling, he clinched the chain, then eased himself free of Geoffrey's embrace and left the room to put the kettle on.

A   L   A   N   B   E   L   L

Corduroy

I N WINGTIPS, CUFFED AND CREASED SLACKS, and shirts buttoned all the way to the Adam's apple, I was a straitlaced boy at Thomas Jefferson Middle School, my clothes so starched and ironed that when I walked, I creaked. A parochial school transfer, I noticed that public school boys wore jeans or cords, sneakers and t-shirts, and windbreakers with the collars turned up. Public school boys were cool and comfortable—everything I was not.

My new classmates quickly dubbed me "The Brain" or "The Walking Encyclopedia," and made fun of my attire. Even so, I was popular, something that mystifies me to this day, but upon reflection I guess I had a few saving graces. I had an ironic sense of humour, and could tell wry, entertaining jokes, and though otherwise athletically clumsy, I was a fast runner. When Coach made us run laps, I was usually in the top three.

And I had one other asset: I was Sean McDonnell's sidekick. The seventh grade's most athletic and best-looking boy, a child television actor who had appeared in breakfast ads for Cheerios and Fruit Loops, Sean helped me fit in. When choosing up sides for sports, none of the team captains had ever selected me first or second, except for Sean. I was his first pick for soccer. "You've got good legs," he explained.

Over the previous year I had slowly grown aware of my attraction to other boys. Homosexuality was my secret shame, but something I was powerless to stop or evade. Virtually every time I came near Sean, a tingling would start in the middle of my belly, spread to the ends of my fingers and toes, and produce a painful erection—which I tried to hide by locking my penis between my thighs.

Of course, I was terrified of being found out, and called a faggot. At Thomas Jefferson Middle School, boys liked to use that word a lot. Any oddness, any sign of deviation—the way you held your books, the way you combed your hair—might be cause for comment, and concluded with the epithet, "Faggot." But Sean, Big Man on Campus, was above suspicion. He attended all the school dances (I never went), and the next day would tell me how he had French-kissed Cindy and Denise (or any of a half-dozen other girls), and slipped a hand inside their blouses and squeezed their breasts. I was in love with Sean, and while he told me these stories I worried that he might sense my jealousy.

During fifth-period science, Sean and I were the only kids seated at a round, plywood table near the front of the classroom, but placed off to the side. One day, while Mr. Smith lectured on the solar system, Sean, to my horror and amazement, stretched out his legs and placed them across my knees. He kept them there for the rest of the class, and every day after that used my legs as a footstool.

The last fifteen minutes of science were normally quiet study time. Sean often neglected to bring his textbook to class, so we'd read the assignment together. Sean would scooch his chair next to mine, and then slowly let his legs drift up against my knees. Sometimes I would look at him out of the corner of my eye and spy a bit of dried shaving cream lodged beneath an earlobe, or smell a still vibrant hint of that morning's splash of Jade East or English Leather. Once I asked him why he never brought his book to class, and he said, "Why should I? You always bring yours."

One afternoon, Mr. Smith wheeled a projector on its beige chassis into the classroom. "Movie today," he muttered, in that faintly cynical tone of voice that let us know he was too tired or unprepared to teach. We all shifted happily in our seats. "Sex ed," Mr. Smith added.

The class giggled nervously, and a couple of boys let out a howl. "Sean, will you get the light?" Mr. Smith asked. Sean bounded out of his chair, flicked the switch, and the class settled into the grey light. The eye of the projector cast a white cone onto the screen. Over cracked and tinny background music, a fulsome voice announced, "Boy to Man."

Sean favoured corduroys, and that day he had on a pair of pale and worn green ones, the white-tipped nubs like sea foam. Lately Sean had been after me to get a pair. "They're cool," he said. "They feel good against your skin." He wanted me to touch his pants so I could feel for myself, but I was too fearful he might see the ensuing erection.

The projector flashed cartoon diagrams of how a boy's body changes during adolescence. Then Sean leaned over and whispered in my ear, "Touch my pants."

"No," I said fiercely.

"Come on," he said. "You know you want to feel my cords."

"No," I hissed again. "No! Why should I?"

"So you can feel what corduroy's like," he said.

"Mom will never let me buy a pair. She wants me to dress up for school."

"Feel them anyway," he said.

"All right," I said, and placed a perspiring hand palm down on his leg.

"Now rub it."

"No," I said.

"Touch it. It feels good."

"Okay," I said reluctantly, and rubbed the length of his thigh.

"Now, don't those cords feel good?" Beneath soft, ribbed cotton I felt the twitch of a muscle, and the radiating warmth of his skin.

"Yes," I agreed. Then he grabbed my wrist and pushed my hand down. I felt his hard-on. Immediately I tried to yank my wrist away, but his grip was too strong.

"Corduroy feels good, doesn't it?" he said. I turned and stared into the liquid quiver of Sean's grey-green eyes.

"Yeah," I said. "It feels good."

D A V I D   G R E I G

First Kiss

THE COLD MUD GLEAMS in the light of a distant street lamp as the gin clears from my head and I find myself stark naked and pissing on the back of your thighs. My aim is off so I miss your firm round ass by mere centimetres. Leering teenage-boy laughter is hushed and our "streak" interrupted by a kid riding his bike through the deserted schoolyard where we're hiding. (What the hell is he doing here at this time of night?) As everyone dresses, you and I discreetly break free from my brother and our friends.

Walking with knowing urgency into the darkened ravine, we decide to "streak" again and run bare-assed through the near pitch-black empty forest. After stripping, we hear a passing dog-walker crunching the late-autumn leaves under his quick-stepping feet. Clutching our clothes, we race along the bank of the muddy creek, balls flapping, finally slowing as we enter the forest proper. Dropping our clothes, we both freeze and stare at one another through the dim grey light, barely able to make out each other's quivering sixteen-year-old bodies. The sudden shock of finding myself alone and naked with you causes my pale skin to flush red. Your dark skin camouflages the deep blush that I know you also wear. The moon flares like a fresh-lit match and I look into your eyes and find them as frightened with anticipation as mine.

I overcome my shyness and reach out my hand to caress you, discovering your cock hard and upright like my own. My hand grasps your dick from the top; the opposite hand position from that which I

22

use to jerk off. I'd never touched a man's penis before. I'd touched Charlie's when we were both nine years old, but that doesn't count. Yours is thicker than mine but only slightly longer. As our fingers stroke each other's pulsing dicks, your eyes lock with mine. Every unspoken moment of desire sits captive in your eyes as if waiting to be freed by some act of acknowledgement. Acknowledgement that we have been fated since that day in grade seven geography class—when you deliberately brushed against my crotch and my brother called you a fag—to finally stand together, naked and hard-dicked, and enact the simmering, anxious longing that we've harboured towards each other for almost three years.

We move off the path, through the bushes and onto a patch of smooth cold ground illuminated by moonlight. As we lie pressed together, holding each other's dicks tightly, I try to talk about sex—about masturbating, cock size, and cum. But you just gaze at my face with such stomach-gripping tenderness that words become intrusive. The turn of your full lips as they spread in a shy smile and press against the fuzzy roughness of your proudly unshaven face causes me to convulse, almost into tears, so moved am I by the strength of my feelings towards you—feelings I had no idea were even possible.

I move slowly down your body, rubbing your smooth, lightly-haired belly, curiously fingering your pubic hair and noticing it much coarser and shorter than my own. My lips surround your cock like arms hugging a lonely child. Having no idea what to do, I simply hold your swollen dick in my mouth, feeling with my tongue the pronounced ridge of the head. You then manoeuvre me and kiss your way down my body, stopping to admire and touch the dark hair on my chest, finally reaching and reciprocating on my raging hard-on.

We lie like this for hours. Stopping once and a while for air. There's no need to try to figure out what's going on. All that matters to me are your eyes and your dick and the heat from your body and the sweet smell of sweat and ass and breath and cock. All that matters is that you are finally here with me alone and naked and hard. Almost until dawn, our fingers trip with the shy hesitancy of inexperienced boys. Boys with rock-hard dicks and smiles that say it all. Boys who for one brief night become for one another the men of their dreams.

Duckie

DUCKIE EASED HIMSELF UPRIGHT, sitting in the middle of the couch as he handed me the joint, then ran this thumbs around the inside of the elastic waistband of his underwear showing above his jeans.

"Okay if I crash here on your couch tonight, man?"

"Sure."

Duckie eased himself forward, unbuckling his belt, popping the metal tab of his jeans, and unzipping his fly as he raised his ass to slide his jeans down his slender thighs and over his knees, letting them drop around his ankles.

"I'm wasted," Duckie said, looking down at his crotch. I looked at it too. Then, not knowing what else to do, I scooted closer to Duckie's feet, undid his tennis shoes and pulled off his socks.

"Thanks, man." He lifted one foot and slid it out of his jeans and leaned over and pulled them off his other foot, letting them lay in a heap between his feet. Duckie leaned back into the couch as I handed him the joint. He took a long draw and looked down, his chin on his chest, staring at the thick bulk in his crotch. He stayed that way for awhile.

Duckie then pulled the waistband of his shorts away from his flat belly and stared into his underwear for a long time. Finally, he let it back.

"Ever think about using your dick for a bong?"

"Nope. Never did."

Duckie pulled down on the waistband of his underwear, exposing his thick pecker that flopped out heavily over his big balls, then slipped the elastic band beneath his nutbag, sitting there with everything hanging out.

He grasped his dick and squeezed the spongy head, making the deep piss slit gape open, and inserted the end of the reefer.

"You're some kind of weirdo, Duckie."

Duckie clasped his thick dick in his fist. The blunt knob was pointing up in the air with the joint jutting out at a jaunty angle.

"Wanna light it?"

"You're kidding."

Duckie reached for the lighter on the coffee table and tossed it to me. He was serious.

I eased in between his spread legs as he held his dick up with the cigarette sticking out towards me. Suddenly I started laughing.

"What's so funny?"

"This is about the funniest thing I've seen in my whole life," I managed to get out. I looked at his long legs spread on either side of me, and him holding his big dick with a reefer stuck in the pink cockhead. Somehow I managed to light the joint.

"Fanfuckingtastic," I murmured.

Sweat was trickling down Duckie's neck and onto his slender chest.

"It went out, Duckie."

"Light it again."

I took hold of his dick and held it up and immediately felt it swell and start stiffening.

"You getting a hard-on?"

"Numbnuts. You would too if you had a joint stuck in your dickhead."

I held his big meaty shaft in my hand and lit the joint. I was really getting turned on feeling Duckie's dick. I figured he was too, by the way he was getting hard.

Duckie's belly tensed and he started breathing in and out real fast, hunching his shoulders and stretching his arms, and flexing his groin muscles. Suddenly Duckie sucked in a sharp breath. His dick jerked up and smacked against his stomach and the joint flew through the air.

"It ain't gonna work," he said.

"It was a good idea."

"I got another idea," he said.

"What?"

"Give me a shotgun."

"In your dick? You want me to give your dick a shotgun?"

"Yeah. You never give a dick a shotgun?"

"No, I never gave a dick a shotgun. Have you?"

"No. But it might work."

I was ecstatic and laughing hysterically again. "A shotgun up your dick, bro! You gotta be kidding."

"Do I look like I'm kidding?"

I lit the joint and took a big toke as I reached for Duckie's hard, heavy dick and pulled the big purplish-pink cockhead to my lips. I started laughing again and had to take the joint out of my mouth.

"This is crazy, Duckie."

"Just take the head in your mouth and blow into it."

I took a big toke, leaned down and put my mouth over the head of his dick and blew as hard as I could. I could see the smoke escaping out around the corners of my mouth. I blew so hard I got choked and the smoke burned my throat and eyes. I straightened up and looked at him.

"Give me another one," he said.

I felt lightheaded and thick-lipped as I took Duckie's dick in my mouth again.

Duckie's body tensed and he gasped. "Suck my dick," he murmured.

I sat there feeling stupid, a dumb grin on my face. I went down on his big dick like a duck taking to water. In moments Duckie's body suddenly stiffened and he gave a lunge with his hips and then pulled my head abruptly off his dick. It slapped hard against his belly, shooting long ribbons of white ball juice through the air, spurting all over his chest and belly. He gasped excitedly, his entire body racking with hard spasms that looked as if they would tear muscle and tendon.

And then, all at once, his body sagged, exhausted, onto the couch.

"That was great, man. That was really a head rush."

And then like he was a lightbulb and somebody had switched him off, he was gone. And we sat that way for a long time. I don't know how long, but when I woke up I just lay down on the floor and went back to sleep. But first I got Duckie's worn jeans and wadded them up and slid them beneath my head.

Polyp

EVERYTHING ON TELEVISION is about the polyps in Reagan's ass. So I wash the carrots I put up mine real good. Not sure if dirty carrots are how you get polyps, or what they are exactly. But I don't want to take any chances. Afraid to ask Mom because she might notice some of her carrots missing from the fridge.

Mom doesn't cook much, so missing carrots are never a problem. Always buys a bag but rarely uses them. I leave a few, they sprout, she buys more on our next trip to Farm Fresh. She looks through the tomatoes, I pick a bag with a bunch of skinny ones. More carrots that way, plus I like to see how many I can get in. Four so far.

In canned goods, my carrots buried under yellow onions and Purdue parts, I ask what they are—polyps. She smiles, looks up from coupons. I don't have to worry about that just yet. Old men get prostate cancer. I flip through *Star Hits*, she tells me my prostate is a gland inside my rectum that all men have. She continues but I can't listen. It's all I can do to not get hard. I offer to push the cart, flip, recite lyrics to "You Spin Me Round," "A View to a Kill," but every line has polyp. I can't wait to tell Billy about it. Maybe he'll let me look for his.

Billy and I jerk off together a lot. I give him wedgies, we wrestle, I pull off his clothes, pull down my pants. We don't talk about it but last week he told me he knows I'm gay and it's cool with him. He won't tell. Today I tell him about the polyps in Reagan's ass, my Mom, *Star Hits*, our prostates. I flip through his records, ask him if I can look for his. Don't hear his answer, but he smiles, takes off his t-shirt. I lock his door since his little brother's home. I'm supposed to keep an eye on him, but he's eight and doesn't need much keeping. I'm only a year older than Billy, anyway, and don't understand why his father pays me to come over afternoons until he gets home. All I do is make lunch for his little brother and jerk off with Billy.

I turn back. Billy's naked, cock already hard. His knee's still banged up from crashing his bike. I sit on his bottom bunk, the one he doesn't sleep on. He mumbles, searches his underwear drawer. The bottom bunk was David's. It was before I'd met Billy, before high school, but everyone—even Mom—seemed to know all about David, hit by a Toyota on Shore Drive. I never ask Billy about him and I think he likes that. Billy tosses me the small jar of vaseline we stole from High's. Points the fan on us. It hums, fills my ears.

He says something else, crawls next to me, hugs his knees. His hole, squinting dark pink and ripples. He smiles as I spread and push in. I put two fingers in at first, poking. He mumbles, turns over. I smell ass on my fingers. He kneels, pulls it apart, points to his hole. I take another scoop from the jar and push between the folds. This time three fingers in his ass wiggle. I ask him how I'm going to find his prostate. He turns his head back and says something. Gets up and leaves his room, vaseline dribbling. The fan cools the vaseline on my cock. I tug. Billy seems to be gone for a while.

He returns with a short plastic tube, a little metal around one end. Like it's from the vacuum cleaner. He shakes water from it, locks his door again, tosses it to me. "Use this." He pushes papers off his desk, mounts, adjusts his fluorescent desk lamp to light his hole, now a bluish pink-grey. I look at the tube, grey and smooth. The attachment on our vacuum Mom uses to get the pretzel pieces from the insides of the couch. I rub it with vaseline and work it in. It takes a little bit, a twist or two, but soon locks into place, its spout opening toward the fluorescence. I look in, my hand fumbling around his desk. I find a red drink stirrer with Bally's in gold lettering on it. I suck on the stirrer, guide it down and in on the plastic. Billy shivers so I jerk his cock, and rub the stirrer back and forth.

I don't hear his fart but feel it. I love the smell. Warm, not like an after-dinner fart. His cock dribbles like melted ice cream. I spread more vaseline inside the plastic, grease my cock and work it inside. He flattens onto his desk, holding the edge. After I come I lay on him until I can hear the fan again.

"You forgot something," he says and wiggles his spout. He grins up at me then looks down to my cock. His grin fades. I look down too. My cock is red with bloody vaseline. Kind of like grenadine, only thicker. Like glue.

"Just get it out." He looks away, murmurs. I twist and slide it out, then place it on his sock. I stare at it and wonder if I cut his prostate, if he'll ever let me in his hole again. He grabs a t-shirt, holds it to his ass, and goes to the bathroom. I fold the sock over, put it in my bag, then follow. I lock the door and peer into the shower. Red glue trickles down his leg and spirals into the drain. He doesn't look. He just backs his head into the steaming water. I turn and lean over, into the sink. My cock, glistening red with gluey pellets, is hard again. I soap my hand and tug it into the sink and watch the bloody suds. Hope they wash off.

Sleeping With the Boogeyman

E VEN THOUGH DUNCAN WAS NOW SEVENTEEN and had been named alternate quarterback on the defending champion football team at his high school and was captain of the wrestling squad and weighed 180 pounds, he continued to be terrorized by periodic recurring nightmares of his childhood nemesis—the Boogeyman.

For as long as he could remember, Duncan could only get to sleep at night if the lights were on. Every night without fail before climbing timidly into bed, he had to look under it just to be sure. Still, he would sometimes lay awake for hours staring at the ceiling light, afraid to go to sleep. If he ever woke up during the night, even with the lights on, Duncan could feel the presence of the Boogeyman nearby, usually at his back, but sometimes lurking beneath the bed. He was sure he could hear it breathing.

The Boogeyman was huge. The sensations that announced its nearness were flushing heat and wetness, as well as a characteristic odour. At first, it had been an intense acrid smell, sort of like cabbage. Eventually this reek had changed to the unmistakable caramel-like smell of burnt sugar.

In his repeating nightmare Duncan was always surprised in his bed by the Boogeyman who would roll on top of him and pin him to the mattress, crushing him and smothering him beneath its heavy hot wet bulk. Immobilized by terror and dread, dreaming Duncan was unable to move even an eyelash. All he could do was lay there helplessly while the Boogeyman mashed down on him. When he finally did wake up,

Duncan was always fever-hot, soaked in sweat and thoroughly entangled in the sheets and blankets. A sweet caramel-candy odour would linger in his nose for hours and he would stay freaked-out for most of the following day.

Duncan was popular at school and a class idol because he was a total jock and had big muscles and was extra good-looking. Though he always got invited to parties and bashes, he tended to shy away from the school social scene and had never had a girlfriend. Football practice and the wrestling team took up most of his free time. His one best buddy was another football jock named Tyler.

Tyler was the biggest-built hunk in the school. He weighed 260 pounds in his jockstrap and had a mammoth chest, massive thighs, and a huge butt. He was the centre on the football team and an aggressive offensive linesman. Tyler was easy-going, friendly, and confident, and felt very protective about shy Duncan. During a game, whenever Tyler was hiking the ball to Duncan, it wasn't so often that an opposing defenceman within his reach could get past his protective blocking shield to tackle or interfere with his bud the quarterback. Tyler's offensive blocking was one big reason that the football team was so unbeatable.

Tyler would often remind his best buddy teasingly that Duncan was the only guy he'd ever let get that close to his great big butt. Duncan would always chuckle of course, but he for sure didn't get what Tyler was hinting at. Tyler was powerfully attracted to retiring, hot-looking Duncan, but he couldn't figure out how to go about getting it on with him. He wanted to a lot.

In the showers after practice or following a game, it took a lot of effort for turned-on Tyler to keep his unit from pointing to the ceiling. He had to struggle to restrain himself from manhandling Duncan's big jutting athlete butt and sporty masculine equipment. Tyler was in love and he realized it, but Duncan didn't have a clue.

Calculating Tyler had managed to arrange several ski trips during the winter to Whistler and Mt. Baker, but these were just day trips so there hadn't been any favourable opportunities for man-to-man, one-on-one contact.

After football season in the late spring, Tyler finally succeeded in luring Duncan away for a long weekend to his family's beachside retreat on one of the Gulf Islands. They took along a mountain of food and snacks, cases and cases of beer and dozens of the latest R&R CDs. Tyler had major plans.

During the first afternoon they drank beers and tore around the backwoods logging roads in Tyler's new 4x4. By nightfall they were starting to get nicely pissed.

When they arrived back at the cabin on the beach it was almost dark. Since the power had not yet been reconnected for the summer season, Tyler lit a couple of candles and they both pigged-out on chocolate chip cookies, potato chips, and other tasty shitfood. Tyler stoked up the fire in the woodstove and they got down to some serious beer drinking to the accompaniment of extra-loud heavy metal R&R.

Tyler kept stuffing the firewood into the woodstove and in no time the little two-room cabin heated-up like a Finnish sauna. Since it was now so totally hot, and because he was feeling dangerous, Tyler stripped off all his clothes, including his jockstrap, so of course Duncan had to get naked too. Tyler's careful planning and clever calculating were beginning to pay off.

Tyler failed to tell Duncan about the other bed up in the little attic of the cabin, so naturally when crashtime arrived they were forced to pass out together on the large double bed in the smaller room. At the foot of the bed a big window looked out onto the dark saltwater beach.

Although he was feeling very loaded, Duncan kept concentrating his attention on the light being cast across the ceiling by the solitary candle. He could feel the familiar undeniable presence and pressing encroachment of the Boogeyman. The tremendous heat in the cabin and the sweaty wetness added to his unease. But, as long as he had the candlelight to hang on to and could stay awake, he could keep the Boogeyman at bay.

Tyler was stretched out next to him on the mattress, nicely toasted and totally sexed up, eating his way to the bottom of a bowlful of caramels. Tyler's dick was rock-hard, pointing at the ceiling.

When Tyler sat up and leaned across Duncan's thighs and blew out the candle on the windowsill at the foot of the bed, Duncan started smelling that scary smell. Caramel-candy.

It was totally dark and fever-hot in the little bedroom.

When Tyler's hand started moving up Duncan's thigh, Duncan knew for sure that it was the Boogeyman's hand. But, for the first time, he didn't feel scared. At all.

Tyler leaned very close to Duncan's face. Duncan could feel Tyler's hot breath on his cheek, and the sweet burnt sugar odour of caramels got all the way up Duncan's nose. He liked it a lot.

Tyler's hand reached Duncan's hard boner and closed tightly around it. Suddenly, Duncan realized that there was no such thing as a boogeyman.

Pop Culture

IT'S MY FRIEND BRIAN'S TWENTIETH BIRTHDAY. We're here to get drunk at the Silver Fox pub where Brian has talked me into going to see the world famous stripper and performer Mitzi Dupree. Mitzi's notoriety has come from doing amazing things with her twat. Things like using it to shoot ping pong balls clear across the bar, playing songs on the recorder with it, and using it to hold large felt markers with which to write her autograph on men's t-shirts who lie on their backs on the stage beneath her gyrating hips.

There are only two empty seats left in the place and they're right up front where a waist-high bar, packed with hard-drinking customers, circles the stage. But the chairs aren't next to each other. Brian grabs the one with the best view so I sit myself down between two guys I don't know. The one on my right offers me one of the half-dozen uncapped Pilsners he has lined up in front of him. He's friendly so we start shooting the shit. He tells me that he and his buddy have driven in to Lethbridge from the even smaller town of Cardston to see Mitzi's act. After a while he introduces me to his friend, Wade, on my left.

Wade shakes my hand in that firm, manly buddy-type way. I look briefly into his dark eyes and say "Hi" with my phony deep manly-type voice. My face betrays nothing but in my head I've just come in the pants of my tailored three-piece emotional outfit.

He's beautiful. He's what my push buttons were designed for. What I wouldn't have to get drunk for to fall into bed with. I know it's lust but it's purer than even my fear of being a nineteen-year-old guy who's just beginning to figure out that this queer thing he's going through isn't just a phase.

I'm talking to Wade and he's telling me that he's a farmer who hates farming. He wants to do something else. I casually remark that he should try modeling.

"You look like you have a good face for it," I say.

I'm rescued from my moronic babbling by the blasting music and cheering men as Mitzi takes the stage.

Her act starts with a quick strip but that's not really what everyone's here for. So she dips her hand into a tin bucket and pulls out a ping pong ball which she licks seductively before pushing it into her vagina. "Pop!" It sails out of her to a roaring cheer and lands in someone's beer mug on the other side of the room. One after another Mitzi fires them off with deadly accuracy to waiting beer mugs and waving hands in every corner of the bar. The testosterone and noise levels rise even higher as she leans back on a stool and drinks the entire contents of a beer bottle into the recesses of her body, and then turns and sprays it all over the Work Wearhouse crowd.

Suddenly, Wade puts his hand on my knee and slowly squeezes. I freeze. Without changing my expression or tone I turn to him and say, "Um, what makes you think it's all right to do that?" He looks in my eyes and says, "I just know." His hand moves to the inside of my thigh and slowly begins caressing my cock until a pearl of pre-cum darkens a spot on my faded Levis.

I'm completely fucked up now. We're surrounded by big, frothing, hairy, ugly men who wouldn't hesitate to beat the living shit out of two fags; a woman is playing ping pong with her vagina in front of us and I'm more turned on than I've ever been in my life.

I get hard. Very hard. Wade's getting off on this almost as much as me.

Mitzi's set ends to the pounding rhythm of Heart's "Crazy on You." Both Wade and I excuse ourselves to go make phone calls. We head to a set of swinging doors that lead to an entrance lobby lined with pay phones.

When the door swings shut I push him against the wall and drive my tongue into his mouth. He grinds his crotch into my leg and slides a moist hand down my jeans and squeezes my cock.

The bass thumps through the walls from inside of the bar. As Wade moves down to blow me I wonder if I will die tonight and if it will have been worth it. And then the doors begin to open as two drunken John Deere caps pour themselves toward the outside. In an instant, Wade turns and takes a shoe-tying posture. I spin around, pressing my cock against the Yellow Pages and pick up the receiver of a telephone, listening to the roar of a dial tone. Moments later we're alone, so we start again and then again and again until we've both taken turns answering every phone and tying every shoe while drunken hets parade by us.

I shoot down the back of his throat in a wild pumping orgasm and then stand over him quietly for a few moments before pulling my dick out of his mouth with a Mitzi Dupree-like "pop." I kneel down and begin kneading the head of his dick with my tongue. He pumps quickly now, pushing my head against the wall with his cock as his fingers tangle in my hair. With a moan he begins to come and come until it dribbles out the side of my mouth and down my chin.

I stand up to face him. He smiles as we do up our pants and then he says "I'm gonna find you again, man. See ya later." Then he's gone back inside the bar as the music swells and becomes the beat of my pulse.

My friend Brian seems entirely too heterosexual right now. I need someone with whom my relationship transcends sexuality altogether to come and collect me. I pick up the phone and call my younger brother Bob, and say, "Bob, I'm out of control. Can you come pick me up at the Silver Fox?"

I count the street lights as we drive home in silence. When the car slows to a stop in front of my apartment I turn to my brother and say, "Bob, I've been giving this gay thing a lot of thought. And I've decided: Fuck it! I'm gonna try being gay for a year. And if it doesn't work out . . . well, if it doesn't work out, then fine . . . . I'll just go to university or something."

"Okay, man," he says. "You still gonna take me to see Mitzi next week?"

"Yeah, sure," I say. I reach into my pocket and pull out a perfume and Pilsner-scented ping pong ball for him before closing the car door behind me.

MATT BERNSTEIN SYCAMORE

Cowboy Boots

MY FINGERS BRUSH AGAINST HIS HAND as I take the pen from under the stall. The note says, "I don't know where the stairwell is." Fuck. I write "Follow me," and pass back the pen. I hear him unroll the note and then he passes it back: "Okay." I breathe. I hear wheels in the hallway, the bathroom door swings open, and the janitor comes in. I unroll some toilet paper and pretend to wipe. I flush the toilet, pull up my jeans, and try to hide my hard-on with my sweater but that doesn't work. I open the stall door, go over to the sink, and wash my hands.

I nod when he walks over to the mirror. He's actually cute—I can't keep myself from smiling. I leave the bathroom and go to the pay phones, try to hide the bulge in my pants by turning toward the wall. He follows me. I catch his eye and walk past the elevators, into the stairwell. The door swings closed and then open; he's right behind me. I hurry downstairs. We get to the last parking level and there's a chain blocking us from going further. I'm sweating.

He stops beside me. "Do you live nearby?" He must not know how old I am.

I look at my watch. "What's today?"

"Wednesday."

I can smell his mouthwash: Scope. Wednesday. My father isn't in his office.

"Okay, just a few blocks away."

We walk back into the mall. I hope I don't run into anyone from school. We walk out the side door, across the street, past Woodie's, across Western, downhill, right, uphill, into the building. I glance back to make sure he's still with me. He is. The guard smiles and buzzes me in. I push the elevator button and stare at it. The elevator stops, we get in and I press nine. Does the guard know? What will I do if he tells my father? The elevator doors open; I see myself next to this guy in the mirror. He's my height, has reddish hair and a brown leather jacket.

"This way," I say, and he follows me. I turn on the lights and he sits down on the couch my father uses for analysis.

"Do you live here?" He slides off his cowboy boots.

"No, it's my father's office. He's a psychiatrist." I drop my backpack and pull off my shoes. He's unbuttoning his shirt. I can see his pale skin and freckles, red chest hair. I'm used to bathrooms; I don't know what to do.

"Come here," he says, and I sit down next to him. "Lay down." I lay down and he gets on top of me. I feel like I'm about to come already.

He slides his hand under my sweater and I giggle. "What's wrong?"

"Nothing. I'm just ticklish." He sits up and takes off his shirt. I reach through his pants for his dick. He's hard. He reaches over and pulls off my t-shirt and sweater as I lift my hands. I bend over and start licking circles around his nipples, like I read about in this sex guide I got from the *Adam and Eve* catalogue. I watch his freckles. He grabs my dick through my pants; I squeeze his dick harder. I look up at him; his eyes are bright blue. I want to kiss him. I look back down.

He unbuttons my pants. I lean back as he unzips them and pulls them off with my boxers. I'm glad I'm not still wearing briefs. He starts licking my balls and I lean back onto the couch. I'm trying not to come yet. He pulls on my cockhead with his lips, then sits up and takes off his jeans. I put one hand under his balls, lean over and slide his cockhead into my mouth, but I don't really know what to do. Usually the guys I meet are old men and I don't want to suck their cocks.

His crotch smells like Dial. He leans back so I guess I'm doing okay, but I don't want to get AIDS so I sit up and reach for his dick. He reaches for mine. His dick points straight out; mine's bigger but I hate the way it curves. We both lean back onto the couch. I grab one of his thighs, just below his balls. I spit on my other hand and start jerking him off. He's teasing my cockhead with two fingers, then he grabs my whole

38

dick and starts jerking fast. I'm trying not to come before he does. I jerk faster and he starts to breathe more heavily, then he comes, squeezes my dick harder and I come.

"Do you have a towel?"

I pull on my boxers and go into the kitchen for a roll of paper towels. When I get back, he's already buckling his belt.

"I got some on the couch, sorry."

"Oh, don't worry about it." He wipes it up and asks what he should do with the towel. I put it on the desk. I pull on my jeans, then my t-shirt and sweater. He's putting on his boots. I've always hated cowboy boots but right now I'm not so sure. I stare at his boots so I'll remember them if I see him in the bathroom. I wonder if he's a Republican; Democrats don't wear cowboy boots. I wonder how old he is, how old does he think I am?

He sits up. "Thanks."

"Yeah, thanks. What's your name?"

"David."

"I'm Matt." I look him in the eyes. He looks down.

"I'd better be going."

He leaves, and I don't feel disgusted like usual. I want to run after him and hold him in my arms, kiss him and say I love you, look him in the eyes for a long time. I can't remember his name.

Sweet Boy

Y O, SWEET BOY! COME ON OVER. I got something for ya!" Julio
shouts across the street.

I used to hate it when he called me Sweet Boy. Now I don't mind
so much. It's like my moms says. Him and his friends just jealous 'cause
I look like an angel, which is what she named me.

Julio grabs his crotch, yells, "Yo, bitch! Your Mamma didn't com-
plain last night!"

Him and his stupid friends all laugh. I ignore him, walk to my
building. Tito's sweeping the steps. He's mad ugly, with a knife scar
right across his cheek. They call him Gorilla but not to his face 'cause
he's huge, with muscles he got in prison. I told my moms he skeeves
me out. She says he keeps the building clean and the heat working and
that's all that matters.

I go up to my apartment, feeling Tito's eyes on me. Inside, I take off
my jacket, head to the window. Julio's still out there, talking to some
girl. He's always got himself a girl. He's real handsome with green eyes
like a tiger. He starts tongue kissing her.

"Slut," I say and go watch TV.

The next day Julio follows me down the block, right up my steps.

"What's up, Sweet Boy?" he says, forcing me down the hall, behind
the stairs.

He gets me against the wall, his breath in my face. I'm scared but
go right to my knees when he pushes me down. He opens his belt and

pants, lowers his boxers, and out plops his cock and balls, huge, growing thick and long, the smell rank yet turning me on.

"Come on, Sweet Boy," he says. "You know you want that shit."

I take it in one gulp, my head going back and forth, my jaw feeling like it's gonna split. He keeps telling me to watch my teeth, grabs my hair with both hands, moves his hips back and forth, my nose in his pubes, keeping me there as he grinds his hips. I can't hardly breathe, but don't want him to stop.

He comes. Tells me to swallow. I do. I look up at his tiger eyes and he smiles, pats my head, says, "Nice job, Sweet Boy."

Then we see Tito standing there. Julio gets the fuck out quick, not saying nothing to Tito. I stay on my knees until Tito walks away, giving me a nasty wink before he goes.

Julio comes back the next day, up to the apartment. Has me suck his balls as I jerk him off. The next day he makes me eat out his ass, which I don't want to do but he says, "You want Julio to keep coming back, don't you, Sweet Boy?" which I do. He tries to fuck me but it hurts too much and he can't get it in, so I blow him.

Then he stops coming. Word is he got himself some Manhattan bitch. I find him. Ask him what's up. He punches me right in the face, says I best keep my faggot ass away or he'll kick it good.

I go home, pass Tito in the hall. My lip's bleeding. I'm putting ice on it when someone knocks. I get excited thinking it's Julio coming to say he's sorry but it's just Tito, standing there all greasy, smelling like sweat and liquor, saying he wants to check the kitchen pipes or some shit. I tell him to knock himself out.

I'm sitting there watching TV and trying not to think about Julio when Tito comes up from behind and touches my hair.

I jump up, say, "What the fuck?"

"Don't worry, Angel," he says, coming near me. "Tito treat you right."

I tell him to get the fuck out but he keeps coming closer, telling me how good he's gonna make me feel, just give him a little bit of what I gave Julio. I go towards the door. He yanks me back by my shirt and throws me into the wall. I tell him my moms is coming home soon but he knows she works late. He grabs my hair, flings me across the room, kicks me in the ass, drags me by the hair into my room.

I'm scared, start telling him it's cool, I'll suck him off real good, lick his balls, eat out his ass, whatever, as long as he chills. But he just slaps me real hard, throws me down on the bed, pulls off my pants, rips off my underwear. I try to fight but it ain't no use 'cause he's three times my size. I scream so he puts my face in the pillow and holds it there until I can't breathe and he pulls my head up and I breathe real quick but he's got my face back down in the pillow and he does this until I ain't screaming or fighting no more.

He shoves his cock into my ass and it hurts worse than when Julio tried except Tito ain't stopping. I bite the pillow, afraid to scream, the pain so bad I think I'm gonna pass out. He fucks me for a long time, pulls out, yanks me up, gets me on my knees, on my back, over the dresser, the pain going away, turning to a good feeling but one I don't want to feel.

He sits on the edge of the bed, lifts me up, puts me back down on his dick, wraps his arms tight around me, kisses my neck and face.

"Don't worry, Angel baby. Tito's gonna take good care of you."

I close my eyes real tight until I hear Julio calling me Sweet Boy.

The Most Important Rule

VINNY WAS THE KIND OF GUY you'd see in a gangster movie: about five-nine with dark hair and eyes, and a nose that belonged on a Roman coin. He wasn't particularly muscular, just lean and well-defined from years of lifting boxes at his father's grocery store in South Philly's Italian Market. He wasn't great looking either, but his thick pouty lips and dark intense gaze drove me nuts.

I liked that he knew exactly what he wanted, too. From that first conversation on the phone line where we met: "I come in, ya get down on yer knees and put your fuckin' face in my crotch. . . ." That's what I did. When he walked over to my sofa, he unzipped his jeans and sat with legs spread, his slightly-larger-than-average cock hard with anticipation. He made me crawl to him: "Start on my balls. . . ." The steady rhythm of his sex talk and his barked orders put me in a frenzy by the time he let me take the head of his cock into my mouth. But he had more on his mind than a quick blowjob.

Vinny fucked me from behind, doggy-style; he grabbed my hips and repeatedly pulled me onto his cock, stopping when he got too close. "It's gotta last," he'd say. When the sweat poured out of him, he smelled like my Sicilian grandfather, a farmer before he came to America.

Vinny liked it often. "Twice a day, three times on Sunday," he'd joke. Sex was his daily nourishment. When he was twelve, a neighbourhood boy, Armando, went down on him when he thought Vinny was asleep. Vinny never let on, but he made Armando suck him off again the next morning. For years, until he moved away to college, Armando serviced Vinny's growing desires.

Vinny wasn't queer. "Guys take care of me better," he'd tell me. Besides, he couldn't order girls to do the things I did, like kneeling beside him while he pissed, then cleaning off his cock with my tongue.

"Ya gotta respect girls," he'd say. "Fags ya respect by letting them do the things girls ain't supposed to do."

Part of me resented Vinny's attitude. Friends told me I was short-changing myself. But growing up in Little Italy not far from where Vinny lived, I endured one teenage crush after another on guys like him. I even sucked off a few of them when I was younger. There was never any danger of getting beaten up, as long as I obeyed the Don't Ask, Don't Tell policy: Don't Ask them to bottom, Don't Tell them they're gay. Most importantly: Don't fall in love. No problem. I was dating Jose, a Filipino guy I met at a gay rights rally.

Vinny usually came over on Thursday nights. Sometimes he'd call late on a Friday or Saturday night if a girl he was out with didn't "put out." Those nights, I purposely took it slowly, knowing he was in heat. I sniffed and licked his underwear, heavy with the smell of overheated crotch, and often still damp from pre-cum. When Vinny became impatient with this, he'd order me to suck his dick or to get down on all fours. My ass and mouth would be sore for a day or two, but it was well worth it.

One Saturday night, I sucked him off but he wasn't satisfied. "Man, I gotta fuck your ass," he said. It was a long ride. He kept stopping himself from coming. By the time he shot, we were both exhausted. "I'm gonna rest my eyes for a few seconds before I take off," he said. It sounded like a good idea.

When I awoke a few hours later, I decided to let him sleep. Around eight, I swallowed his morning hard-on. He opened his eyes, pleased at what I was doing. "I gotta piss," he said. I laughed. "Go ahead."

Reluctant at first, he finally let go in my mouth, still hard. Then he rammed his cock down my throat until he shot. When he noticed the time, he grabbed his clothes. "I gotta get to church."

"Church?" I laughed.

He became immediately defensive: "Ya got a problem wit dat?"

"You don't strike me as the church-going type."

"I gotta get communion."

"Wait a minute—you just—"

"Papa's an usher, if I don't—" He didn't have to finish.

Vinny still came around after he got married to a girl I went to school with. I'm sure she didn't know the score. Jose and I finally decided to move in together; seeing Vinny was out of the question.

"Hey, it's cool," he said the night I told him about my plans. "I'll see you Thursday."

"I just told you, I can't see you no more."

"Why?"

"I'm moving in with Jose."

"I ain't got no problem with that." He smiled. "You just call me when Jose's not gonna be home."

I couldn't believe what he was suggesting.

"You can find somebody else—a lotta guys would—" I started to say.

"I don't want a lotta guys. I want you."

From the look in his eyes I could tell he had broken the most important rule.

Under
the Bridge

THE MAN SAT AT THE BAR, legs apart. He was very well-built, with a shaved head. I suffered an instant attraction. I eyed him, cautiously at first. In my mind's eye I undressed him, undoing his white shirt, button by button, and sliding down his formal grey trousers. It became difficult to stop myself from staring at him.

He noticed, and stared back with his piercing blue eyes. He smiled a few times, but I didn't smile back. It was the first time I had ever found a man so attractive. He raised an eyebrow and my cock went stiff, then turned to rock. I smiled, but I found it impossible to approach him.

Closing time approached. The barman rang the bell and shouted last orders as the man put on his coat and made his way out of the bar. I pondered for a second, thought I was going mad, but decided to chase after him.

It didn't take long for me to catch up. He heard my footsteps behind him, and turned round. I didn't know what reaction to expect. I felt a bit pathetic to be honest, but the alcohol had given me bravado.

We exchanged names. His name was Steven. The softness of Steven's voice surprised me, and I began to feel at ease with my new-found friend.

"You're gagging for a shagging, aren't you?" He smiled.

I couldn't believe the corniness of the line but I was turned on with the idea of shagging with him.

"Yes sir, I am."

"I've got a big, thick cock."

The conversation stopped as I imagined his fat cock in all its meatiness, veins and all. I stepped closer to him as we walked, stumbling slightly and bumping into his side.

"How big is yours?" he asked.

I tried to laugh the question off. His frankness was embarrassing.

"It's tiny," I giggled, and a slightly irritated expression crossed his face.

"How big is it?"

"Big enough to make a greedy man happy."

We were walking under a bridge when he grabbed my bollocks. He had a beautiful thin mouth, a sign of a cruel man, my mother would say, but his kiss was warm and wet. His other hand made its way inside my shirt and stroked my chest.

He went to put his hand through my hair and his ring caught in my chest hair. It was a ring I normally would have hated, with a ruby stone, but I loved it because it was his. He forced his hand through my hair, and it hurt as he grabbed my ponytail and pulled me down to my knees.

I opened the zip on his trousers with shaking hands and he watched me take his weighty cock out. I kissed the end; it was wet, warm, and sticky. I looked up at his beautiful face. I couldn't believe this was happening.

He smiled at me, then slapped me hard round the face. He guided his wet, wide cock into my mouth and I felt him place both his hands on the back of my head. My face was stinging and I moaned. I was hungry for it.

He eased his cock into my mouth, holding me steady with his hands. Then, he began to thrust, roughly fucking my throat, pulling my head forward as he pushed himself deeper into me.

He smelled of fresh sweat, and his hard muscled legs were warm as I wrapped my arms around them in the cool night air. I closed my eyes and submitted totally until he groaned. I felt his cock shoot warm salty spunk down my throat, and as he withdrew, I closed my lips around his member and gently sucked.

I stood up, awkwardly, and he told me to drop my trousers. I pulled my trousers down, grasped my throbbing cock and tugged it over the top of my pants. It had left a sticky patch on my underwear. From behind, he put one arm tightly round my waist and held me with a fierceness that I welcomed.

He wanked me hard. My breathing became erratic and I shook with ecstasy. The friction of his hand made me sore but happy as I came, spurting into the cold night-time air. I shot two, three times then turned round to kiss him, but he turned away.

We walked on together for a mile. I was more content than I had been for ages, until we got to a junction.

"We have to part now. It's been fun."

I felt desperation sink in, for I wanted him again. I wanted him in my bed that night. I wanted the dream to continue.

"Stay with me. I only live a road away."

"I'm married, darling. I love my wife."

I watched him walk away. I stood watching until he was out of sight. I still think of him, and wonder if we'll ever meet again.

P A U L   V E I T C H

Glands

I'M NOT GAY," he says.

When finally my cock enters his bowels, he makes no sound. I move in deeper, feel a silken resistance, then stop.

"And I'm not straight," I whisper in his ear. I bite it. He lets out a little cry. Then I move down and close my lips around the side of his neck and kiss him there.

"No one's kissed my neck like you do," he says.

"This hollow bit here," I say, taking breath, "it's where the lymph drains out from the glands in your neck."

"Okay," he says, interested.

"When I roll my lips against it, it stimulates the lymph system in your body."

"Lymph . . . system."

I feel the jaws of his asshole twitch—a message in Morse code—and I raise myself ready to move further inside him.

"It stimulates the cleansing of your body. You do good, strong chews, no teeth—like this." Sheathing my teeth behind my lips for force, I embed my face in his neck. He rolls his head back softly. His jaw presses hard into my shoulder.

"It's good," he says, so blissed he's inarticulate. Almost involuntarily he, or his ass, allows access, and I draw my cock up past the pelvic bones, pressing the tip into the recesses of his belly. It's hot in there, hot and wet and slowly, glowingly relaxing and relaxing.

"Take it out," he says.

49

I take it out. I watch his asshole re-pucker. My condom brushes his thigh and he twitches. This really *is* his first time.

He gets his breath back.

"Why does it feel so good, then?" he asks.

"I told you, because of the lymph system."

"No, your dick up my ass."

"Men have a gland in their ass." I find it for him and press hard with the pad of my left index finger.

"I want to pee."

"It just feels that way. . . . That feel okay?"

"Good," he nods, moving himself against my motionless finger. "Really good."

After a moment he sighs a bit. "All these glands," he says. "I thought it was just the cock, yeah?"

"All these glands," I say, and I chuckle.

The noises of the dorms around us remind us of our situation. We're losing the sexual energy. But just as I slip my finger out with a sound like the smacking of lips, he turns around, ignoring my cock, and feels my butt. I start to get excited again, and he finds the hole.

He spits. My breath quickens.

"It's like a pussy," he says, his lips close to mine, his chin on my neck.

"Just like it. Just as willing and just as nice."

"Can I fuck you?" he asks.

I don't say a word as he pushes me against the wall, in his urgency forgetting me. He slips the condom over his cock. I look under my legs and see it swaying, swollen and white and smooth with a ring of red skin where his foreskin was cut off. Thirty minutes ago he had only just wondered what my foreskin might look like. "I've often wondered what it'd be like . . . " he'd said.

His cock presses against my ass. I hear him spit, then again. He pushes, sandwiching me between the wall of our shared room and his hard, clean and white rubberised cock.

"I'm not gay," I say.

"I'm not straight," he says.

I stretch my neck to see a wry smile, a curved eyebrow half cut off in the shadow of the bedside lamp. His cock enters my asshole.

M I C · H A E L   W Y N N E

The Mitcher

S HAMIE COULDN'T HAVE SAID how he knew. But as soon as the
vest disappeared, the one with the tear at the back that showed
his mole, the one that had gone without a wash for ages, he thought
straightaway of the boy with the townie accent who, most days, sat
and watched him as he ate by the pub. Shamie tried to tell himself it
was fuckwitted, senseless, this feeling of a link between his missing
work-rag, with its colour and feel of dead skin, and the boy with
rust-coloured hair and smokey eyes that came out to Carney to mitch
during these last sun-flooded days of his term. But the feeling stayed,
in part because he willed it to.

All the builders knew the undutiful student to see at this stage.
Shlyser, Mikey, and Padraig affectionately called him the young dosser,
the little waster, whenever he would appear down the shining slope
of the street wheeling his mountain bike with his navy school blazer
slung over the crossbar.

"Ah, here he is, yer young fella on the doss yet again," Mikey would
announce, one Wellingtoned boot propped on a block, his hard hat
pushed back off his brow and a World Cup mug halfway to his lips. A
chorus would start up on how well it was for the young fucker to be
able to get away with skiving when others his age were killing themselves doing exams in glass class-halls that in this weather were like
hothouses.

The first time Shamie had seen the boy was after Easter, when
renovations on Quigley's pub had begun in earnest. From early on he'd

an idea of the silent youngster's atte ion. Indeed, he remembered the first afternoon they had sighted each other, and his immediate notion of having been found interesting, in se ne way, by this unlikely source.

That day the cement mixer had broken down a little before the Angelus bells had signalled the second official break of the day. Shlyser and Mikey had examined it throughout, and tried all sorts of ways to get it going again, but there was no joy. The consensus was that they would have to work around it, or at least do their best to, for the rest of the day. Shamie had left them to it and was sitting against the wall of the farrier's house opposite to where they worked. He was talking to the farrier's wife who, for a small charge, served the builders simple refreshments at one of a pair of pine benches at the front of her bungalow.

With one foot propped on the edge of a tub of calla lillies and a fat-draped arm crooked on her hip, the farrier's wife, whom Padraig called *mantachán* because of her gapped teeth, talked down to him with zealous assurance about her husband's mechanical know-how, and how he "would have that micheen goin' in no length," while Shamie nodded and "Oh aye-ed" over the ham sandwiches she'd provided and squeezed his eyes against the noon sun to see past her thighs to the boy who sat drinking at her bench, watching him. As his glance lazily moved from the face of the woman to the unblinking eyes of the boy, he gripped in his lap the vest which the young stranger had observed him use to wipe the fresh sweat from his armpits and chest and across his faintly convex midriff, with its stripe of hair that ran from the navel to below the waist of his moleskins. There was something tacit going on between them, a budding sensual sympathy that made each erotically conscious of the other. Each felt this connection in the other's stance, or way of looking off into the distance, even in the other's way of chewing a mouthful. Rarely after the first sighting, though, did they look at one another directly. The boy particularly was careful of this. There was, however, that gusty day some weeks after he'd begun escaping from the heavy afternoon atmosphere of Abbey-view Academy when he deliberately followed Shamie around the back of a tucked-away ruin and stood at the opposite end of the tumble-down gable, pissing in synchronicity with the dusty and soiled older man. As Shamie squeezed dribbles from his chute-like foreskin he glanced across and met the smokey eyes of the silent teenager; his stare

apprehended, the boy hitched his head in a panicky nod of acknowledgement, prematurely finished micturating, and, buckling up his
school slacks, ambled off through the thistles and dock.

■ ■ ■

Men such as Shamie, broad-backed and thick-bottomed, the boy,
Austin, had hungrily eyed from late childhood, puzzling always at
their irresistible draw. Even though their attraction was only now
beginning to make sense, he still opted for a dreamlike kind of pursuit
without formulating any idea of what it would mean should the
chance to follow things through arise. The desire, by and large, was
more sensed than fully understood by him. He was a little confounded,
also, that he should meet with such a vision as Shamie at Carney, a
place he had randomly chosen to doss for no reason other than its
being a pleasant backwater he remembered vaguely from infanthood.

He had decided to take the vest on the morning that the Christian
Doctrine priest—the corpulent one who talked as though his tongue
was paralyzed—had advised the boys emphatically to regularly wash
their penises, but to take care not to become excited while towelling
themselves dry. These cautionary words, by some nameless associa-
tion, were the ones that spurred him to filch the rag from the mixer
where each of the recent sweltering afternoons Austin had seen Shamie
toss it before his tea-break, a time which usually corresponded with
Austin's arrival at the village.

When he had found that the men had cleared away, and that the
rag was where it more than likely would be, he had secretively stowed
it in his satchel, and, skirting by the site, passed with his bike across
the street from where he caught a fleeting sight of Shamie's smooth
swollen arms and legs among those of his comrades, and beyond to
the ruin. Here, at a rubble-strewn, weed-bordered semi-clearing, he
loosened his school slacks and, leaning back against the broken stone
wall, alternately breathing from or stroking his falling balls with the
rag the colour of sloughed skin, he brought himself to jerking, snorting
release, and closer to clearer and braver self-knowing.

DAVID   GARNES

The Back
of the Bus

A S HOWARD ENTERED THE BUS TERMINAL in downtown
Providence, he was engulfed by a cloud of warm air reeking of
cigarette smoke and disinfectant. The air conditioning mustn't be
working properly, he thought, glancing wryly at the flaking decal that
proclaimed in icicle-shaped letters, AIR-COOLED FOR YOUR COM-
FORT. At least he wouldn't get a chill as his sweat-drenched shirt dried;
he had run the whole distance down the hill from campus.

It was midnight, and the nearly empty waiting room was quiet except
for the buzz of the harsh fluorescent lights and the snoring of an old man
slumped in one of the red plastic chairs. Howard bought a ticket from the
clerk standing behind the dirty glass partition at the counter.

"The coach for Worcester will be departing in about ten minutes
from Track 2," the man said. "We're waiting on the Newport bus."
Howard knew that meant there would be a lot of sailors travelling with
him to Massachusetts.

Howard walked over to the men's room and pushed open the door.
Here the smell of bleach was overpowering. A short man with a mottled
red face and matted hair was washing his hands at one of the sinks. As
Howard stood at the urinal, the man moved to the adjoining one and
leaned over towards him.

"Let's see," whispered the man. His breath smelled of whiskey. "Let
me see."

Howard quickly finished and moved away. Last week someone

about his own age had been at the very same urinal. Howard had been tempted to linger, but he had been too frightened.

Howard returned to the waiting room just as the passengers from Newport arrived. He joined the line outside waiting to board the bus for Worcester.

Howard focused his attention on the young man standing in front of him. He was wearing jeans and a white t-shirt that hugged his torso and muscular arms. His bushy eyebrows nearly met over the bridge of his nose, and his thick dark hair rose stiffly in a short brush cut. Howard knew he was a sailor because of his black shoes that shone, reflecting the dim light from the terminal doorway.

Howard gave his ticket to the driver and climbed the steep steps into the bus, a big old Trailways "luxury" coach that had probably been in service since just after the war. The seats in front were taken. Howard followed the sailor and climbed a few more steps to the elevated section in the rear.

He waited until the sailor had chosen one of the few unoccupied double seats. Then he asked, "Okay if I sit here?"

The sailor looked up and half-smiled. "Sure," he said.

Howard sank into the plush of the cushioned seat, so high-backed that his lanky frame was enveloped, his neck resting well below the worn headrest. He was immediately aware of the sailor's body next to his. He could feel the hair on the sailor's arm brushing against his own bare skin.

The doors of the bus closed with a whoosh, the overhead lights went out, and the cooling system blasted on.

"Smoke?" asked the sailor, offering Howard a pack of Lucky Strikes.

"No, but thank you," said Howard.

"You a college kid? Brown?" The light from the sailor's match shone on the silver chain around his neck. Howard caught a glimpse of black chest hair curling over the top of his shirt.

"Yes, I'm a freshman, class of '68," said Howard. "Are you at Newport?"

"Yeah, for now. Maybe soon in 'Nam. Who knows."

They sat in silence in the darkness. The air was turning cold, and the heat from the sailor's body felt good. The sailor bent over to stomp out his cigarette, and his leg pushed up against Howard's. Howard didn't move away, and when the sailor leaned back their knees remained touching.

After a while Howard could tell by his breathing that the sailor was asleep. Howard remained wide awake. He gradually inched his foot and lower leg against the sailor's. When the bus stopped occasionally to let passengers off, Howard pretended to be jostled even closer to the sleeping sailor.

The bus swerved suddenly, and Howard could sense the sailor wake up. He held his breath. "It's fuckin' freezin'," the sailor murmured, moving his head closer to Howard's shoulder.

Soon Howard could feel the sailor's steady breath against his arm. His hair felt bristly but soft under Howard's chin. Howard closed his eyes and breathed in the heavy smell of the sailor's Old Spice.

By now there were no passengers left in the rear section of the bus. Slowly, Howard shifted, manoeuvering his body so that he was almost facing the sailor. Carefully, he moved his hand so that it rested against the sailor's leg.

Suddenly he felt the sailor start. Howard remained perfectly still, his heart pounding. Finally, he said, "I'm sorry."

The sailor didn't respond. After a moment, he reached over and grasped Howard's hand. He moved it to where Howard could feel the warmth and dampness of the sailor's jeans and then the cool metal of his zipper.

"Come on, kid," the sailor whispered in Howard's ear. "We ain't got much time."

R O B E R T   C H O M I A K

All Done
with Mirrors

I BRING HIM TO MY BED. Like many who have visited my sheets, he has come straight off the conveyor belt of the Calvin Klein factory, searing the air with Joop! and straddling my face with ivory-coloured thigh-length undershorts.

"Oh, buddy, you're so aggressive," he sighs when I tug the waistband down with my teeth.

I've freed the long-anticipated cock and it joyfully springs out like a surprise gadget from a Swiss Army knife.

"Not a bad size, uh? Bet you thought I was lying."

I've ungirdled the trick of his skivvies and he rhythmically pumps my mouth in a syncopation gleaned from faithful patronage of the porn industry. Even with a lubed hand, I remain stubbornly limp, and so I close my eyes. Beneath the lids I search for inspiration.

My car has been pulled over by this irate cop who hates rich boys with Daddy's Porsches. He speaks in that polite cop talk underscored with friendly sarcasm. But I've been giving him some lip because of the twenty-sixer in my bloodstream, and he loses his politeness.

"Sir, step out of the car."

I take my royal time climbing out onto the highway's edge. The officer grabs me by the scruff of the neck and hauls me to a nearby grove of trees. His partner sits in the cop car, wearing a smirk. Now I'm really afraid.

"Sir, I'm going to teach you to behave properly when addressing an officer of the law." He throws me to the ground. Before I can protest, he's slid his cock out and is straddling my shoulders.

"Show it some good manners and we'll forget about the ticket."

"You like it when I do that? Huh?" The trick grins. "Your balls are hot for action, man. I can feel it."

I slap my hand onto his hard buttock.

"Oo, man," he says.

I tug his loins and position his equipment over my face.

"Yeah, man. Be aggressive with me. Oh! I wanna do you, too."

I feel his denture-less clamp nipping my own fleshy extension, like a praying mantis turning on her spent mate. I gaze at his bare foot by my head. My eyes are locked on that marble foot, its toes curled, its heel poised.

I've interviewed some of the players after their Stanley Cup win. The proximity of their sweaty jock bodies and the ghostly nude apparitions heading for the shower nearly make me buckle at the knees. The camera crew heads off.

"Hey," says one of the Adonis players to me, "the heat's done a number on you. Look at him sweating, boys. Why don't you join us for a quick shower?"

I gladly strip down and join the victorious bodies for a dip under the spraying shower heads. The tiled room is steamy and ethereal.

"Playing sports always gets me going," says a hunky player as he soaps up his massive dick.

"You're not the only one," chimes another. Suddenly the shower room is a surge of testosterone and erotica. I'm dragged down to the warm puddles. A pair of legs climbs over me and an anonymous cock plunges mercilessly into my mouth. My view is blocked. All I can see is the hockey jock's bare foot by my head, its toes curled, its heel poised. Yet I know that a wealth of homoerotic activity of sucking and fucking is all around me.

He rises up in ecstasy. "Fuck, no one's ever blown me like that before. Jesus. How're you doing that? Oh, God, that's so good. Buddy! Man!"

I slap my hand on his thigh and tug on his balls. He whimpers and breathes in deeply. Without warning, I spit him out and bear-hug his stomach.

"Whoa!" he says, as I flip him onto his back. He laughs deeply. "What're we doing?"

Everyone has left the gym, except for the pair of us. Determined to win the national Greco-Roman championships, we've been practicing our tech-

niques over and over—for hours. Between rounds we talk about the ancient Olympic Games and how contestants used to wrestle naked.

I begin: "Do you want to . . . ?"

He acts innocent. "What, naked?"

"There's no one around. The janitor doesn't come in 'til late."

We strip, looking away. When we turn back, it's awkward, both of us sheepishly staring at one another's semi-erections. I decide not to waste this moment. I lunge for his stomach and drop him down. There we are, a flurry of naked skin grappling, our erections filling out and batting each other. I flip up his legs.

He's startled. "Hey!"

"The Greeks did this, too." I hoist up his rock-hard ass and slide my cock slowly into him. He grimaces at first, but I can see his cock swelling even larger.

"Push it in, buddy, all the way in. I can take it. You like that?"

The trick has his legs spread up in the air, which I find too accommodating, and I lower his feet down to my buttocks.

"Whoa! That's good! That's good! How's that feel for you?"

My moment approaches.

The rough cop. The hockey jock. The nude wrestler.

The trick lies beside me, both of us with pounding breaths. "You shot so hard. That was amazing," he says. "Man, I know this sounds like a line, but I really mean it. That was the best I've ever felt. Really. How about you?"

There's a slight pause, and I agree.

He looks at me dreamily. "It's like we're so connected. Completely in tune with each other. Each other's bodies. Man, I think I'm in love!"

I calm him down. I lie there. Relieved and satisfied, yet feeling strangely cheated. Why not in the here and now, like him? I lament. Why can't you be where you are, like everyone else?

Minutes later I lock the front door and crumple his phone number. I climb back under the sheets, alone. A sad coldness permeates my bed, like a dark carnival under a starless night sky, and I am lost between a smile and a sob. I tumble into the outer space of sleep—quickly, to avoid further deliberation—and yet, before the plunge through the Looking Glass, I swear I hear the sound of my phantoms already snoring.

One True Cowboy

THE OLD BUS BARRELED down the highway, and I worried my balls every dusty mile of the way. Sweaty, burnin' and itchin' to beat the band, my crotch needed a lot of attending to, whether the old lady sitting next to me liked it or not. She clucked her tongue and gave me all kind of farmwife frowns every time my fingers went near my jeans.

I tried to keep my hands on my knees or wherever, but that darn inner seam never felt so tight nor so irritating in all my life.

Finally, Mrs. Busybody could stand it no more.

"Where are you from, boy?" she asked, just as if she were the queen bee.

"I'm goin' to see the doctor, 'cause I got a rash," I blurted out. My own words embarrassed me so bad, I jumped out of my seat, stepped all over her fat toes, and charged into the toilet. Once the jeans came down, my poor raw nuts dangled free at last.

They looked like hamburger meat.

Somebody knocked on the door, but I wasn't budgin'. The fresh air felt good and whoever was out there could just tie it in a knot, far as I was concerned.

We pulled into a station in a few minutes anyway. The driver announced lunch, and gave us forty-five minutes. I couldn't have eaten a cracker, but I did get off the bus, after everybody else cleared out.

The bus depot smelled like grease, coffee, and farts. I thanked the Lord that all I wanted was a long drink of water, but I never made it to the drinking fountain.

I got ambushed by a pair of eyes, so sad and blue—so wide open—I fell right in and forgot I was ever thirsty.

He was a real cowboy. His brown suede jacket sported fringe on the sleeves and the yoke. His hair had the colour and texture of hayseed. The air about him seemed to carry the memory of an older time, of cattle, dust, campfires, and horseshit. He stood there, looking somewhat confused, as if he couldn't figure how he'd gotten where he was.

To me, he looked like he was caught in a ray of light streaming out of a crack in heaven. He didn't smile, when he saw me, but his eyes changed. He knew.

Turning on a dime, this beautiful cowboy shuffled off with such a bowlegged gait, I had to wonder what happened to his horse. I followed, of course; I never did like gettin' left behind.

Before I could even stop to think, I found myself back in another toilet. We were alone, and Cowboy had left the door to his stall half open. By the time I snuck into view, his shirt was already undone, his dungarees were down around his ankles, and his hand was wrapped around his cock. He tried to grin but only managed to look sheepish, in spite of a body more akin to a bull. His balls alone would have fit on some buffalo, that skin was so thick and heavy and wrinkled, not to mention the size. I thought about those nuts filling me up and I was on my knees in no time.

His cock was hard and fat and musty. My mouth got so wet, it seemed like I was born to suck his dick, to make him shake and shiver and grab my head with his big hands. He started pounding my face, jamming my cheeks, riding me like a pony. We crossed a border and then we were gone.

The blood pounding in my temples painted a picture of the old West: red sky, red river, red dust. We were cookin'; we were exploring the range of each other's dirt, root, and branch. Cowboy did everything but yodel.

He would have fallen over, but I held on as if this blood sunset might be our last day on earth.

Suddenly he flooded my mouth with the ropy white heat of his jack, his juice, his seed. We were lovers then, making our bedroll in a wilderness outside of time, under the stars.

Cowboy picked me up and kissed me so hard, those same stars could've spun out of the sky. Then he dropped to his knees, fumbled around with my jeans, and—lo and behold!—Cowboy proved himself to be a cocksucker too.

He chowed down with enough gusto to blow me into next week. His tongue was everywhere. The fire in my balls came back in a rush, and a horrible groan rose out of me. He heard, he saw, he knew, and he went right back to work.

Whimpering and hollering, with my knees shaking and arms flailing, I shot my load down his throat, a real gusher. It was a miracle we didn't get arrested on the spot. I plain and simple forgot where we were. It had seemed as if there were only the two of us in all the world: just two cowboys in love.

We never said one word to each other.

Damn.

I could still smell him, though—back on that godforsaken bus again—smell him and taste him, too. His stuff was becoming my stuff, down there in my belly.

A guy sitting behind me jibber-jabbered on and on, about the future and America and Swiss cheese and how he was gonna blow up all the lawn ornaments in the suburbs so people could see the holes in their lives. It all seemed just like a dream. Even later on, when the doctor told me it was poison oak on my testicles, it seemed like a dream.

It was only a ten-minute trick, but it sustained me, somehow, knowing I had myself one true cowboy.

I don't know what piece of the sky he fell out of, but that night, and many nights thereafter, I thanked Heaven for the holes in the fabric.

MATTHEW R. K. HAYNES

Kink

THE STREETS ARE BARE. No cars or buses. No people, only me and a few hundred empty beer bottles. I stand smoking; needing something or someone to want and take me. The sky is clean. Every star hangs individually. Each twinkle a call. I hear no music. I try to tap my feet to keep a rhythm in my head, but I am too drunk. I do a dance and hum half a song that I learned in grade school. Although the night is thus filled with solitary fun, I proceed to walk home because it is getting cold. And it isn't worth the wait.

A car passes me. Slowly. The driver glances in my direction. He or she I can't tell. It's a white car with license plates that read, GOFORIT. Really makes me laugh—the pretentiousness of it. My voice echoes down the street. The exhaust fumes taper, and I continue my walk home. The silence is here again. I whistle to drive it out. It works momentarily. I light a cigarette to give me something. It tastes fantastic. Warm when I inhale. Cold and dusty when I exhale. New.

I hear a car stop at the corner I crossed about a half a block before. I don't look back. I just keep walking. Fear, mostly, prompts my actions, but being a curious cat I finally turn and look. The same white car turns the corner and starts my way. Moving slowly. I walk. I speed up but don't go too fast. The car moves closer then pulls alongside me. I glance at the car. I put my head down, watching my feet. The little voice in my head screams, "Don't look 'em in the eye. Just keep walking." I hear a noise, and I look. The window rolls down.

"Hey there."

A man's voice. I peer through the passenger hole and see nothing. "Hi." I keep walking, increasing my pace to strides.

"Stop there a second." I stop. "You look cold." I'm sure I look cold. Freezing. Frozen. Petrified.

"Yeah well, it's pretty cold out here."

"Yeah. So do you need a ride?"

I walk towards the car. As I get closer, the face becomes clearer. I smile and think happy, horny thoughts. I slide into the car. Sit for a moment and laugh.

"What?"

"Nothing." I pause, too nervous to really explain anything. "I just think this is really weird. Getting into a person's car. That is—I mean—it's pretty late, and I don't know you, and I don't know, but hey, here I am." I glance his way. He smiles. He has a moustache and red baseball cap.

There is silence.

The car moves.

■ ■ ■

His apartment is beautiful. Large. Warm. Black and white photographs. Candlesticks. Porcelain lamps. Television. Chair. Vase. Coffee table. Bottles of beer. It has wooden floors and a picture window that looks out onto the city. I want to smoke and drink and listen to jazz.

He takes his coat off and offers me a seat. I decline and stand my ground by the window.

"What are you looking at?"

It takes me a moment to answer. "It's a beautiful view. Not so quiet from up here."

"You're dark. What are you?" he asks, his left leg over his right at the knee. Left arm extended over the back of the black leather couch.

"Pardon me?" I don't know exactly how to answer.

"What are you?"

I grind my teeth and my eyes dry until I am forced to blink them wet.

"What do you mean?"

"Your ethnicity? What are you?"

"What does it matter? So, I'm dark. So what?" I take a defensive swing and miss.

"It doesn't. You're just really beautiful."

I turn away to rediscover the view. I am flattered. He is smooth. He has me.

I can feel his breath and his scent that lingers between my body and the window. Sweet. Alive and moist.

He puts his hand on my shoulder and kisses the right side of my neck. He grabs my hands and pushs them to the window. It is cold and drains my warmth. His warmth. He kisses my head and massages my shoulders and puts his hands up my shirt. They touch my back, move to my chest. He grabs my nipples, softly pinches, then lets go. It is a ritual at most. I am sullen. Depleted.

"Pretty view, isn't it?"

My pants drop.

"Beautiful view."

I see our reflection and my breathing on the window. I grip the glass. He hits hard. I wait. He moans. I lick the glass. Taste it and relax.

D A M I E N   B A R L O W

Octopus

THE BOY I'VE BEEN KISSING wears too much Jazz. I have an overwhelming desire to rip his Calvin Kleins—and I do. The tearing cotton has an almost sacrificial sound. I kneel down to feed on this newly exposed flesh. His arse even smells sweet, and as I prod with tongue and finger a bottle of amyl hits my ear. Standing above me is a French-looking sailor with hands that smell of brine. As I inhale the proffered poppers, his big cock thumps against my scalp, acting out some mildly irritating form of discipline. The sailor smiles as if he knows me, bends down, and whispers conspiratorial obscenities in my drug-fucked ear. I only hear, "Oh yeah! . . . fuck that . . . big . . . yeah," as he simultaneously rubs my cock and pokes the boy's moist arse. Upon closer inspection, my foul-mouthed sailor more clearly resembles a porn-obsessed waiter, and yes, that is shit on his white trousers.

I know that with boys like this you cannot touch their hair, but the waiter is now fucking the boy's face, pushing the gelled head further down his cock. The boy slaps the hands away. Already I feel a little bored with the whole scenario. The amyl has killed my erection. Before I've even buttoned up, the waiter's cum-call cuts through the semi-darkness like a frenetic foghorn.

■ ■ ■

The boy I want to kiss goes walking past me, indifferent. He looks like an accountant, sensibly dressed in those ironed clothes with his neatly parted hair. I start having wicked thoughts about corrupting this accountant, of making him dirty. And as he passes me again, I think I can smell fresh soap in the air. I fantasize that his balls, lolling in my mouth, would have that squeaky clean taste, almost like licking plastic. My accountant stops his laps and hovers outside an aromatic candlelit cubicle. A large hairy man, dressed only in a leather fishmonger's apron, stands in the doorway. The accountant looks past the fishmonger to a thin man suspended in a series of nets. He looks like a sprawled out crab with his glowing red skin. I catch my accountant's soapy scent outside the closed door, then quickly forget it.

Tired of pretty-boy posturing, I walk down the stairs in step to rhythmic moans from below. Under the stairwell, a man is receiving, with a kind of drug-induced bliss, a fierce ramming by an unseen cock. I pause under one of the dim lights to watch, then enter a drum-made cove. The air is damp, but my throat feels dry, my lips encrusted with salt. In the darkness, a pair of disembodied hands slide under my arms and pinch my nipples. My eyes begin adjusting to the murky darkness as these extra hands start to undress me. The body they belong to sticks to my back, and I feel, even for the fleeting minutes we are together, that this stranger and I are inseparable. A second cock, much larger than mine, emerges from between my legs. With my doubling complete, I feel like an octopus. I start to masturbate my new cock, which already seems moist and well-used, at a stage of numbed erection. A man appears with really white teeth and begins sucking my chest. Two faceless mouths take my cocks, and I hear saliva or semen splat across my boots. I look up and see a crowd, men hammering into my little cove eager to watch the spectacle. Some have their cocks out, so I reach with avid tentacles, swiping knobs, grazing unknown skin.

■ ■ ■

The boy I really want to kiss is in the small crowd, watching my fleshy tentacles pursue hard cock, noting my now perfected dual thrusts. I pretend not to see him. But he lights a cigarette, and momentarily exposes my creation as imperfect bodies, sloppy mouths gasping. My chest is illuminated with bruises. I remove the man now biting my stomach. Disengage myself from the salty smelling body behind me. I pull up my jeans, stumble through my fleshy cove, and quickly escape.

His name is Dimitri. He is the boy I constantly lust after during tutorials, as he deconstructs White Australian imperialist discourses, recapitulates Edward Said with flair. I always seem to be nodding my head in agreement when he talks, to the point where I feel as if I've been sucking him off. But that is in another world.

■ ■ ■

The cold early morning air starts a minor coughing fit. The orange glow of the streetlights makes Melbourne barely visible in this thick fog. I wander down an alley bordered by old derelict factories, all with the promise of pink dollar conversion. Nearby cries could be a bashing, but most probably are stray sounds from the S & M bed and breakfast. My cock is still hard, so I divert to a small alcove and begin jerking off. In the foggy dark, I'm once again an octopus; my suckerbearing arms tasting the darkness, my sperm-smeared tentacles ravishing newly acquired flesh. I cum on the bonnet of a BMW and rub the remainder into my raw skin. Through the fog, a figure emerges. Dimitri walks towards me and places a warm hand on my limp cock.

"Nice show. I guess I put you off back there."

His lips look swollen, recently chewed.

"Sort of," I reply, as my cock grows against his palm.

Dimitri smiles and thrusts a bottle of amyl up close to my nose. It is only then that I notice his hands smell of brine and smeared shit decorates his white trousers.

"Come on, I'll drive you to the ocean," he says, as my head swims with chemicals.

Six Positions

I'M MAKING LOVE TO THE OLDEST MAN I've ever been with. His hair is white as Egyptian silk, his skin is translucent, blue and pink, I can see his heart beating from excitement. I am drawing an arrow down with my tongue, shoulder to opposite hip, a ribbon of saliva like a banner from a beauty pageant. This one says, "This man has tasted and been tasted by men for decades." Blood ricochets around his body and builds at his surprising erection. The wrinkles on his face, arms, hands, so loose, a multitude of scrotums all over his body, which I take up into my mouth like dinosaur eggs, rare plums, a tulip's head unopened. With veneration, I lift, squeeze softly, hear a gasp like an ocean caught in shells. It is the last ocean. It is wet. The tide recedes like sadness.

I'm making love to the fattest man I've ever been with. His anus cannot be found amidst the mounds of flesh, but his mouth, pink, red, puckering, surrounded by two round cheeks, has a passing resemblance. He laughs a great thrusting belly laugh the whole time we grapple, him turning and flopping, me dodging the weight whirling all around for my own safety. Every part of my body is a phallus, my fingers, hands, arms, legs, head. I press these into skin that says, yes! and takes me in, out, in, out, sweating, sliding, surrounded by warmth, by darkness. Somewhere in this maze I find a cock that is fat and round like a root vegetable. I punch at it, grasp it with my hungry hands. Hear a voice as if outside of a room or all around, of god, or a pregnant mother, *huh huh huh*. The sticky fat flood smells of appetite.

I'm making love to the most exotic man I've ever been with. He has eyes like jungle animals. Tigers, wildebeests, possums, crocodiles, sloths, night owls. His skin turns colour depending on the angle of light: dark as petroleum, as the centre of your skull then yellow as the eyes of jungle animals—tigers, night owls, crocodiles. As slight as a bamboo reed, then a tight round muscularity on fire with bound up strength. Then two breasted and big cocked and more pictures, pretty pictures, so many I'm almost blind and I fuck him I fuck him I fuck him until I am covered in the fluids of my own exertion, thigh muscles, stomach, arms, still tensed, energy hanging on me still. Shivering, and when the thought returns to my head, I understand him not a bit more.

I'm making love to the thinnest man I've ever been with. He is so thin and long that he is sharp. I bleed with pleasure. He places his fingers down on me and leaves a lovely symmetrical arc, five small half-moon-shaped pricks. The air on my skin, and my cuts, feels spiny like a cactus, a tall spindly one with a downy white veil of spikes. Like pins and needles, when a part of your body has fallen asleep, and you have to shake and shake to get the blood back in. I am in a desert of sensation, so quiet that every grain of sand is noticeable. But I do not notice as he clothes himself head to foot in rubber and enters me from behind. I don't know if it's his penis, his arm, his leg, his whole body. I just remember he's thin. It's suddenly an Arizona night and the stars are twinkling in time with an orgasm soon to arrive. Sensation pours through the star-holes, the rest is black. Each time I exhale, one of the stars goes out.

I'm making love to the smallest man I've ever been with. Small is beautiful. He has attached his mouth to my cock, his legs dangling down, I feel *enormous*. I am enormous in comparison. He leaps and lands on my tit, and bounces on my nipple like a trampoline, does cartwheels and somersaults up my stomach, around my neck. My touch on him is crude but large; he rubs into it like a cat, then returns to my crotch where he gives special attention to each square millimetre. When he finishes the last, I explode. I worry I've drowned him, but he shakes himself off in a triumphant dance, slides down my leg and disappears.

I'm making love to myself. Really. With elasticity and extra parts. I am seeing what all the others have seen before me, I am tasting my nipples, which come alive and harden, punctuation marks in the air all around me. My voice. *Oh oh oh*—periods. *Uh uh uh*—commas. *Awuhaaahh*—question mark. Gasping hyphens, sighing slants, I grunt out underlines. I am writing myself onto my page as my cock extends long, so long, I'm entered. I'm thrusting into myself. I have ten hands. I have eight tongues. A line between my balls and thigh. The slit in my throbbing head. A dimple where chest meets abdominals. All fingered. All stroked. All tongued. The skin of the page curves into its wet stain. Words run into each other.

S H A U N   D E   W A A L

Swallowed

I CAME AND, once the shuddering was over, withdrew my cock. With one hand I began to peel off the condom, making sure I didn't release the little gobbet of cum in its tip. With the other hand, I reached for the cock of the man before me, the man lying on his back on a rough table, legs in the air, having just been fucked in the dull glare of a single red bulb. Around us, shadowy figures hovered, watching in the gloom. I didn't look at them.

The face of the man I'd just fucked was hidden by a black mask, and his cock was still hard. His body jerked: he wanted me to continue, was probably close to coming. His arms were spread out, cruciform, on either side of his body; he seemed not to want to touch himself, but it was clear from his movements that he did not want to stop.

I got the condom off, neatly, and flicked it under the table. The air was filled with loud music, but I imagined I heard the condom's plop. My cock was wholly limp now. I ran my left hand up, over the masked man's hard belly and swelling, heaving chest. My right went to his asshole, and a finger went into the hot, wet orifice, where my cock had been; I pulled my finger out, and two went in, easily.

I intended to do no more. Pulling his cock with one hand, two fingers of the other rhythmically moving up his ass, I felt his climax building. In the half-darkness, I could see the muscles of his gut clenching and unclenching, and could feel the suck of his anus on my fingers, tensing and opening like a mouth.

Then something seemed to ripple, and my whole hand was inside him. The asshole was swallowing my forearm, up to the elbow. It—or he, if it was him—did not pause there, but continued to suck, to pull, at my arm, and suddenly I was wedged against his buttocks, my neck pressed hard against the perineum, my right ear stuck between his balls, and my whole arm, up to the shoulder, deep within his body. Where did it go?

I could hardly breathe. I felt trapped; I couldn't move. The music seemed to have become more frantic; my mind was dazzled, my head spinning as though I was about to lose consciousness. And his anus kept sucking at me, my head twisted at an uncomfortable angle as the orifice pulled ferociously on my arm.

It—he, the man in the black leather mask, whose whole body seemed to have become a giant anus—convulsed, and suddenly my head was inside it, in some succulent darkness, and I could not breathe at all. My mouth opened madly, trying to gulp air, but there was none.

Still it sucked, rippling like an anaconda must ripple as it swallows its prey, pulling me in, ingesting me. My lungs bursting, I felt it, he, this man's body, close around my shoulders, and my whole torso slid in, held tightly in this slimed passage, caught in the suffocating embrace of his inner muscles.

My hips were sucked in, and I could feel my legs follow easily, an afterthought. At the same time I felt, as if very distantly, my own cock throbbing—I didn't know if it was hard or soft, but it felt as though it were on the verge of such a stupendous ejaculation it might come free of its moorings altogether.

In a brief vision, my head exploding, I sensed or imagined his erect phallus, huge as a man, towering over me. My whole body was inside him, crushed, as if I were being digested, being squeezed convulsively. There was a painful roaring in my ears, a waterfall of blood. My mind began to fade, to flicker out into nothingness, my body's every bone broken, pulped.

Then—I don't know how long it was—I was awakening again, rising to awareness, but still seemed unable quite to breathe, to move even, and there was a great shuddering in the juiced walls that held me, and a pounding. I was being squeezed again, harder, more violently than before, thrust this way and that, battered, and I seemed to be rushing through a tunnel, at nauseating speed, fighting to get out, struggling to breathe, to be, to—

And I was out in the air, flying, gasping, slammed against the wall. I thudded to the floor, crumpling. Covered in some kind of reeking ooze, from head to foot, wet, hot, streaming. My head felt as though it had been kicked. My body ached, feeling its bruises. I screamed and saw my cock, somehow as hard as the wall itself, pumping and pumping and pumping.

J O N A T H A N   S T R O N G

Letter Without an Address

DEAR SAM,
I did try to find you that next week when I got home. I called every beauty salon in the North Shore phonebook, in Lynn and Danvers and Peabody and Salem, but no one knew you. Well, one guy said he knew a Sam but he didn't work there. He hung up, suspicious. Are you really training to cut hair somewhere, shampooing and sweeping up? Is Sam your real name?

All I have of you is the pink cigarette lighter you left beside my hotel bed. And these thoughts: walking back and forth on the road to Winter Island, brisk January afternoon, my tight faded blue sweatpants, hardly anyone out there to take notice, a few cars in the lot at the end. I sauntered past, nothing happened. Walking back to Salem and your car went by heading to the island, caught a glimpse of your skinny face. Nuts, I thought. But down the road your clunker of a rusted-out Pontiac pulled over then swung around, came back my way making lots of noise. I thought: what if it's some punk with a tire iron? You stopped, rolled the window down. You were half my age. Just stared at the bulge in my sweatpants, said you wanted to see it close. The closer I got the sweeter you looked.

I said it was cold and you said you'd drive me back to town. I got in and said I had a room, and you told me you had to drive careful because the brakes were bad. You didn't want to do a lot, just look, watch, maybe touch. Be totally safe. I was happy suddenly. By then we were talking like pals. We told each other our names, Tom and Sam.

Only a bed in an empty room with cruddy green carpeting in a welfare hotel. I was spending a few days there cheap to get a job done. We lay down, held each other, kissed delicately; soon the smell and softness of your skin made me feel faint and then I was licking your neck and saying, "You're so pretty, you're so pretty," which you liked to hear. We got naked and now it was your whole body. But careful. You held my cock in your slender hands and stared at me and I stared back. That hour you were everything in the world. Our skin was hot, we wrestled and tumbled and rubbed, our blood pounding through us chest to chest.

Your cock was stiff, boyish, just enough smaller than mine to let you say, "I want your big cock," and "Your cock is so thick." I was thinking of how you wanted us to be safe, and I wanted you to be safe in all ways, safe from the cold too. We jerked each other off with hand cream. You came in powerful shots, along your thin flat pink chest. It hit the corner of my right eye as I nestled close to your cheek, flushed from my own flood that had dappled your thigh.

"Tom, Tom, Tom," you said in the voice of someone who had known and loved me a long time. I tried for the same tone, "Sam, Sam, Sam."

I dabbed at my eye with the pillowcase, you lit a cigarette. We lay naked, all entangled, and we talked. I told you some things about me. Do you remember any of that? You talked about your parents knowing about you but not understanding, about living with your sister and her husband and them understanding better, about being laid off from G.E. in Lynn and training at the salon. You didn't like to "pahty" (I hear your North Shore accent, softer than Boston), you liked TV and going to "bahs" sometimes. You smoked several cigarettes, calming down, didn't let go of me. I had you in my arms for that long.

Then we found our bodies moving against each other. Our cocks were coming back to life. I kissed everywhere around your face but then gingerly on your lips, you kissed back hard. The second time was all passionate, as if we were together again after a long separation. You wanted me to lay my cock against your ass, just press it there so you could imagine getting fucked, and I wanted to fuck you the way you imagined. When we came that time it wasn't so spectacular but like hearts melting.

We showered, soaping each other up, balls, nipples, slick, delicious. I washed out my eye better. It got dark outside. You had to get your sister's car home, hoped the brakes wouldn't give. I walked you down the creaking stairs, past the sleepy lady at the desk in the laundromat. I reminded you where you could find me. "Call," I said. You were looking sadly at me. I watched you getting into that rustbucket and chugging off down Route 1A.

Next two days I walked out to Winter Island, hoping. Then, from back at home, I annoyed every beauty salon up in those four towns. Slowly, I had to tuck you away in a memory.

In March I got a bad fever. I went for my yearly checkup in April. Now I know, Sam, that our first time making love was my last without the virus, that our last time was my first with it. I want to tell you that I love you. But who will look after you? Do you even know what danger you're in? You wanted to be careful with me but there was so much power in that young cock of yours letting go. Are you eating right? Seeing a doctor? I should go up and search for you. Why don't I? Would I even recognize you in different clothes, in a different car, maybe with a different name? I belong to you, you to me, but we have a secret we're left keeping from each other for the rest of our lives.

Your
Tom

The God
of the Sea

MEN HURTLE LIKE STALLIONS across the pool; arms whip up, crash forward, black-capped heads smack the chlorinated water like cannonballs. When it's my turn, I dive, startled as a rush of wetness bubbles along my skin. Beneath, muscled legs thrash, thick arms curve, swimsuits pass holding dangling wands or curled snails. At the pool end we wait, panting, a chest against mine, an arm on my stomach.

The coach yells, "Six laps freestyle."

How I yearn for water without walls, my body flying in an unbroken trajectory.

The change room is a wet towel slapped across my face. There, the swim-team, fish-naked, shipwrecked on wood benches—talk.

"I gotta visit my girlfriend's mom. . . ."

"I was fixing my old pick-up. . . ."

My mind wraps around their words, squeezing as I'd wring a towel. But there are no secrets. When I stare in their eyes, they do not flicker back. I am looking down empty wells. I wonder why I live in this landlocked town.

I think: the pool is not water as the ocean is water. It is imprisoned water. A water zoo. I swim to the square drain vent at the bottom and gaze up at the constellation of bodies. I open my mouth and say a word. A bubble rises to the surface and explodes.

■ ■ ■

One day I'm clutching the pool's edge, adjusting my goggle-strap, when I see on the deck a new man snapping on a cap. He is watching me. His head is square as a shark fin; his eyes, kelp green. When they don't slide from mine, I am thunderstruck. The smell of sea salt penetrates the chlorine-filled air, and I realize—he is from the Ocean. I drop my goggles, lose grip of the side, nearly sink underwater. He still stares, and I wonder: If I throw my life to him, will he catch it?

He walks over to me, smiles. "How're you doing, I'm Pete." His chest is bevelled like an island cliffside, his stomach, soft surely from his diet of lobster and clams.

"John."

"I heard there was a Masters' swim club. Well, if you're the master, where are the slaves . . . ? Sorry, bad joke."

Unlike the others he doesn't show off and dive but slips in. I think of his skin touching water that touches me and I shiver. My voice is choked.

"We're doing 400-metre freestyle."

He grins and plunges forward, his arms smack at waves, legs paddle, the oars of a Viking ship. I follow, swallow water; ahead his swimsuit beckons like a matador's cape.

At the pool end I must stop. He's waiting.

"You're amazing," I say between breaths; my goggles are full of water. "I can't believe how you swim."

"Thanks." Then he ducks below and shoots to the pool centre like a torpedo. I put my face down and blow a long row of bubbles. Then another. And another.

In the change room my voice is too loud. "I really enjoyed that swim." I know my eyes are blazing. I use the towel to cover myself. The others watch me—the man who never speaks—their eyes slitted thin as razors.

That night I dream of waterfalls, tidal waves, and flash floods. All the next day there is a roaring in my ears.

I gaze at the computer screen.

"Mr. Jones, are you all right?"

Waves crash against rocks.

"Yes, I am."

Before me the rows of digits seem too ordered to be related to anything real.

Next practice I wait as Pete swims. A wave precedes him. It crashes against my chest, shoulders, face, subsides into bubbles and foam.

"Your butterfly," I'm shaking, "is incredible. I can barely get my chest out of the water."

And for the first time, someone teaches me.

When he closes his hand around my wrist, my arm trembles. He guides my fingers into the water, "the arms curve as they enter, the chest drops"—his hand presses my upper back—"on an angle, like this."

I feel my body gradually break apart, dissolving to water beneath his strong hands.

"The torso leads. Don't divide yourself in pieces, one part moving one way while the rest goes elsewhere."

All my muscles are trembling.

"Tighten your back, and swing with"—he touches them—"your hips—"

"Oh, Poseidon!" I cry.

"What?!"

"I mean, Pete—this is great."

Then a voice like acid: "You two seem to be enjoying yourselves."

We push away from the side. As I do the back crawl, ceiling bulbs glare in my eyes like search lights.

"That was wonderful," I bubble. "We can practice again tomorrow. And you'll want to come Thursdays. They have a public swim that goes all year."

His forehead suddenly creases. "Sure."

Eating dinner I decide: I will invite him to my house. The kitchen floor will tremble at the touch of his feet; the living room lights will glow bright when he smiles. When he sits on the bed, it'll burst into flame, soft tongues of fire curling round him. I don't need to lock the door; he won't want to escape. I have caught and pulled him from the sea and he will live with me forever.

I fill my rooms with long twisting corals, wave-worn rocks, curled shells, and starfish. Dried seaweed hangs across the walls and mantel. The smell of baked trout fills the air. I depart with my swimsuit and towel.

Outside the pool Pete holds luggage and wears a suit. He waves and half-smiles. "Hi, John. Can't talk long. I've just come to say goodbye. My boss wants me back in Vancouver tomorrow."

My jaw drops.

"I mean, I was only supposed to be here a week. . . . I just wanted to say I really enjoyed meeting you and, well . . . I've got a partner, a guy at home. And this place, these guys . . . I just want to say thanks and good luck."

He looks at me, smiles. Then he quickly shakes my hand and vanishes like a mirage.

Suddenly the air is parched. I open my mouth and discover my tongue is glued to my palate. I scratch my arm and skin flakes off. I go home and turn on the taps and all the water runs brown.

Far away the ocean roars, and immediately I know: I will leave. Next month or next week. I have waited too long for the sea.

That night I stare at the sky. I open my mouth and release a word in a bubble. It rises higher and higher.

Waiting

THE SKY ABOVE IS BABY BLUE and the sun slants through distant mountains to slap awake the West End. This early May morning in Vancouver should make me happy, but it doesn't.

At first coffee I spot this man across Denman Street. He's big, mid-twenties, dirty yellow hair slicked back as if wet, as if rushed from a steamy shower to the bus stop. He stares impatiently up the empty road and when the bus doesn't show, he paces around, swinging his legs out straight to a rhythm only he can hear.

I like them like that: helpless. Waiting for greater powers to descend. Compelled to wait. Locked into place. He may have the looks of a god but suddenly his limitations are starkly revealed. Every time a taxicab whizzes by, his head turns and his eyes follow longingly. His blue jeans look thin, even from a distance. Knee-bumps poke out and white has faded in a block along the back of his thighs.

I like them like that: at a distance. Far enough to shrivel their power to reject with their cavalier frowns. I'm middle-aged. Chinese. Lived in Canada all my life. I've had my share of men, but never anyone like him. I'd have to pay money to get him into my apartment. Only money would stifle his snickering. I'm clean. If he wants, we can toss aside the condom. That's how much I want him. I'd risk my life for one night with him.

I like them like that: big and volcanic. Craggy head, barrel chest, soccer thighs. A cleft in his chin, hawkish nose for a dramatic silhouette, and eyelashes generous enough to brush away years of hurt.

In my fantasy, my car squeals around the corner and jolts to a stop beside him. "Need a ride?"

"Hey thanks, man." He has a gruff but friendly voice and his face relaxes. He's so relieved to start moving that he doesn't notice my face. Later, he lies in my bed with eyes closed and lets me worship his body. My fingers twirl idle knots in his chest hair, my heel massages the sheen of his thighs, my nose is buried in a warm armpit.

In reality, I stroll to the beach on solitary mornings and follow three-point seagull tracks through the ocean debris. Whole trees are swept in, their roots and branches blackened by saltwater. Waves crash forward, liquid walls rise a metre high, then drop and drop until flattened fingers of foam are pulled back into the sea.

■ ■ ■

Now that my retirement has started, I can sit by the beach all morning, sipping mineral water and praying he'll show up. When he saunters by, we're close enough to touch and my chest tightens slightly, but he never notices me. He's Chinese, about forty, with a full head of neatly-styled salt and pepper hair. His confident strides testify to regular workouts at the gym, and a nice firm ass pokes out behind him.

I like men smooth and hairless, with tanned skin clear as a woman's. Some chests are reminiscent of muscular breasts.

I like men small-boned and slight. Light enough to wriggle atop me as a baby playing astride his father. A hole small enough to grip me tight, then milk me dry.

I like men sweet-smelling despite the grunting heat of sex. They don't perspire and if they do, their sweat-pearls are teardrops for the licking.

I like men with faces flat and uncomplicated, so my belly simultaneously absorbs nub of nose and pucker of lips, twitch of eye and lick of tongue, velvety cheeks and tickle of air.

I like men deceivingly young and rejuvenating. If he looks twenty-five, he's thirty-six and I lose two decades at least. If he looks forty, he's fifty-five, and I lose a decade. We will have shared men in common and visited many familiar landmarks.

Men label me *Rice Queen* and accuse me of objectification. I would not silence them; I hear every word, respect each argument, understand all issues. Their bodies are crowded temples to be revered and I will travel the world on my knees to complete the pilgrimage. For now, I'm an ocean freighter moored in restless waters waiting for a harbour berth.

■ ■ ■

If I stop at the beach to nap after work, the old guy on the bench will sneak glances my way but always turn away as if ashamed. He must be a retired professor or a gallery curator, someone with a distinguished reputation. Silky white hair frames a ruddy face and lively eyes that dance with wit and delight. He never wears shorts, not even on hot days, probably because his long legs have lost their muscle tone. But his sandaled feet are slim and long, and the manicured nails are pink with good health. When we weary of debate, I will suck his toes for hours.

His body is lean and lanky, one that eagerly and easily bounded through the Himalayas or up Kilimanjaro. He's travelled far to find men, but I want to reassure him it's safe to play here now. We're the same height, so we can kiss and savour each other as fingers travel down chests and ribs to thrusting crotches.

I can't blame him if he avoids me and assumes I'm a male bimbo. I didn't ask to be born with the body of a sex toy. Truth is, I have a Ph.D. in philosophy and there's no one to talk to. Older men take me to bed and serve me fresh coffee for breakfast, but the slightest hint of gravity frightens them. They suspect I'm casting for a sugar daddy if I admire their degrees, they conclude I'm too needy if the barbwire attitude doesn't stay fortified, they worry I'm moving too fast if earnest questions are asked. I work in a mega-bookstore in Surrey (no gay Mecca) and it takes an early bus to get there. I'm so sleepy I march around the bus stanchion to get my blood going in the mornings.

D E N N I S   D E N I S O F F

Club Me

IT'S FINALLY HIT ME. I moved here for money, and that means
I'm old. It's been a couple of months now and, while I'd been
forewarned about the absence of gay clubs, I couldn't believe that there
aren't any cruising areas either. A thin, Englishy kind of guy at
work—Dexter—told me that, apparently back in the '70s, guys used to
cruise at the Zippy. That's the connector train to the main Amtrack
train that then delivers you to the throbbing, oily heart of New York
in less than an hour. Locals will straight-facedly give you the time
down to the minute—"It only takes fifty-two minutes to reach Grand
Central Station!"—apparently not recognizing the anxiety in their
own voices. But it takes me forty-five minutes to slog over to little
Zippy himself, which somehow neither Dexter nor anybody else ever
bothers to factor into the equation.

Dexter is the only guy at work that I've met. He's been working here
for over a decade, but he lives in New York and raves about the clubs
as if they were life preservers. He's written the lesbian and gay history
of this town. It filled one whole column on the back page of an issue
of *The Body Politic*. Dexter isn't really my kind of guy but I followed his
suggestion and went and hung around the Zippy station in the freezing
cold—this was '96, the winter of blizzards—for a whole week and
didn't bring anything home except piles from sitting too long on the
frozen cement. One should not be embarrassed to call one's mom to
ask her how to get rid of them. So Zippy failed me big time, but I
couldn't afford the extra hours it takes to trip into New York. I was just

starting the job and all and having to spend over-time setting up the computer systems for my sector and down-loading, down-loading, down-loading so much shit, I feel like my job title should be "down-loader guy." So I went for the next option—cruising bathrooms. Not too surprisingly, there wasn't anybody waiting there either.

After checking out every public bathroom I could find, including the one at the Salvation Army, I found no life and only two pieces of graffiti. The piece in the library says, "God is my thing." Yeah, whatever. And the one at the university says, in those scary, perfectly square letters, "Suck my pulsing hard-on," to which somebody else has tagged, "I agree with you in theory, but why so small and bashful?" You can tell if a bathroom is a happening place by the graffiti—or lack thereof. Things definitely aren't happening here. Things *are* happening—Dexter is sure to remind me every Monday morning—fifty-two minutes away in the throbbing, oily heart of New York.

I briefly considered phone-sex, but my phone isn't connected yet, and "Jersey Bell"—the name always makes me think of a cow wearing lipstick—wants a two-hundred dollar deposit and another hundred-fifty-two in connecting fees and other stuff for an answering service and an internal repair guarantee and something else I don't remember but I have it written down somewhere. Anyway, I can't afford a phone until the paycheque after next week, which the government is taking for student loans so old I can't remember getting them, by which time I'll no doubt have followed Dexter to the city.

So here I am, reduced to level three—buying porn and masturbating, which is what Havelock Ellis had recommended for his patients back in the 1880s, although not as a money-saving strategy. Imagine my sense of weirdness upon discovering that this town only offers pornography directed at heterosexual men. This should've been my measure of the town before I'd considered taking the job. I check each of the magazines, but there aren't even pictures of men laying *behind* the naked women, not even a man's hairy leg kind of sticking out as background landscape, or male hands holding up the pert and rosy breasts, or some hunky ruffled guy acting surprised as he walks in the door to find a sexy woman doing erotic things on a couch, or even a tiny, black and white ad in the back showing a picture of an "exotic wrestler" that you can order for only fifteen dollars or whatever, or even an ad for cologne, underwear, or golf that might have an erotically workable graphic, if one has the imagination to work it, and I don't.

Slogging through the snow back to my stupid cold apartment, I begin to understand the source of the desperation behind the town chant "fifty-two minutes away, fifty-two minutes away, fifty-two minutes away." I feel like I'm in one of those ads for tropical vacations, where they show a person in an overcoat puddling through a blizzard but just about to step off the curb into a warm blue ocean dotted with beach balls and life preservers. There really is no way of surviving out on this island. It's clear to me now that, when various acquaintances suggested that I might think of living in New York and commuting in everyday, they were more than just trying to appear urbane. Chilled through by the dampness, I stop on the almost deserted street and listen. Yes, yes, I can almost imagine that I hear the throbbing, throbbing oily heart of New York. It sounds something like a Grace Jones album from the '80s. I guess for the younger boys, it would sound like electronica. This keen sense of distance (fifty-two minutes, fifty-two minutes) makes it clear to me that, if New York is indeed the heart, them I'm stuck somewhere between the toes, jammed somewhere under the cold and dirty nail of a big toe. Alone except for the lanky, young worker with the perfectly round ass who is hanging up a "CLUB MED" sign, all the letters cut separately from blue and orange glittery paper. He's almost finished when the "D" falls from his grasp and flutters down spastically into the slush-filled street. Before he can retrieve the letter, a Volvo squashes it under its tires—oh, the carnage. It's the first letter of my first name. It's the first letter of my last name. The worker looks at me like he knows this, like I might have some advice about resuscitating the "D." Then he stares at the mangled letter running disco blue into the street and, unsympathetic, saunters away, splashing through the slush in a pair of those orange work boots that everybody's wearing. That's another fad I'll never understand.

Reflections in a Dry Fountain

THE SUN WAS GLORIOUSLY WARM for November. Crisp brown leaves swirled in eddies around small dogs and sneakered children. Washington Square was bathed that afternoon in the clearest, cleanest light. It cast hard-edged shadows onto the ground like pieces missing from some giant jigsaw puzzle. They splashed over steps and sidewalks and into the grass, still green from summer.

Alan sat alone in his discontent on the inside ledge of the great fountain. Out of use for what seemed like forever, it was bone dry, the charcoal stone of its outer wall comfortably warmed by the midday sun. There was just the slightest hint of meaner days yet to come hanging in the air; an unwelcome portent to be ignored at all cost.

He had found himself by the fountain, like waking from a dream—an ongoing nightmare, really, too cumbersome to cast off. It had not been his intent, his destination, when he left his room, but here he was all the same.

"Isn't it odd?"

Alan turned his head to look at the man beside him. The source of the comment was reading a book.

"Did you say something?" Alan asked.

"Yes. I said, Isn't it odd?"

"Isn't what odd?"

"Life."

The park attracted all types. "I suppose," Alan said, to be polite, and turned away. He wasn't in the mood to make conversation. Not today.

"Oh, it is. Trust me on this. Steve Wilson," he said, holding out his hand.

Alan shook it. Again, to be polite. He wanted to be left alone.

"And you are?"

"Alan."

"Just plain Alan?"

"Alan Banks."

"There now, that wasn't so difficult, was it?"

Alan had to smile. It wasn't the line itself, the sarcasm or the delivery, but the look on his face. There was something almost comical about it, although he hadn't a clue as to what that was. It simply made him smile—and he hadn't wanted to.

"I'm harmless," he reassured Alan. "That's just my opening line, 'life is odd.' Sort of an ice-breaker. I use it when there's nothing else to talk about, short of the weather. I suppose I could have said, 'nice day, huh?'"

"I suppose," Alan answered, dryly. He was not going to be pulled into a conversation.

"Life *is* odd, though."

Alan refused to respond.

"You're not much of a conversationalist, are you?"

"I have my moments," Alan said, and looked out over the crowd. Perhaps if he ignored the genial Mr. Wilson, he'd go away or just go back to reading his book.

"I bet you do," he said, this time without the sarcasm in his voice. "I bet you do have your moments." He was being sincere, and just a bit seductive.

Alan hadn't really looked at him until then, but he quickly took it all in: nice face, good body, strong hands. There was potential here. Definite potential. Perhaps Steve Wilson was worth his time.

"I'm sorry," Alan said. "I guess I'm being rude."

"No. Not at all. You're entitled to your privacy," he said, and went back to reading his book.

Alan continued to stare at him. He was well-dressed, clean-shaven, articulate. In fact, he was quite attractive. Why hadn't he noticed him right away?

Steve Wilson stopped reading his book. He looked back up at Alan and smiled. "Now you're being impolite," he said. "It's not nice to stare. But please don't stop on my account. I'm flattered."

"Are you trying to hit on me?" Alan suddenly asked, feeling a little foolish and somewhat presumptuous. He hadn't considered the question, it just sort of popped out of his mouth like a hiccup.

"Is that what you think?"

"Yes. It is."

"I see. Is it what you'd like?"

Alan didn't answer the question, but continued to stare.

"Well, you can think about it for a while. I'm not going any where. Take your time."

"You *are* hitting on me, aren't you?"

"Am I? I thought I was being friendly."

"How did you know I was . . . ?"

"Was what?"

Alan couldn't decide what to say. Had he not judged correctly?

"Please, don't get all self-conscious on me. It's not tattooed across your forehead or anything. No lavender 'H' or pink triangle sewn conspicuously on your shoulder that you don't know about. I took a chance. Nothing ventured, nothing gained. Right?"

"Why?"

"Why what?"

"Why are you coming on to me?" Alan was beginning to feel out of control.

"Don't you ever look in the mirror?"

"Not if I can help it."

"Why is that?"

"Maybe because I don't like what I see."

"I find that hard to believe."

"You can believe whatever you'd like," Alan said, sharply.

"What's the matter? I was giving you a compliment. You're a good-looking guy."

"Am I?"

"Yes, of course you are."

"Well, it's your fantasy. But don't ask too many questions. The more you know about me, the less exciting it's going to be. Right?"

Steve Wilson closed his book. He stood up and buttoned his navy blazer. "It's always enlightening talking to strangers, Alan Banks. A real learning experience. Thanks for the conversation. I'll leave you alone now."

"What about . . . ?"

"What?"

"You know."

"I suppose I've changed my mind. It was a mistake. My mistake. I thought I saw what I wanted, but I was mistaken. I'm sorry. I'm *really* sorry."

"Sure you are. You're really weird."

"Am I?"

"Trust me. You're weird."

"Odd, perhaps?"

"Most definitely!"

"Yes. Well, life's odd. I told you that at the beginning." Steve Wilson looked off into the city, at the sky, the cloudless blue sky; the sun ablaze overhead. "But it's still quite a nice day, unless you choose not to see it." He nodded to Alan and walked away.

"Fuck you," Alan mumbled under his breath. "This city sucks!"

L A W R E N C E   W.   C L O A K E

Scruff the Puff

CRUFF PEERS INTO THE BLACK BOWELS of the jaks buried deep beneath the pavement of Dublin's city streets. In the midday sanitized gloom, the public toilets are empty and cold. The tiled walls echo like Hades' cavern.

A long line of cubicles face a bank of patient urinals. Scruff picks a centre cubicle and slips into its narrow width, like a sentry taking his post. He drops his 501s around his ankles and eases himself onto the cold toilet seat. The graffiti-covered door has a crotch-level spy hole which some privacy-minded patron has bunged up with tissue.

Ears cocked, Scruff leans back against the cistern, reaches down with one hand and gently cups his balls. With his other hand he begins to stroke the slowly growing length of his dick.

Last night had started out so well. Scruff had been drinking alone at his favourite bar when a dark stranger approached him from the smoke-filled shadows.

"May I sit here?" asked the handsome stranger.

Scruff, enthralled by the man's liquid brown eyes, had stammered an affirmative. For the next two hours, Scruff and his companion had sat huddled together like conspirators, talking, laughing, drinking, and kissing. Scruff was sure he had met the man of his dreams.

Happy, horny, and bleary-eyed, they had staggered home together. Everything had been fine until they reached Scruff's flat.

They had stripped and tumbled together onto Scruff's narrow bed where they rolled, wrestled, groped and pinched, kissed and caressed until the moment of truth—the moment when Scruff had tried, unsuccessfully, to manoeuvre himself to the bottom position. While Scruff scrabbled for his rubbers and KY, his tall, dark stranger had rolled onto his back, placed his ankles behind his ears, and aimed the cavernous abyss of his arse heavenward.

Scruff groaned and rolled off the bed onto the floor, where he lay and bemoaned his cursed state—another night wasted on a big, brawling man-queen! The big bottom just lay there, waiting. What was Scruff to do?

Then Scruff remembered his present and started to giggle. Hidden beneath his bed lay a huge dildo that his best friend had given him for his birthday. He scrabbled under the bed until he found it, still in its wrapper, all covered in dust. He tore away the clear plastic wrapping, raised himself up, leaned over the edge of the bed and brandished the humongous rib-tickler.

"Will this do?" he asked, chuckling.

The dark Adonis opened his eyes, blinked twice, shrieked, leaped from the bed, grabbed his clothes and stormed out of the flat. What a night!

■ ■ ■

The shuffle of feet descending the tiled steps interrupts Scruff's reverie. Scruff's hand slows its movement around his now-hard shaft. He smiles, a shiver of delight coursing through his body. Scruff listens as the whispering feet roam the loo. Then, from beyond the cubicle door, a phlegmatic cough precedes the sound of piss tinkling against the tiles.

Eyes half closed, Scruff regards the door. The piece of tissue blocking the hole sparkles in pristine whiteness. Scruff splays his legs wide and slowly begins to masturbate again, wondering who is out there on the other side. He feels the toilet seat cut into his clenching buttocks as his arse and balls grind against the plastic rim.

The tissue plug pops from the spy hole and Scruff's gaze snaps suddenly back into focus. He watches it bounce once, roll, and come to a standstill near his feet. When he looks back up to the hole, he sees the glistening eye of the cough's owner, its rheumy pallor a clear sign of its owner's age. No lusty knight in shining armor here, either.

Scruff hears a light knocking and looks down again to see the man's left foot intrude beneath the door. For a moment, but only for a moment, he thinks about letting the old fella in.

In his imagination Scruff sees the door push back into the cubicle and the man slip in. The old man leans back against the door, revealing himself in all his cock-ringed and limp glory. He smiles a toothless smile and reaches out for Scruff's dick. Scruff stands and waits for the old git to go down on him. Then, with a practiced slurp, the old man takes Scruff's dick into his gaping maw. Scruff looks down at the balding pate beneath him. The old man sniffles through his nose while he slurps and licks around the shaft buried deep within his throat. Sighs of pleasure gurgle from his meat-filled mouth. Scruff feels his balls tighten as the impending tingle of orgasm races up his dick.

Scruff lets out a gasp of surprise as he shoots his load. He looks back at the spy hole, sees the eye retreat and hears the old man mutter, "Ya stingy bastard." Scruff shudders at the thought of the ancient flesh touching him.

After a few moments, Scruff stands, cleans himself quickly and leaves the jaks, guilt burning his already flushed face.

MICHAEL MacLENNAN

Coming Clean

IT'S LATE IN THE AFTERNOON, but the sun still rages on the decks outside as the cruise ship plies the Caribbean toward tomorrow's port-of-call. I'm weak from the heat of today's excursion which has left my fellow passengers wide-eyed and puffing, sweat soaking their camera straps. It's been hot, probably the hottest day I've ever known, but my skinny frame thrives in this torrid environment. I decide to push things further—sweat it out even longer before dressing for cocktails. So I find the ship's sauna—the men's sauna.

I push the door open to find a small dark room with one feeble light. Sitting under it is the drummer for the cruise ship's orchestra, reading a paperback. It's his break, I guess. I've watched him on stage each night as I sat alone sipping martinis in the Rosario Lounge. I've been fascinated by the bored, almost suffering look he has as he keeps time for the ensemble rendering big band tunes for the geriatrics around me.

I take small gasps of the sauna's searing air until I can breathe normally without coughing. I look at the drummer, smile a silent greeting, but he won't lift his eyes from the book. I steal glances across the bench, admiring his delicate sparrow's chest and small tight muscles. He must work out or eat like a bird to stay so lean amid the ship's constant feasting. He sits there unmoving, save for the syncopated staccato of his eyes that follow the lines on the page. He is naked, his thick penis limp, its tip just touching the bench between his legs which buttress him into the corner.

We are down so deep in the ship it feels as if the engine is beside us. Its muffled shivers throb through the wall into my back. I rest my head in my hands, catch my breath, and wipe the sweat that has begun to form on my forehead.

The drummer's body is slick with sweat. How long has he been in here? Why would anyone want to read in here of all places, dripping onto the pages, wrinkling and staining them with your sweat?

"Hot," I say. *Oh, good start.*

"Yeah," he says, his eyes never leaving the page.

I shift my back into the corner. The baked wood stings my skin. I urge him telepathically to look up, to see me, take me into his warm drummer's arms. He turns the page and sighs. I wilt into my hands and mournfully watch sweat pool in the crook of my arm.

When I look up again, he's absolutely still; even his eyes have stopped moving. Everything has stopped in that room except one thing: the bobbing of his cock as it slowly fills up and arcs hard onto his flat belly. I sit and watch his flesh grow rigid. He still doesn't look at me. He turns to face the wall, to stare at a knot while he spreads his legs at the knees, offering.

When I lick his stomach I taste slippery desire, breathe a scent like hot buttered cabbage. He takes my skull and massages my wet hair, firmly pressing me down. I inhale him deep, arousing a viscous saliva which covers his hard, urgent organ and mingles with sweat where the base of his cock meets his tight abdomen. He moans and lifts his narrow hips to my chin as I devour him, his shaven pubic hair a thistle against my lip. He bucks and moans and whispers words like promises to me. "Yes, yes, yes. . . ."

This is it, I think, as my parched throat takes him in deeper—hungrily, my hands seizing and scratching his slick, perfect ass: *I've found someone. He is mine, someone beautiful who will call my name and will desire—desire me as I desire him. For the rest of the cruise at least, for four more days I've found it, I've found him. . . .*

I hear his brief, astounded groans as his balls shrink into his pelvis and the hot bolts knock the back of my throat. I think, *Yes, I'm going to, I'm going to* . . . and I do. And in the shudder of my gulp, in his final shudder into me, he reaches, *please,* to touch me, barely. Barely. *No.* I stay small, drawn close up under him.

"That was great," he says. A slight drawl. His fingers stumble over my shoulders as I shift up, trying to reach his eyes, to meet him there. And when I see that won't happen, I settle for a look just to remember his face for a while.

He does give me a kiss. Our salts mingle and then mutely slip past one another, a tongueless kiss. He slowly hoists himself up from the bench.

He says, "Thanks—see you."

The door bounces twice on its spring. I catch glimpses of him through the small smeared window, slowly dressing. He doesn't even shower. My tongue plies my acrid mouth, parched and empty. Soon I stop looking out. But I can still smell him on me, just above my lip.

I stay in too long, until he is coming out of me, coming out of my pores, until the dead air around me smells of him. I stay in here, in the belly of this ship, until I am dry inside, sweating clear in a dark wooden box.

Heroes

ONCE THE EVILDOERS ARE INCARCERATED, *once the City has been patrolled several times over, once peace again reigns over your jurisdiction, when the threatening tsunamis have been waylaid, when the stylish girl reporter has yet again been rescued, when you're resting now in your hidden sanctuary, when all your responsibilities as a hero have been met, all that remains is. . . .*

You've always wanted to be a super-hero. Nothing fueled your pre-teen fantasies more than the sight of the muscle-bound do-gooders, clad in their bright colours and spandex, showing their every curve, every contour, every bulge. These men who were more than ordinary mortals, who were bound and gagged on a monthly basis in their very own comics, tortured by the sadistic villains, caught in deathtraps from which only their mighty powers and Holmes-like cunning could free them. With little imagination on your part, hot, erotic fantasies were played out in the pages of *Action, Adventure,* and *Detective Comics,* or through the orgiastic groupings to be found amongst the *Fantastic Four,* the *Justice League,* the *Avengers,* and the *Legion of Super-Heroes.*

You became a super-hero for the sex. Your mother wanted you to study accounting, but let's face it: how often does the average CPA get laid?

You straighten your crimson cape, adjust your utility belt, and decide it's time to head over to the after-hours club. The rest of the heroes will be congregating there. You then free yourself from the planet's gravitational pull and soar towards Supertown, the local hero ghetto.

As you descend, you hear the beat of a recent dance mix coming up from the club. Arriving at the entrance you check your cape and move through the steroid-pumped crowd to the bar, where you order a dark rum and coke and, leaning against the bar, survey your surroundings.

Across the bar you spot the Golden Hawk, as hot as ever with his sculptured physique, plumed half-helmet and wings strapped to his bare chest by a stunning leather harness. You saunter up to him and engage him in conversation. Soon your hands are all over each other, and your cheek brushes against his. You adjust your head slightly until your lips find his and you lock him in a kiss. It doesn't last long; he tastes of birdseed. Undaunted, you free yourself from his mouth and move up the side of his face to where his ear lies nestled under his feathered helmet—feathers that rapidly find their way into your mouth. Spitting them out you decide this isn't working and, making an excuse, you head back to the bar.

Looking around on your way, you see Superiorman. You would consider coming on to him, except that you've heard stories of his superiorsperm, ejaculated at superiorspeed during the height of or-gasm, doing terrible damage to his sexmates. The Scarlet Speedster leans against the bar close to where you are. You cross him off your list as well. Rumour goes that he has a terrible problem with premature ejaculation. Beside him, the Bulk flexes his unbeatable muscles, but people have told you that he has this wicked temper—don't make him angry—and besides, his cock, you're told, was the only part of him not affected by the gamma rays that made him the Bulk.

Sitting on a barstool at a table, his back towards you, you spot the Fledermaus, pointed ears on his cowl, cloak hanging down like huge bat wings. You move up to him from behind, wrap your arms around him and caress his muscled torso, feeling his every ripple beneath the silk-thin, skin-tight costume—and you discover he has no nipples. You feel for them again. None. Bizarre. It's no wonder he's taken to having them moulded into his rubber costumes in the movies.

You take a few steps back, squint and glance around at the other heroes close by who are topless: the Dark Condor, Nemo the Mariner, the Bulk, and even the Golden Hawk, who you can see clearly now that your eyes have fully adjusted to the dim lighting. All without nipples.

This is weird, but it kind of makes sense. Why hadn't you noticed this before? In all the comics you read as a youth, none of the super-heroes had nipples. Shit. You should have realized this right from the beginning. Well, you'll just have to cope.

But fuck, you're horny. Lieutenant Marvel stands at the other end of the bar, giving you the once-over with those Fred MacMurray eyes of his. You decide to go for it. You suggest that the two of you blow this joint, and grabbing your capes from the coat-check, you fly together to the roof of a nearby, abandoned building. You forego foreplay, getting down to the rough and tumble of super-sex. Two sets of spandex tights are rumpled beside you as Marvel demonstrates his prowess by giving you a god-like blowjob, simultaneously rummaging through your utility belt for a condom. Before long, he's behind you, holding you tight with the strength of Hercules, and you feel him filling you up. It doesn't take long for the Lieutenant to come, yelling out "Shazbot!" as he does. *Boom!* Lightning strikes at the sound of his magic word, and as soon as the smoke clears, you turn your head to see if he's all right. A twelve-year-old boy lays on your back, a look of bliss on his face.

This is too much. You grab your tights and fly back home.

Back at the Sanctuary, you come to the conclusion that super-hero sex may not be your speed after all. You consider switching your genre to war comics, or westerns. Perhaps Howard Cruse has an opening. Or maybe down at Archie Comics.

You always thought that Reggie Mantle was kind of cute. Hmmm.

. . .

DAVID MUELLER

Air Disasters

I AWAKE WITH A PAIN IN MY ASS and the startling, cream-coloured face of a French-Canadian refrigerator staring at me. Slowly the details fade in: its skin is marred and infested, crawling with magnets and photos of a kid named Jean. It occurs to me that I don't normally sleep in the kitchen.

"Christ!" I say to myself as young atheists sometimes do when they wake up in the wrong room in the wrong country.

There's more: it dawns on me I am unfucked, de-fucked in fact—my ass still tight and dick-hungry.

On my left the clock radio is giving off news of an exploding plane. On occasion the green sea of shivering cornstalks that stretches across the great crotch of this continent is pelted with fuselage, along with the tanned and Rolexed arms of marketing directors, or bits of tourists unsuccessfully returning from vacations in Anaheim. It's not a frequent occurrence, and it's not good for the corn, but it has been known to happen. And as it hits the 7,900-mile-wide clod of dirt below, it points out that air disasters really happen on the ground.

In the other room there's a man who will not kiss me, typing. That's a long story.

A shorter one is that I've just had this warm, piss-coloured dream that I was drinking back in San Francisco. I can still feel the night sky, wet and glowing amber. In my dream I'm talking to a smooth-chested dreamboy, who for some reason is wearing nothing but a pair of white spandex shorts. This is not something I would go for in a waking state so it must be fraught with deeper meaning. I'll have to look up "spandex" in the dream symbolism index.

"I was warned," I say to him, "but a week ago I got on a plane with a bag of my warmest clothes and a strange, distended e-crush for a man I knew through a keyboard and I swear by my 14.4 fax/modem that I'll never type again."

I empty my beer down my throat. "It made some gutsy sense at first, but somewhere over Kansas I realized that I wasn't in San Francisco anymore and began to sweat a little puddle into the sanitary seat cover, but then the plane hit the tarmac and there I was, abroad even—dumbstruck, dislocated, and full of senseless love for this guy who turned out to be not quite ugly."

My dreamboy somehow takes this as a cue to move closer. I move my hand up the back of his thigh and over his ass with a squeeze.

"So, what happened?" he asks.

"Well, I'll try and make it brief but picture this: a French-Canadian Tuesday passes. Two dinners go well. A hard, fast screw in an armchair and my thoughts drift towards expatriation. But somewhere in the gentle closing of my lips there's been a threatening tenderness, the desperate detail work they've done clinging to the curve of his ear. And hanging in the eyes there's been a slight, unforgivable sadness stabbing through the lusty leers. And then in tiny gestures I'd revealed the need, the vast necessity of those moments and the million more appended in my mind. And, well, that shit's just too much for mere men. Alarms go off, doors slam shut, his dick goes perma-limp, and he begins mumbling something about space. A trail of havoc stretched out inside of me."

"So what did you do?"

"I did what I had to: I started drinking like some kind of alcoholic fish on a bender. My recollection is a little warped but I remember standing in the rain on rue Sainte-Catherine holding my ninth Polar Beer screaming, 'Space! You want space! You'd think 43.8 percent of North America would be enough! I travelled 3,000 miles,' etc. etc. It was stupid. I don't think our neighbours to the North have the same taste for schlocky melodrama. I felt like Carmen Maura in a Bergman film. It soon became clear I had no choice but to fire the casting director and start over. So I ran off alone. I ended up at a leather bar standing on a stool, singing along to 'Super Freak' and drowning as much of my my self-pity as I could before loss of consciousness. Then I fell off the stool and into the arms of some big daddy who kept calling me *cochon*, which I think was a compliment. I must've had a good time and for all I know I got laid even. Yeah that! Or maybe I just walked around for a while until I found my way back to what's-his-name's apartment. I'm not sure, actually."

Dreamboy gives my nipple a tweak. He's really very cute and I feel this immediate warmth and connection with him. He slides off his spandex shorts and moves around in back of me kissing my neck gently and folding me in his arms. His dick is starting to stiffen against my ass. "I'm gonna fuck you," he says, and no sooner, he's got me down on the floor and he's pounding into me like all the dick I ever wanted; that's when I woke up in the kitchen.

Cigar Angel

IT WAS HARD NOT TO STARE. Everything about him seemed larger than life. I'm sure he caught me a couple of times, gazing at his basket. The bulge between his thick thighs seemed ready to burst through the thinning denim.

He sat directly across from where I worked behind the counter. Every twenty minutes he'd order another coffee. He had been there for the last two hours.

He was older than me. My guess would be late thirties, early forties. He was handsome, large, very tall. Six-four, easily. He had a stern look on his face. Not mean, but stern. His salt and pepper hair was shortly cropped, bristly—as was the bushy moustache that crowned his ruddy, full, and sensuous mouth.

His hands were godly, with thick digits, and cushion palms—real paws.

The lit cigar he held was the largest I've ever seen. It was wrapped in heavy green leaves with vascular streams gracing the top in ornamental detail. It trailed a thick, milky fog. I figured his prick must be as large as that cigar; it was so proportionate to the size of his towering body.

He rarely put the smouldering phallus down, but when he did, the uncircumcised end was drowning in spittle. He'd leave the stogie only seconds in the ashtray, then he'd notice me staring and whisk it back into his mouth, rolling the tip across his steak-rare tongue. He smiled for the first time in one of these moments.

The vision of this cigar-puffing daddyanimal had my cock going. Luckily, my burgeoning tent was concealed behind the counter where I shamelessly humped and pushed it to its extreme. As I watched, I could feel my cock pulsate—radiate energy into space. It ached.

He sent ring after ring of smoke sailing into the air. They gyrated like crazy compasses in all directions at once. Some of them would hover above my head—Havana halos of smoke that would fade slowly, sink around my neck, and with a final wisp seem to strangle me, leaving me breathless, wanting more.

I wanted to touch my cock so badly, longed to set it free, out into the smoky room, but feared that if I did that I would somehow break the spell—cast this religious experience into ruin. So I just gazed into his eyes that now looked back steadily and deeper into mine. I knew he knew exactly how I was feeling.

He frowned slightly. A pout pursed his lips—brought my hormones to heel. I willed my hands away from temptation and folded them reverently on the counter. I was his.

Every time I tried to break from his stare, tried to shift my body sideways, or focus my eyes elsewhere, a mesmerizing stench would flood my nostrils. I couldn't be sure if it was his cigar or him, but that smell, wave upon wave of invisible molecules of lust, held me firmly rooted where I stood, gulping for air.

Still holding me in his gaze, the man dropped his smouldering cigar into the ashtray, rose slowly, and ambled towards the counter. The closer he approached, the more I wanted to avert my tearing eyes—but I couldn't.

Was he going to say something? Would he give me his phone number?

In that split-second, the spell snapped. I tumbled back into reality. Fell from grace. Just at the moment an angel of ecstasy had been ready to rain blessings more than I could imagine or endure, I had wanted his phone number? What blasphemy!

When we were face to face he reached deep into his pocket, dropped some loose change into my tip bowl, then without a word disappeared through the door out into the brittle winter night.

I stood transfixed, staring at the door for a few more seconds then, exhausted, staggered toward the still-smoking relic waiting in the ashtray.

Puppy Love

WANNA PLAY CATCH? You game?"

He pants—whimpers.

"Good puppy! Now let's just move my jock over to the side. There you go! Don't touch it, not yet, just look at it. Study it, yeah, look at the power puppy, nice big boner for you to slobber. Watch me flex . . . . Wait, look. Whoa yeah, look at that! Look how it just bobs and twitches in front of your face. Yeah, you like that puppy, you're my puppy, you're such a good boy! Gives me a kiss, yeah that's my boy. What's that? You want my jock, you want it? Here it is, here you go boy. Fetch! Go get it, go get it. Bring it back here. Good puppy. Here boy, here. Let me have it. Here, here, bring it here."

"Grrrrrrrrr!"

"Let it go."

"Grrrrrrrrr!"

"Yeah, yeah you love that jock, don'tcha boy! Whoops! Where'd it go? Where'd it go, boy, find it! Go find it! Oh you think I still have it, do you? Smart puppy. Look. Look, here it is! No. No. Sit. Sit. Stay. I said stay. Don't move. Good boy. I'm gonna hang these straps off my dick. Stay. Yeah, that's my puppy, whimper. Whimper for my dick. Yeah, it's okay. I understand."

I take my dick, circle it around the kid's mouth, smack it into my palm. "Stay," I order, hold it down and release. It slaps my stomach. The kid goes crazy.

"What? What do you want, puppy? Oh, you want that big drop of pre-cum, don'tcha? Yeah, look at it just hang there. Whew, yeah, open your mouth. Stick out your tongue. Pant. C'mon boy, pant! Let me hear you. What's that? Speak! Speak! That's my boy! Good pup! Just a lick. Just that drop. There you go!"

The kid, so obedient his tongue barely swipes the head of my prick, expertly retrieves his reward. A strand of fluid momentarily connects us. I flex my cock. The fluid cord breaks.

"Remember how to play Catch? Good boy. Go get your leash!"

He should remember. Catch is basically me swinging my dick in front of his face, while the kid's tied to a rad trying to reach for and catch the head. I won't let him touch it unless I see his entire body strain for a taste. Usually he's beet-red, eyes bulging, in a puddle from the sweat. The kid loves it. Last time, he popped his lips off my prick for nearly an hour before I shot in his face. Better make sure his water dish is fresh.

"What's the matter, you're not tired, are you, puppy? Reach for it."

After ten minutes, I'm bored. I'm standing as close as I can to his lips, just a fraction out of reach, bobbing my head ever so slightly to coax his tongue that extra inch to release. The kid's working hard and is hard as a rock. I keep disciplining him to take breaks, lap some water, build up gradually, not wear himself out too fast. I know it's work, believe me, I did my own strict time as a cock slave puppy. But it shouldn't be all work. It must be pleasurable, unpredictable, exhilarating. Time to change the game.

"Do you wanna be a puppy? Or do you wanna be my baby boy?"

Ah, that's what I thought. The kid loves being a big baby for my big dick. I first clued into this when he started making these gurgling sounds over the pouch of my jock. I laid him out onto a towel on his back next to my gym bag, then knelt over his face, t-shirt hanging off my dick. "Where's Billy? Where'd Billy go? I can't see him anywhere, where'd Billy go? Peek-a-boo! Ah, there you are."

The kid laughs, staring up at my dick like some big toy.

"So big! Soooooooo BIG!" The kid covers his face, hides, waits for me to find him again. "Peek-a-boo! There's my big boy." Eventually my balls replace the shirt. And repeat ad infinity. "Where'd you go?" I grab the talc out of my bag, sprinkling some on the kid's crotch and bum, caressing him while he drools. He begins to sob. I go to move, but the kid stops me and continues to cry and sob over my dick. I hold the back of his head and stroke myself off as he buries his wet face. My cock softens, calms him. He shifts back and forth between nursing my foreskin and hovelling beneath my balls.

"Kneel. Stay. Give me your arms. That's my boy. Yeah, time to teach you something new. A new game. Would you like that puppy? Good. I'm just gonna take your leash and tie your hands behind your back."

In the bath, I'm his uncle. The kid's brought over these washable soap markers to draw all over my cock and body. I have a big purple head, red shaft with blue highlights, and green balls. I paint his face and nipples. I take pictures of my calico cock over his clownish girlface. He wants to play Up Periscope as my head surfaces through the foam.

"We're gonna play Ring-toss. You ever play Ring-toss before in school? Good. Okay, well these are the rules. You stay right there on your knees and I'm gonna stand over here a coupla feet away from you. When I say 'go,' I want your mouth to reach for my dick until you start to fall forward and try to catch yourself on my cock. Got it? I want you to feel the power of my cock and body hold you up by your throat. You won't hit the floor, I promise—that is, if you catch my dick. Ready? Set. . . ."

We've been meeting on and off for a couple of years now. I'd say he's about thirty-six, probably in business, maybe design. Says he loves what we do together. Means a lot to him. He'd like to "go public." Serve me in front of a group of guys, in a toilet perhaps—that is, if I think he's good enough. I like his devotion.

The kid's mouth is wide open, determined—with a look I've never seen before—a mixture of joy and panic as he starts to fall.

C H A D   O W E N S

Willingness for Sale

OR THREE HOURS I WATCHED HIM, trying to work up my nerve. A kid, really, couldn't have been more than eighteen or nineteen—young and slim. The fact that he would suck any man off, no matter who they were or what they looked like, was what made him so tempting.

An executive type stopped to talk to him, looking over his shoulder every few seconds nervously. The kid nodded, leading him toward the alley. Unable to resist, I repositioned myself, and caught sight of them between a dumpster and the dirty bricks of some building wall.

The guy already had his cock out, pushing it at the kid's face. I was close enough to see the lips part, the foreskin pulled back from the head. The kid leaned forward and took it into his mouth.

Watching seemed worse than doing it myself, but it made me incredibly hard. My hand was in my pocket, clenching my money, and pushing up against my erection, trying to relieve some of the ache.

The executive suddenly pushed forward, shoving his cock deep into the kids mouth, down into his throat. I could tell he was coming, saw the kid swallowing, before pulling away and wiping the traces of the sperm from his face with the back of his arm.

As the kid took the money, he glanced in my direction. I quickly looked away, but what I had seen on his face embarrassed me. He knew exactly what I was up to, that I was too scared to approach yet.

When I looked back, he was adding the twenty to a wad of money.

I wondered how many blowjobs that amounted to, what else he had done to make it.

A man pulled up in a car. The kid got in. My gut clenched, afraid he'd disappear and I'd never find him again. But then they pulled into the alley, and I took up my vantage point not more than ten yards away, gripping the corner of the building while his head bobbed up and down in the man's lap.

I could hear the groans, saw him playing with the kid's cock as he watched his own getting sucked. The kid let him, knowing if he did, the guy would come that much quicker. He came up, more cum streaks on his lips, took his money, and got out.

The third that night wanted more. At first I thought it was just another blowjob. The kid went down to his knees, started sucking the man's cock. But then he got up and turned around.

I watched, confused, until he undid his own jeans and dropped them over his ass. My cock throbbed as the man pulled apart the stark white buttocks in front of him and shoved his cock in between. It took him a moment to get the angle right. I saw the expression on his face as he penetrated the tiny orifice, then started thrusting with long, deep strokes.

Once again my cock responded. This time I reached into my pants and rubbed myself openly, no longer caring who might see. The kid visibly gritted his teeth as he pushed back against the thrusts. He whispered encouragements, asking the guy if he was going to come in his ass, telling him how good it felt having it shoved up into his bowels.

The thrusts came faster, harder. The kid bucked against them, determined to get him off. When the guy came, relief washed over the kid's face. He waited until the cock dwindled in his ass before pulling off of it.

This time when he looked at me, I couldn't look away. My cock hurt too much. I was too desperate for what he offered.

He made no move to come out of the alley. I approached, but when I came up to him, couldn't bring myself to ask.

My mind fumbled for something to say. I came up with, "How old are you?"

"How old do you want me to be?"

My cock throbbed painfully in response to his young voice, the willingness in it. His hand reached out, making me jump as he touched it, squeezing, encouraging its growth. Anything to get me to take my cock out, to let him suck it. To get the money.

"How much?"

"What do you want?"

I wanted what I'd watched the last do, to bend him over, stick my cock in his ass. I just couldn't get the words out.

"Twenty," he said, seeing that I was too nervous to answer.

I pulled out the money, handed him a twenty. He took it, dropped to his knees, undid my jeans.

The ecstasy that hit the moment his lips touched my cock caused my body to jerk. He slid down my shaft without hesitancy, his tongue pressing against the vein, teasing it. His fingers squeezed the base, jerking me off at the same time.

He looked up at me then, and the sight of my cock buried in his mouth caused my body to shudder and my hips to twitch. Encouraged by my response, he started sucking harder, holding my gaze.

I wanted to sustain it, to keep watching and feeling him sucking my cock, but he didn't let me. He sensed I was close, forced himself down my entire length. His mouth and throat tightened around me as he struggled not to gag, and I lost it, gripping his head in ecstasy as the first ejaculation hit.

He swallowed the first stream of cum, quickly backed off for the second and let it squirt onto his tongue. My cock twitched and jerked, flooding his mouth with sperm. When my body finally relaxed, he let me slip from his mouth, not caring that some of my cum dribbled down his lips.

It was all part of the hustle.

I left quickly, nervously, afraid someone had seen. But I knew I'd be back. What he offered none of my boyfriends could, a willingness that could be bought. And the thrill of taking advantage of it.

Sneakers

BART: CUTE. **NOT CLASSICALLY GOOD-LOOKING,** but cute, very, very cute. What, twenty-five? Not too tall, not too well-built. Blond Dutch-boy bob. Wire-rimmed glasses. Broad smile, too-big teeth. Not just boyish, which was Steve's style, but mildly effeminate, which wasn't. Still. . . .

Steve: Leatherman. Late thirties. Big. Butch. Buff. Bearded. Buzz-cut. Handsome. Hairy. Which wasn't Bart's style. Still. . . .

Still, Steve found himself wanting that cute, femmy blond boy. He didn't quite know why. Youth? Innocence? Vulnerability? Didn't much matter. He wanted him. So he made the first move. Chatted him up in the lobby of the Castro Theatre. And Bart found himself agreeing to ditch his friends after the movie and meet Steve on the corner of Castro and 17th.

They made quite a pair standing there. The big guy in black jeans, black leather jacket, motorcycle cap. Black-leather, knee-high boots. And the blond kid with limp wrists in baggy shorts and t-shirt, white socks, red low-top sneakers.

In a few minutes, Bart was on the back of Steve's big BMW, headed for Pacific Heights. It was his first time on a motorcycle. The chilly wind ruffled his long hair. At times like this, the helmet law didn't count for much. He snuggled his swelling crotch up against Steve's butt.

All of Bart's apartment could have fit into Steve's dungeon. Bart glanced around at the display of costly floggers on the wall, the polished St. Andrew's cross in the corner, the leather-topped bondage table.

Steve figured it turned the kid on.

"You like leather, Bart?"

"I'm a vegetarian. Don't wear leather."

"But you like these boots, don't you, boy? You want to get down on your knees and service these big, black boots?"

Bart smiled. Big white teeth. "Not as much as you want to get down on all fours and service these sneakers . . ."

"Huh?"

" . . . right, daddy?" Bart grabbed the hard-on in his shorts.

Steve just stood there. Because, by damn, the kid was right . . .

"I said *down on all fours,* daddy."

. . . the kid was fucking right.

Steve hit the floor.

"Kiss my sneakers, daddy. Kiss 'em."

Steve nuzzled the canvas. The faintly sour smell of sweaty sneakers filled his nostrils.

"I said *kiss 'em!*"

Steve kissed the canvas. He ran his tongue over the red sneakers, leaving a dark trail of saliva. He tongued the cold metal grommets, then the laces. The thick rubber toepiece became slick with spit. He worshipped the Boy's sneakers. His dick was throbbing hard.

"You like those sneakers, daddy?"

"Yes, I do."

"That's 'Yes, I do, *Boy.'*"

"Yes, I do, Boy. I'm sorry, Boy."

"That's better. Now roll my socks down and lick my ankles."

Steve ran his cheek down the golden hair on Bart's leg, licked and kissed his ankles, burrowed his nose inside the Boy's white socks like a pig rooting for truffles.

"Okay, daddy. Untie the laces. With your teeth."

Eagerly, the big leatherman did as he was told.

"You want these sneakers, daddy?"

"Yes, Boy."

Bart stepped out of his red sneakers. The smell of sweaty feet hit Steve full force. He buried his face in Bart's feet, rubbing his black beard against the Boy's damp white socks.

"What do you think of your Boy now, daddy?"

Steve looked up at the blond Boy. He opened his mouth wide. Bart smiled down at him and slid a musky, moist foot between Steve's lips.

"You're gonna suck on your Boy's toes good, daddy." And the muscular leatherman did. He sucked the toes real good, 'til the bulky white athletic sock was wringing wet with spit.

Why the fuck was he doing this? What had brought him down to his knees? Oh well, like they say, "Hard dicks don't lie."

"And now, for being such a good, good daddy, you can have your Boy's sneakers." The Boy grinned. Big white teeth.

Bart knelt, picked up a red sneaker, unlaced it partway down. He opened it out, pulled down the tongue, and jammed the open sneaker over Steve's nose and mouth. He pulled the laces around Steve's head and, tying a big bow, tightened his shoe up against Steve's face. The leatherman breathed in the musky, intoxicating smell of the canvas, the rubber, the blond Boy's foot.

"Stay there on all fours, daddy." And Bart took the other sneaker and brought it down on the leatherman's hairy butt. Not too hard. But hard enough. Steve gasped. Gasped in air from Bart's red sneaker. It was better than a bong. Better than a bottle of poppers. Better than being a top.

A couple more whacks on the butt.

"What's that, daddy?"

Steve's voice was muffled. "More . . . please . . . Boy."

But instead of whacking daddy's butt, Bart reached between Steve's big, muscular thighs, grabbed hold of Steve's big, hard dick, and wrapped the sneaker's lace around the base of daddy's dick, tying it off and letting the sneaker dangle like a perverted pendulum. The leatherman's cock got even harder, bulging purple.

"Now watch this, daddy. Watch your Boy." The smelly sneaker came off Steve's face. He looked up. The boy was standing above him, hard golden Boydick in one hand, open red sneaker in the other. Bart stroked his dick slowly, deliberately, a big shit-eating Boygrin on his pretty Boyface.

"You like this, daddy? You like your sneakerboy's boner?"

"Yes, Boy."

"And you're hungry, daddy?"

"Yes, Boy. I am."

Harder stroking, faster. And cum flowed, thick and hot, from Bart's piss-slit. Straight into the red low-top sneaker. Bart knelt down and set the open sneaker before the leatherman. And Steve stuck his face deep into the shoe and tongued every trace of salty cum from the smelly canvas insole.

Lapped up the cum like a hungry pussybottom, like the fagdog pervert he knew, deep down, he was. There was no way around it: he cherished that hunger. Hungry for sneakers. Hungry for Boy.

"Yum," said Steve.

"That's 'Yum, *Sir,*'" said Bart, still hard, grinning broadly with his big, white teeth.

Good Head is
Hard to Come By

I DON'T KNOW HOW OTHER GUYS DO THIS. Could this kill me? The heat? It don't seem natural to breathe air that's this fuckin' hot. But if this is how I'm gonna go, fuck it, I'll go. It'd beat going back to that fuckin' office. Sometimes I think I only took that job because it was so close. And they wonder why I'm better in the afternoon.

"Oh, don't stop that, please."

This dude is making me crazy. I didn't know lips could do what these are doing on my shaft. He's gotta be a pro. Gotta be. Else he's missed his fuckin' calling. If I don't come soon, this is gonna make my head explode. The mouth expanding and shutting as he makes his way down the full length don't seem natural. Seems like maybe he's some freak of nature. How the hell does he control his breathing when it's gotta be a hundred degrees in this fuckin' cube?

"Pinch my tit."

Somebody opens the door. The movement on my cock stops. The new guy slides along the tile shelf to the corner. I can barely see him through the thick hot mist filling the room. I'm straining to get a look at his piece while the guy who's been suckin' me off keeps playin' with the head of my cock to keep me ready. There's another burst from the spigot and the cloud gets even more dense. The new guy has slid another foot closer. Sly fuck. Like we aren't gonna know he's trying to get in on the action. Now, I'm feeling his toes on my thigh. A hell of a courtship. I give Wonder Mouth a pat on the ass and his head falls back into my lap. I reach forward in the fog and take hold of New Boy's

116

nine inches of steel and give him a few off-handed strokes. His legs shoot open and his pelvis rises from the dripping tiles. This guy's a real slut. He'd let me fuck him right here in public if I wanted. I'm tempted. Real tempted. But, why would I want to give up the best fuckin' head I've had in years for just another probe in some guy's ass? Ass is cheap these days. Good head is hard to come by.

"Oh, man, you are the best."

New Boy has his mouth at my chest and is giving my nipples a good workout with his teeth. I don't know who taught him biting was a good thing. It's making me wanna slap him off. But I let him 'cause it's keeping me from shootin' my load too soon. I can barely keep my mind on keepin' his cock happy. I'm lost in the pleasure of Wonder Mouth, who seems to have fallen in love with my cock. I slide a finger up New Boy's bung hole and he quivers like he's already reached his peak. Knowing how some guys are about getting fucked, I know New Boy is just gettin' started. He's advertising the kind of ride he'd give my dick if I would be so kind as to place it inside that snapping asshole of his. I give him three on my left hand and start to finger fuck him.

"Oh, shit, this is it."

I don't know how it crept up on me. But suddenly I'm pulling Wonder Mouth up by the hair. He's given out a cry of pain and disappointment and my load is bouncin' off his chin. New Boy is playing in the mess and using it to lather up his own cock. Both these guys are gonna be pissed in a second when I get my legs working. I've got a one o'clock meeting and I can't wait around to finish them off. I hate being late and time flies in a steamroom. The way this place operates, they'll be here same time tomorrow.

Sucking is Not Permitted

THE SIGN SAID IT plainly. SUCKING IS NOT PERMITTED. There was one in every cubicle. I got into mine, undressed, and waited. The door had been drilled, so there was a large eyehole near the top. Also, the light, kept dim, had to be on at all times. Those were the rules. I had not been to a place like this in a decade, but I was in a strange city in a strange place and I had heard about it through the local gay rag. It was a short drive from the hotel where I was staying, one of those business hotels with an atrium and real, caged birds in it, but nothing else was real, not even the air. I was on business myself. I'm a salesman for a New York publishing house, which means I deal with books, a strange commodity nowadays in the I-never-read generation. I can't tell you how many kids I've met in post-urbia land—which is almost every place now—who tell me that. Or they'll ask me about my favourite author and look lost when I don't mention Danielle Steele or Stephen King.

New York had closed all its bathhouses, and everyone was pretending to give up bath sex, like you were only supposed to make it with respectable men who might on a sunnier day be your business partners. I was not interested in a business partner. But the sign was really a scream. As funny as the place itself—called The Quarters. It was actually part of a cinderblock off-the-road strip mall. Other occupants included a hairdresser, what looked like the only "adult" bookstore in a hundred-mile radius, and an "alternative music" shop, which meant loud sounds and teenagers with pierced tongues.

So getting out of the rental car and coming into this place was no sweat, even feeling as queer as I did here in white bread country, where even "Banana Republic" sounded flatout sexy. At the desk, behind bulletproof glass, I gave the man my license to show him I was from out of town—it's run as a club—and paid him and he gave me a clean towel. The lighting in the halls was very retro-'70s: bathhouse-pink; dim. Everybody looked fetal. The music was regulation *dreck*—too loud, too disco. But this was what I wanted; you pays your money and takes—

For a second, I wondered what the chances were of me catching something here. No sucking, obviously no anal stuff. Maybe a little kissing, if I'm really lucky. A guy came to my door. He was built nicely; medium height; plain, corn-fed, middle-American features that New Yorkers lust for and then become bored with. I nodded for him to come in. "New here?" I told him I was—just passing through. He smiled. The new boy in class gets attention. He pulled off his towel and was, by the attention he was showing below, ready. I tried to turn off the light. "Uh-uh," he said. "That stays on. They have guys who walk around to make sure your light is on and that there's no—"

"Sucking?"

"Yeah. That."

He got onto the narrow cot and we started stroking each other. I found his neck sexy—smooth, muscular, strong. My mouth hit it, but he pulled away when I tried to kiss him. "No kissing, either?" I asked. He got up and walked out, like I had mentioned his mother. A few minutes later another man came in. He was older and getting paunchy, but smiled a lot, which I liked. We started again, stroking and pulling at various parts. I put my mouth next to his and he had no problems with that. We went into some very deep kissing. I got very hot and for a moment control was difficult. He yanked me up from a southern direction. "They're strict here," he warned. "They'll throw you out if they catch you doing something against the rules." I asked him if we could go someplace else—my hotel? "No . . . wife." I understood that; she was probably busy at Banana Republic. Then he got up. "Gotta leave. It's too close in here."

I looked up as he disappeared. Then a face peered through the door hole. "Everything okay?" I told him it was: "Just dandy!" The face left. Several other men came in. Each stayed only a few minutes; each began a certain amount of foreplay that stopped—frustrating the hell out of me. I noticed that the length of each stay shortened, like I was a cab driver charging ever more per short trip. Finally, a trim, black-haired young man came in. He was scrumptiously pretty. He took off his towel and started with me, then got up, too. I grabbed his arm. "Why does everybody jump out of here?"

He shrugged, then said, "We know you're from out of town. I guess everybody's scared you'll bring us something we don't want."

I let him go. Other men approached and I just shook my head. It had all come down to this—fear. There was nothing left except that. This was not "safe" anything—it was more dangerous than sucking; than fucking without a rubber. The sheer, numbing, faceless fear of it. "It." Or *me*? Was I so obviously a spy from the outside? I got up and dressed myself. "No, I never read," I remembered a kid saying in a bar in Houston. "Seems like a waste of time. I'd rather watch TV, at least you learn something." Sure, I thought: what *they* want you to know. Now I felt like *I* was the virus. An alien retro-thing—infecting everybody with something much deeper, and troubling, something from outside.

Paranoia

HE CALLS WHEN YOU LEAST EXPECT, while you're "entertaining yourself," and it takes several minutes to clear Mr. Grey
Turtleneck from your mind and recognize who you're talking to—"We
met at a conference—I gave you my card, remember?"—and you do
remember, because you put the card in the people-I-don't-expect-to-
see-again pile, among cocktail napkins smeared with illegible names,
unused matchbooks, postcards ripped in half, an entire heap of men
you didn't have the heart to throw away, yes, he's in there, even though
it's futile to document every single person who's approached you since
you swore off sex *for good*, citing heartache, too many close encounters
of the wrong kind: wrong place, wrong person, wrong situation, wrong
reason, a series of mistakes (and one big mistake) leading to the
iron-clad promise that this last time would be *the last time*—you meant
it, too, can't be too careful nowadays, psychopaths everywhere, but if
you recall correctly, he looked more sociology professor than so-
ciopath: brown, short-cropped hair, oval glasses hinting intellectual-
ism, the trimmed beard of an aloof hipster—introductory chatter
revealed someone you would have liked to have known better; you
remember the way he pushed his glasses up the bridge of his nose with
his thumb, his stuttering while talking to you—this after delivering a
speech on the latest theory on developmental linguistics—and you
wonder why you didn't call him before—oh, that's right, your no-sex
rule—but he's not asking for sex, just a date on Thursday, your "reruns
and pizza" night gladly interrupted by his arrival—he's wearing those

glasses, a goofy grin, and his turtleneck feels soft against your neck as he hugs you, awkwardly, before launching into the "What do you want to do/I don't know, what do you want to do?" conversation, when he remembers, Damn! he forgot his coat at his apartment, maybe his wallet, some pretext to get you back to his place, where he urges you to "Make yourself comfortable," and "Relax for a bit," clearing a space next to him on the couch, inviting you to sit and massaging your shoulders, his hands sliding under your shirt and across your back, his breath behind one ear, then the other as you turn to say, "Wait," but his lips catch the word mid-utterance, holding you there; after your fingers fumble through belt loops and buttonholes, pulling elastic bands out and down, clothes collecting clothes on the floor, suckling him pacifies you, a soothing insistence that it feels good, that you're doing right—he reaches over to reciprocate, but the angle is wrong, and you don't want to relinquish this warm spot between his thighs, his hair on either leg brushing against your body as he tries different approaches, almost writhing, until he settles back and relegates him- self to rubbing your scalp, fingertips stroking your temples in a soft, calming motion, until—boom!—it happens, catches you off-guard, no warning gasp, no shudder, and before you have time to assess the situation, you're swallowing, gulping air (and burping later, surely) while trying to get it down your esophagus, all of it, ignoring the taste—nothing at all like your last boyfriend's, a flavour you allowed so long ago, it seems, to linger on your tongue, all those months ago, seven to be exact, back when you were *in love*, before it turned sour, never fully disappearing even six months to the day after breaking up, when, after swallowing your pride, you tested negative—but all this swallowing makes your cheeks hurt, and, mouth gone dry, you avoid kissing him, since you don't remember the last time you brushed, but he holds you anyway, eyes closed, as if he's ready to fall asleep, at which point you pull away and dress, hoping that your inner monk immo- lating will cause your stomach to work overtime, when, as if on cue, he perks up and asks, "So what do you want to eat tonight?"—a simple enough question, but given your circumstance, you shrug, allowing him to decide on an Indian restaurant, where, like the ceramic ele- phants holding miniature palm trees on their backs, the hollow, upraised trunks feeding into the soil, you drink water as if your life depended on it, as if you had just survived a trek through the Thar

PARANOIA

Desert, letting the water filter through the gaps in your teeth and, later, calling the waiter to refill your glass, because you'd ordered the spiciest items on the menu so that the peppers and curries could strengthen your gastrointestinal juices, ending up, however, fanning your mouth between sips of water—he finds your intolerance of hot peppers amusing, but that's only because he thinks he knows what, *for now*, is going into his mouth, the consequences—heartburn—coming later, maybe sooner, because you already feel it welling up inside your chest, too much worrying, perhaps, but you maintain control of your bodily functions long enough to refrain from belching when kissing him good-night or when he insists you call him—you already know you won't, not without some sort of reassurance that you can't find alone back in your apartment, where, before the bathroom mirror, lips pulled back like a corpse's rictus, you have trouble recognizing your own mouth: gums with unfamiliar dips and valleys, a tongue jaundiced from curry, fillings that look like cavities; out of habit, you brush—scour, really—rinsing the foam dripping off your bottom lip, then sawing around each tooth with cinnamon floss, dislodging leftovers, remnants, traces; the taste makes you spit, and in doing so, you curse yourself, because, even though the floss was a good idea at the time, mouth tasting clean and minty-fresh, there are red streaks in your saliva—you watch it slide down the bone-white porcelain, into the drain—and you can't tell whether those streaks are cinnamon-flavoured dyes—or blood.

Part of
the Problem

AFTER DINNER HE TOOK ME back to his place, a large house in an affluent area with a view of the city. The entrance, on the back side, led to a large, open concept living room, with window seats, an adjacent dining room and kitchen. Stairs led down to the bedrooms, den and yard. It reminded me of the pseudo Frank Lloyd Wright creation in "A Summer Place." The house that Arthur Kennedy and Dorothy McGuire move into once they marry. It had all the spaciousness and feel of a very fine 1950s design, but the decor was a hodgepodge of antiques, real antiques, and Danish Modern.

"I've been trying to update everything to the feel of the architecture, but the cost of fifties furniture has skyrocketed."

We stood in the living room overlooking the flickering of distant city lights. Julian undid his fly, took out his penis and turned towards me. I dropped down on my knees and crawled to him, reaching for his cock.

"What are you doing?" he asked, somewhat shocked.

"Going down on you. I'm going to put your cock in my mouth." What sort of question was that? Didn't we come back here for sex?

"I'm going to the bathroom," he said. "I've got to take a piss. That's why I've got my cock out." He walked across the living room, with his cock out and ready, leaving me on all fours, telling me to make myself comfortable and to help myself to a drink. There was a bar in the living room. Like, who has a bar anymore? I crawled over. There was some green Chartreuse open. I always wondered what Chartreuse tasted like, so I poured myself two fingers. It poured out thick and syrupy. It tasted awful.

Julian returned to the living room with his penis in his pants. He took me by the hand and we went downstairs to one of the bedrooms. I was wondering whether we would have sex in his bedroom or the sex bedroom, presuming of course he must have multiple bedrooms in such a big house, and I wondered if he was going to play the tease again by pulling his dick out in front of me and then walking away.

We went into a large bedroom, collapsed on the mattress, and began having sex with our clothes on, like in the movies. Like in the movies where the man screws the woman with his pants on. (How many times have I cursed Hollywood directors for undressing leading ladies and giving us no leading male butt.) First we rolled around in our clothes, but as we started to unbutton our shirts they got twisted around us until eventually we had to sit up and take them off properly. We went back to hugging and kissing and rubbing until my cock was pushing up out of my boxers and through the tops of my khakis. Julian's erection was going down the side of his left leg. I started to undo his jeans, which were button-fly, but it was difficult. He pushed my hand away, grabbed me by the legs, threw my legs into the air, and pressed his hard cock against my butt as though to rape me. But we were still dressed, so he tried undoing my belt, which seemed to be stuck, or too tight to loosen in this contorted position. Again, we stopped what we were doing. He left me in that awkward, vulnerable position, with my legs upright, over my head, to pull down his jeans. As I rolled my legs back down I heard a slight crunch in my hip and a shooting pain coursed across my right side. Age and versatility were catching up to me. Lack of versatility, I should say. I should have done a warm-up for sex. That's not in the manuals, that's not something Camille Paglia has ever talked about. I stood up and struggled out of my khakis, but Julian just lay sideways on the bed, half-undressed, too excited to get up I guess. His cock was bulging out of his jockeys. I lay down beside him and we began to kiss, shoving our tongues down each other's throat. I pushed his jeans down to his ankles with my toes—I still had my socks on—and as I did so they bunched up in a knot, tangled over his feet. He shoved me backward, pinned me onto the bed, ran his tongue around my neck and down to my nipples. This was erotic, but I could feel the denim at his ankles scratching my legs, and the pressure of one of the metal rivets pushing into my calf as he straddled me, pressing his body against mine. It was then I realized with his full weight against my gut, that I was going to pass gas. The Chartreuse was upsetting my stomach. God knows what my breath was like. With considerable effort I pushed him off, rolled him over face down, and struggled to completely pull off his jeans. I was clenching my buttocks tight, stifling the inevitable. What a hazardous second date.

I lay down on his back and rubbed my cock up against the crack of his ass. With the pressure off my gut I felt much more at ease. But I now smelled, clearly, the odour from his armpits that I'd only noticed faintly before. It was sweat pure and simple, but an unusual sweaty smell, not markedly offensive, sort of like sweet roots, like the steam off boiled sweet potatoes or turnips. With my nose up against his pit I began to wonder if his crotch would also be, well, er, neglected. I am not into the rank odour of sweaty shit slits. Maybe he was into smelly guys and fetid foreplay, or maybe he just forgot to shower. With hesitation I began the trek down his back. Preparing for the worst I pulled his ass up in the air, doggy style, and grabbed his erection so that it came back through his legs. The flavour note below was decidedly different than above. His groin was seductive and fresh, with the air of a commercial soap—the sort of soap you would imagine having a green colour, a fern or forest or fresh type smell, and then it occurred to me that he probably had a wash in the bidet before coming out, but not a shower.

Julian reacted negatively, however, to me pulling his erection upside down. He removed my hand, rolled over and positioned himself underneath me, sort of in a sixty-nine, but awkwardly—comfortable sixty-nine requires two people of not only equal height, but of equal proportion. We had similar bodies in height, but he had longer legs than I, and consequently had to sit up partially to get his mouth near my cock and balls, which hung over him like baubles on a charm bracelet.

"Are you not into this?" he asked.

What did he mean, I thought to myself, pulling my tongue off his balls and scanning his attractive lean flesh. Then it hit me. I realized I'd lost my erection. I'd lost it thinking about his sweat and his smell and worrying that his crotch would turn me off, and paying too much attention to the scrape on my legs and the indent the rivet left on my calf and the way my hip felt after he shoved my legs in the air.

"I'm having a great time. This is hot. I don't know what happened." I tried to say, "This is hot," in a sexy way, but it came out affected. I do my best gay impressions without even trying. No doubt Julian thought he'd dragged home Siegfried. Or Roy. He bent forward and pulled my head to his mouth.

"I've been thinking about this all night, and I'd really like to fuck you."

Oh Jesus, how could I tell him? When it comes to fucking I'm a bit like the Peking Duck in a Chinese restaurant: I need twenty-four hours' notice.

"Well, uh, how about you fuck me in the mouth?" I asked rather hopefully, using the negotiating skill gleaned from my Peace and Conflict course.

"Lovely," he replied, with seeming sincerity. Applied knowledge, I thought, it's rescued me I don't know how many times.

Julian makes a lot of noise while having sex, so I'm sure he missed the two or three belches of Chartreuse residual during his orgasm. As it turned out his cum—which I swallowed, which may be unsafe sex, but there you go, life has its unsafe moments—his cum was a welcome digestive after that indigestible liqueur. He rolled over afterward like an archetypal straight male, with no concern for my needs or my now very hard cock, and fell asleep. Fast asleep. So I let out the gas I'd been holding in and stayed the night hoping for morning sex.

Warren

THE PLACE WHERE THIS GUY WARREN LIVED was just like you'd expect it to be: a dark, rundown, flea-bag place that smelled like piss and old men. But I guess I've been in worse places. And anyway, he'd sounded okay on the phone. I mean, he didn't sound crazy or anything, like he might cut me up or try something kinky on me.

So I go on up the narrow stairs to number twelve like he said. You never know what you'll find when these guys open the door for you, but I've learned not to expect a lot. Sometimes, though, the guy will be pretty hot. Like maybe he's just a regular guy caught in some bad shit and doing this until things start looking up again.

Anyway, I'm feeling pretty dangerous. I stopped in at Buck's and had a few after work. It was pretty dead there so I picked up one of those papers with the ads in the back and that's how I found out about Warren. His "free massage" didn't sound too bad so I called him from the pay phone at Buck's. Pretty soon I'm at his door, number twelve, and his locks are snapping open on the other side, one by one, four in all.

Like I said, I didn't expect much. It's dark in the hallway, but I can see he's not much to look at. His ad said he was thirty-seven, but he looks older. He's pale and thin and wears glasses, thick and gold-rimmed, making his grey eyes look huge.

I go, Warren? He nods and seems real nervous. He lets me in and I figure right there I'll just stay a few minutes then make some excuse about not feeling up for a massage after all. Something. So I motion to one of his two chairs and go, You mind if I sit?

He shrugs and I sit down. He just stands there watching me. I notice he swallows a lot too. I'm thinking I could use a shot right now and ask him what he has to drink. From a closet he takes out a half-gone pint of whiskey and a plastic cup. He hands them to me and I go, What about you, Warren?

He goes, No. You go ahead.

So I pour myself a shot and drink it. On the street below, a woman is singing. Every couple seconds, the neon sign outside his window blue-splatters ROOMS and WEEKLY RATES across bare, yellowed walls. A bed is pushed to one corner and a few odd tables around the room hold knick-knacks and pictures Warren cut out of magazines and placed in little frames. The smell takes some getting used to. It is the smell of a place the same person spends a lot of time in. It's hot in Warren's room. I pour a second shot and drink it down.

Finally, I hear myself say, You have a table or do we use the bed?

Warren looks at me funny and goes, A table?

I go, You know—a massage table. The reason I'm here, remember? He goes, Oh.

He goes, No. I don't have one of those. He was really nervous.

I go, Most guys charge for a massage. How come you do it for free? He goes, Well, I've never done one before. You're the first one.

I stand and walk over to the window. I go, You mind if I open this and let a little air in here?

He goes, I don't know if it'll open, but you can try.

It takes a few hard pulls, but finally the windows slides up with a loud shudder. The thin curtain puffs up in the sudden rush of air and the room seems to puff up right along with it, filling with street sounds and music. I turn and look at Warren. He is looking at me in this way that makes me think it wouldn't do any harm to stay a little while and give him some company. I don't have anything else to do on this particular night. So I go, Warren? What would you like me to do?

He swallows hard. I go, Would you like me to undress?

I don't wait for his answer. I pull off my jacket and lay it across the chair. He watches while I remove the rest of my clothes, slowly and deliberately, first my t-shirt, then my shoes and socks and finally my jeans. Standing in front of him in my briefs, I can't figure it out. I'm a little nervous now too. I mean, I've done this kind of thing a hundred times, but I'm not sure if I should pull off my briefs. The blue neon is flashing across us. I can hear Warren breathing and swallowing. He is looking at me like no man has ever looked at me before. The woman on the street is singing. The whiskey in my gut burns. It is midnight, and I am a thousand miles from everywhere, waiting.

J U S T I N   C H I N

Death of
a John

I T WAS ALL A HORRIBLE ACCIDENT, of course. There was this
john called Bob Smith—really, it was Smith, I checked—that I see
on a regular basis. This was our meeting night and when I went over,
Bob was in a great state of excitement. He had just obtained a new toy.
Came in the mail that afternoon, he told me excitedly as he ushered
me into the room. We don't waste our time with silly formalities of
trying to be cordial and coy about why we're in each other's company.
It's beer from the fridge, clink of bottle, one good swig, and off to the
bedroom.

And there it was, lying amidst its carton and brown mail wrappings
in the middle of the bed: the Flesh Toned 5-Speed King Dong Super
Dildo Deluxe. But more than that, Bob, being an engineer and a
buttfuck enthusiast, had souped up the Flesh Toned 5-Speed King
Dong Super Dildo Deluxe. No more four "C" batteries, the Flesh Toned
5-Speed King Dong Super Dildo Deluxe was now one lean mean highly
charged AC socket power plugger.

Well, everything was going fine, but in the middle of the session,
Bob had to go take a beer piss. He got out of bed and waddled to the
bathroom with the Flesh Toned 5-Speed King Dong Super Dildo Deluxe
still firmly tucked into his anus. He was talking to me from the
bathroom and I guess he said *unplug* but somehow I thought he said
buttplug. The next thing I knew, there was this loud spark, the lights
in the room blinked evilly and there was a heavy thud in the bathroom.
Bob had fried himself on the can with the Flesh Toned 5-Speed King

131

Dong Super Dildo Deluxe. When you have the Flesh Toned 5-Speed King Dong Super Dildo Deluxe in your arse, you have to sit to piss, I guess.

With the benefit of hindsight, I guess it may have been my fault. After all, I should have known that he said *unplug* and not *buttplug*, because quite simply, if you have the Flesh Toned 5-Speed King Dong Super Dildo Deluxe in you, why on earth would you need a buttplug? It's like going out for a damp McDonald's hamburger when you have your boyfriend cooking filet mignon with a tarragon pepper sauce for you at home. Stupid stupid stupid. I should have known.

I wiped off what few fingerprints I had in the place, an easy task because I was wearing rubber gloves for most part of that sordid, unfortunate evening. Then I sat on the sofa, finished my beer at a leisurely pace, watched some cable TV, and left. At least Bob Smith died kind of happy, which is more than what some people can ever hope for. Cheers, Bob, this one's on the house.

Robbery

OUT **A BIT TOO LATE**, I plop down on the couch for a snooze. Later, I awake to the sound of someone going through my things. I sit up, turn on the lamp, find a boy standing in my living room, my VCR in his arms. He jumps at the click of the lamp like a child caught with a cigarette. "Fuck!" he says. Tall, olive-skinned, t-shirt, jeans, belt, sneakers. Hair girl-long in the back, moustache starting.

"I didn't hear you come in," I say, feigning a smile. His eyes scan the room for an exit, the front door wide open in the foyer. I rise from the sofa before he can get any ideas, turn his chin toward me, kiss him flat on his rough mouth. He swallows, hanging onto my VCR like a life raft.

"I—I—" he goes, eyes trapped and dark.

"When did you get here?"

"Uh—"

"Were you planning on taking that up to your room?"

"Uh—"

"If you wanted to watch videos you could have just done it, I wouldn't have minded. You know what a heavy sleeper I am."

"Uh-huh." Nice voice; masculine, resonant.

"Aw, come here, baby—" I take the VCR away from him, and place it on the coffee table. "Give your daddy some sugar."

He stands there like a statue as I grip his neck and kiss his cute young face. His lips don't move.

"Why, baby, you're all uptight. Something the matter?"

"Uh, yeah."

"Come over to the couch and tell me about it," I say, pushing him by the chest until he falls backwards on the cushions. I step out of my pants, pull my shirt over my head, walk over to the foyer, slam the door shut, and turn the lock.

Last time I forget to lock that goddamn door.

I climb onto the cushions, dick swelling branch-like in my shorts. He shrinks against the opposite arm of the couch.

"Come on, baby. Let me make it all better. You've been away for weeks." I yank him horizontal by the belt, then peel off his scrap of a t-shirt.

He has a sour, nervous smell. He moans as I tongue his sternum, nipples tough as raisins. His hands push against my shoulders to keep me at bay.

"I'm going to think you don't like me anymore if you don't give it to me. You wouldn't want me to get mean, would you?"

"Unh-unh."

"Well, then." I unbuckle his belt, shuck his jeans right down to his knees, his big hard cock flopping up against his navel.

"See, I knew you wanted it." I lever it up by the base, thinking Christ Mary Joseph and all the saints, but not out loud, and stick the whole thing in my mouth and hum with pleasure. I gobble and jack, gobble and jack. He's going, "Aw, fuck, man!" and writhing against the cushions. I pop it out of my mouth—"That's right, baby, talk dirty"—then lean down and lick his crotch from crack to sack.

"Oh, you—*fuck!*"

"You've done something bad. Now I get to punish you for it." Hugging ass and hips to my face, cock buried deep in my throat, I roll off the sofa with him. I'm on the floor, on my back, underneath him, sucking upwards. He gets up on his hands and knees, panting and desperate, a fucking motion coming natural to him. I peel off then kick away my own shorts, let his wet cock flop out of my mouth then scramble underneath him to hook my knees around his neck.

"Come on, baby. Let's do it nasty."

"Oh, no, no, no—"

"Oh, yes, yes, yes. You came here, let's finish what you've started," I say, getting that wet cock of his lined up with my butthole.

When he doesn't co-operate, I give him a few solid whacks to the ass like I mean business; then I lean all the way back, tugging down on his neck with my ankles, and push my hole at him just right 'til he pops in and gasps. He's all the way inside me now, moving it around before he even knows what's happening.

"That's right, baby, fuck your daddy."

He's up on his toes, trying to bring it off fast like a bunny. I yell "Ow!," yank on his long hair, and scooch along the floor to align his cock so it doesn't kink up but just goes straight in. I lay back and become wide for him. He's thrusting good now, then suddenly it gets real slick; he tenses up, quivers, turns his head away, grimaces: "Aw, fuck!"

He's laid out face-first on the floor, breathing still heavy but subsiding. I get his pants back up around his hips, sit there and stroke that dark hair gently like the good daddy he thinks I am; then when I see his eyes haven't opened for several minutes, I get up, go into my bedroom, pick up the telephone, and dial 911.

The Proselyte

THE BELL IS LOUD. Very loud.

And it's early. Very early.

Why does the alarm clock go off so early?

Especially on Sunday. Sunday?

Sheesh! It's not the alarm, it's the doorbell!

I hit the buzzer to open the front door and grab a robe so that I can offer at least the appearance of modesty. Opening my apartment door, I hear an unfamiliar voice.

"I'm here with good news from the Lord!"

A goddamned revivalist! Golden blond hair, cornflower blue eyes, engaging grin, slender body with an ill-fitting suit and a crooked tie. Who was his designer, Norman Rockwell?

"I knew God would send me to a receptive home. Have you been saved?"

"Well, the lifeguard pulled me out of the lake at camp."

Polite laughter. At least he's diplomatic. "No, brother, I mean saved for all eternity. Have you given yourself to Jesus?"

"Not that I know of." After all, I don't get a business card from every trick.

"Oh, you'd know it! Giving yourself to Jesus gives you a great big load of joy!"

My turn to be diplomatic. "Why don't you come in?"

Sweeping the leather pants and red bikini briefs off the couch, I invite him to take off his jacket and sit down. "Would you like some coffee?"

"I . . . I'd like that," he decides. The sun streaming through the windows seems to recharge his godly batteries. "Days like this make me feel so close to the Lord! His creation all aglow in the light of His blessed sun." I go into the kitchen while he continues to exult. The hypnotic rhythm of his speech starts to turn me on. Just to keep him talking, I ask, "Are you one of the champion soul-savers?"

"Saving souls isn't a contest! It's the duty of every Christian to prepare all mankind for the judgment to come. Womankind, too!" He must have just spotted the *Village Voice*. Wonder what he makes of *Honcho*. "We all need to reach out to one another in love."

My cock is beginning to reach out through my open robe. I arrange the coffee cups on a tray and walk into the living room, wondering how my guest will react. But he is searching through his briefcase.

"There's a wonderful article here," he bellows, assuming that I'm still in the kitchen. "I can leave this . . ." Turning around, he finds my groin at eye-level.

"Cream and sugar?"

"Ye . . . uh . . . yes, thank you."

"What was that article about?" Leaning over to see, I press my body against his and place a casual hand on his now-bulging crotch.

"It's a powerful testimony by a man who lived in sin for years, just like . . . just like so many of us—until the day a messenger came to save him."

"And you're my messenger?" I place a fraternal arm around his shoulder, resisting the temptation to kiss the pink curve of his ear.

"I . . . I may be. That's for the Lord to decide."

"I see." I begin to playfully undo his tie. "Why do you run around in so many clothes in this hot weather?"

"I always dress proper, to show respect."

"In my house, people show their respect by dressing comfortably." I begin to unbutton his shirt. He makes no effort to stop me. No undershirt. A well-muscled chest, light peach fuzz, then a gym rat's stomach. "You must work very hard," I observe, stroking his breast-bone, his navel, stomach, stopping at the belt buckle. He's focussing very intently on my conversational lead.

"I work in the printing plant," he explained. "It's an honour and a privilege to do the Lord's work. I've been dreaming of this—doing the Lord's work—since I was eight years old and the preacher took me in his arms to baptize me. I knew back then what I really wanted." His tightening grip on the arm and the back of the couch heighten the definition of his pecs.

I open his belt buckle, but his eyes focus on the windows, the bookcase, the stereo, the coffee cups—everywhere but my face. "Do you have any friends back at the dorm?"

"I have a friend in Jesus!" This platitude comes with unexpected vehemence. I gently open his fly and release its treasure from white cotton briefs. Uncut, tall, pale, and handsome. I kneel on the floor and take it in my mouth.

"The Lord is my shepherd, I shall not want." He begins so quietly I can hardly hear him. "He leadeth me beside the still waters. He annointeth my head with oil." A pause here, for breath. "He prepareth a table before me in the presence of mine enemies. He restoreth my soul. Yeah, though I walk through the valley of the shadow of death, I shall fear no evil." Another breath. Two. Three. "Thy rod and thy staff, they comfort me. Surely . . . surely . . . surely . . . *surely . . . surely . . .*"

Warm, salty, and plentiful. It will take the rest of the coffee to wash this down.

He jumps up, knocking me against the coffee table. He zips up, grabs his jacket, and bolts for the door. Figuring out the locks slows him for a moment.

"Didn't you like the coffee?" I ask, noticing his untouched cup. "I can make tea or cocoa if you want."

He finally succeeds in opening the door and runs down the stairs. "Come again," I call after him, unsure if he understands my words are not just a polite cliché. "We hardly had a chance to talk!"

J. R. G. DE MARCO

Enthralled

SIMON WAS ENTHRALLED. He had never imagined that his computer could bring him into contact with the type of men he desired. Two weeks before, Adonis II, the man of his fantasies, the man he had waited for these thirty-five years, appeared through the online service. Adonis II, whose real name was Anthony, was an art-loving, poetry-quoting dream of a man. Italian, short, only twenty-seven, and in decently average shape, Adonis II was everything Simon longed for; there was even an electronic picture to confirm it all. Anthony loved the ancient poets like Theocritus and Catullus and could even quote them; the words of Lorca, O'Hara and Pasolini also tripped lightly through the ether to Simon's screen. All their chats were dream-like and beautiful. When the time had come to speak on the telephone, Simon fell in love all over again with Anthony's resonant voice; he seemed shy and reluctant, even coy. And so they planned to meet.

Simon was cautioned by his friends to meet on neutral ground, but dismissed their concern and ignored their warnings. He put on his new yellow shirt, the one with the faint green pattern; bought a colourful bouquet of flowers and chose a book of verse wrapped in pink foil paper.

Anthony's apartment building, looking as if it had seen better days, gave Simon an uneasy feeling. Ignoring it, he pressed the buzzer and was admitted. Cooking smells and cat litter odour accompanied him through the halls. This was certainly not the apartment building he had imagined as the home of Anthony, lover of words.

He knocked and the door opened almost too quickly. This was not the Anthony of the electronic photograph. Simon wanted to drop the flowers and turn away, but, feeling obliged to be polite, he smiled. This man could indeed have been twenty-seven; but twenty-seven years hung on his out-of-shape frame like two-hundred-twenty-seven. As he continued studying his host, Simon noted other discrepancies. Anthony was taller, six feet five inches or more, not the compact Italian figure he had boasted. He wore nothing but a leather harness connected to a leather jockstrap nearly hidden by the overlap of hairy, unappealing beer gut. Anthony also had a tattoo, which, if it had been small and tasteful, would not have bothered Simon. Anthony's tattoo covered his entire right arm from wrist to shoulder then arched over his back in thick and muddy blue, red, and green. When Anthony turned to lead the way in, Simon saw that the tattoo was a huge boa constrictor slithering down his back; its head, sporting beady, evil eyes, pointed to Anthony's flabby ass. The snake's forked tongue licked the very beginning of the crack and seemed to flicker delightedly when Anthony moved.

When the door slammed behind Simon, Anthony smiled. Two of his front teeth were missing. His eyes were bloodshot, his face unshaven, and his skin was pitted like the moon's surface. This was definitely not the man in the picture.

Simon managed a weak smile, while quickly but unsuccessfully trying to hide the flowers behind his back.

"For me?" Anthony grabbed around Simon's waist and took them. "Lovely colours," he said. "Reminds me of some artist or other. I don't have my book here or I could tell you which one. It's easier when I'm on the computer, I can look things up as we chat."

Simon felt his heart sink even further at this.

Then, tossing the flowers across the room, Anthony grabbed Simon and squeezed him to his chest. Overwhelmed by the giant's embrace, the wind went out of him and he found himself staring into Anthony's ruined smile. Simon fought the panic he felt and attempted to wriggle free. It was a vise-like grip that nothing short of a few good kicks to the groin would break. He decided to try diplomacy.

"Anthony, you're too strong for me. How about a little talk before—y'know." He tried winking and felt a tear forming. Anthony winked back and, carrying Simon, moved to the bedroom. Simon's breathing was laboured, squashed as he was; his feet dangled inches from the floor while his mind raced, looking for a way out.

At the foot of the bed, Anthony deftly tossed Simon onto the king-sized, rubber-sheeted surface. Simon bounced; his head felt as if he were being rolled down a hill in a barrel. When his vision cleared, he saw Anthony approach and just managed to jump up as his would-be friend hopped onto the bed bearing silvery handcuffs.

Bounding off the bed, Simon made it quickly to the bedroom door before Anthony could get to his feet.

"There are two tragedies in life. One is not to get your heart's desire," he said; it was the voice Simon had fallen for on the telephone.

Now he's quoting Shaw, Simon thought and hesitated just a second too long. He heard the bed squeak behind him and as he regained his senses, he tried to open the door. Before he could turn the knob he felt the metal and heard the click of the silvery handcuffs as they encircled his wrist.

"The other tragedy," Anthony breathed into Simon's ear, "is to get your heart's desire."

C H A R L E S   L.   R O S S

Paperboy

I'T'S FIVE O'CLOCK IN THE MORNING and I'm sitting—na-ked—at my computer. The monitor casts an eerie light reflected in the chrome clamps pinching my nipples. A leather cord connects the clamps to my erect cock: every time my dick moves it pulls the clamps, sending joyful pain to my tits. My erection is so hard the head of my dick hits the underside of my desk.

The desk is in a bay window. No curtains. Anyone could look in and see my nakedness, but my neighbours are asleep. I slap my cock against the front of the desk, each whack tingling my nipples. My balls get rounder and more solid. I savagely pull on them and my cockhead responds by enlarging even more. I am so hot I would like to stand up and shoot my load against the window pane. But I am waiting for the yellow Volkswagen.

Pre-cum oozes out of my pisshole, glistening in the radiation. Suddenly, twin headlights turn onto my street. I hear the thump, thump, thump as the young man in the yellow Volkswagen tosses newspapers on the lawns of neighbours on the opposite side of the road from my house. Thump. Thump. Thump.

He U-turns at the corner and tosses papers toward homes on my side of the road. I walk into the night air wearing only black boots. I stand in my driveway so that a streetlamp shines on my eight-inch cock. Thump. Thump.

The Volkswagen headlights go out. As I walk to the curb the car pulls up next to me. Only the instrument panel lights the boy. He is good-looking, just eighteen. His blond hair is cropped above his ears, but long, thick strands fall over his forehead. He is not wearing a shirt on this summer night, and his jeans are crunched below his knees. He has no chest hair, but a thick mass of blond pubes surrounds his hard cock. It is not big, yet pretty with its pale pink head. It looks virginal, as though it's not been up any dark holes or inside any wet mouths. But we both know we are not here tonight to service his penis.

I stick my cock into his waiting mouth. He caresses the head, biting the loose skin underneath. He is young but sucks like a pro. He teases my dick until I am out of control and ram it down his throat. It's what he wanted all along. I fuck his face, my balls slapping his chin. As my breath quickens, he yanks the leather cord stretching my nipples almost beyond endurance.

I look around, stimulated by the scene: I stand naked in the street; at any moment someone could look out a window and see us, or a car could approach, exposing us with its harsh headlights. The boy slurps my meat like a favourite piece of candy. I arch my back and slip my cock free before shooting semen across his tanned chest.

He rubs my cum on his dick. His excitement is so intense he only needs a few strokes before his juices mix with mine. He closes his eyes, takes a deep breath, and exhales.

Then he flashes me a sly smile, hands me my newspaper, and moves on.

Thump. Thump. Thump.

ALLEN   BORCHERDING

Truck-Driving Man

THE ENTIRE CAB SHUDDERS as the diesel engine cranks once, twice, then fires. It settles into a pulsing vibration that spreads up my thighs, back, and into my chest. I alternately watch his leg as it flexes and extends, pumping the clutch in, out, then in again, and his dark forearm, where the taut muscles contract successively as he yanks on the gear shift. The rig eases out of the lot.

This guy I just met, Chet, acts embarrassed about driving us back to his place in the cab of an eighteen-wheeler. He makes his living hauling freight up and down the coast, and tells me he heads south tomorrow, once he gets his load.

Gets his load off, is what I think and start chuckling to myself. But I stop abruptly because I've got the sort of buzz going where I'm not quite sure what stays inside my head and what comes out my mouth.

"It's a little weird driving this to the bars," he says apologetically. But then, he has no idea he's rolled right out of my fantasy archives.

This one dates back to when I was about twenty-two and for months and months dreamt day and night of making it with a trucker. For a time I pursued it ardently. First by periodic visits to highway waysides where everyone knew that legions of broad-backed, moustached brutes, with mammoth biceps and swollen crotches fought like gladiators for the honour of pleasuring someone like me. But whenever I positioned myself in an "invitation only" stall for two, a steady stream of vacationing families would begin arriving with droves of kids who played for hours in the sinks and punched the hand drier until it neared meltdown.

As my frustrated desire gnawed away, I became more daring. I would refuse sleep for thirty-six hours, skip shaving—what little difference that made back then—and smoke half a pack of Luckies on the way to a local truck stop, where, looking, I thought, convincingly road weary, I'd saunter up to the attendant and inquire about use of the trucker's shower.

Whether driving a powder-blue Ford Pinto gave me away or what, I never knew, but "Them's reserved for the truckers, boy," was the most polite response I ever got. So I never soaped down any burly chest, thick with dusty, coarse hair, nor crawled into a sleeping compartment with some driver steeped in caffeine and testosterone.

Where all around us, in those days, boys played in costume—policeman, soldier, construction worker, cowboy—no one I met approached the authenticity I craved. Subsequent fantasies buried that one. And it might have stayed buried had I not ended up on a barstool next to Chet.

I begin the evening with a delightful, potent joint that puts me in a blissful, lava lamp state of mind, where every thought takes on heightened poignancy and imagination outpaces reality. A couple of bracing gin and tonics keeps the buzz going. A third comes unsolicited, sliding down the bar, trailed by Chet's infectious grin.

We fall into a graceful, effortless conversation, one that turns tactile with growing familiarity. Soon we are grabbing arms, nudging shoulders, squeezing knees.

The hours left until closing evaporate. I blather on while my brain begins inventing circumstances to privatize this party. Then I feel Chet's forearm on my shoulder. He fingers my collar as if to straighten it, clamps his hand on the back of my neck and pulls my mouth to his.

"Let's get out of here," he says, in a voice raspy from shouting over the bar din. I squeeze his knee between mine. He slides from the stool, riding his crotch over my leg. I foam with desire. As I follow him out, I notice in his hip pocket a zippered wallet, chained to a belt loop. But I assume nothing. Outside he hooks a finger on my waistband and pulls me close.

"I'm at a motel," he says. "It isn't far." He turns to face me, hugs my waist and presses his thighs tight against mine. I ache. "Hope you don't mind what I'm driving." We open hinge-like and round the corner of the building. I follow his gaze to the far side of the lot where it falls on the cab of a White Freightliner. The dust rolls off my fantasy and I am twenty-two again, in pursuit of my trucker.

He boosts me into the cab with both hands on my ass. We sit high and erect above the rows of cars, the air inside a smear of grease and smoke, dust and miles of asphalt. My bones vibrate from the throbbing engine. As we accelerate onto the highway, the throbbing evens into a powerful, steady drone.

He slows and turns onto a frontage road. The motel driveway is narrow and winds tight under a low overhang. I close my eyes, lean back and began to imagine what's to come. I see Chet sweaty, stripped and supine on the taut white bed sheet. The blankets are pulled free of their moorings and entwined between our legs. My chest presses against his. I pin his arms overhead, suck the air from his lungs. The truck lurches as he downshifts, slowing almost to a standstill. My cock swells under the taut web of my jeans and pokes itself along my left leg.

We inch ahead with emphatic thrusts. Each jerk of the cab strokes me, and my pelvis amplifies the rhythm. My breathing quickens. I brace myself against the edge of the seat, losing all awareness, save that of my groin. The truck pushes deeper under the overhang, nudges ahead again and again. One long pull forward and I shoot hard. I gasp for breath, then shudder.

The truck brakes suddenly. My head flies forward, eyes spring open. Sheepishly, I turn and look to my left. Chet stares. His mouth falls open, eyes widen. "Goddamn," he mutters. With a puff of exhaust, my fantasy dissipates into the night air. He punches in the clutch and grinds the transmission into reverse.

Logger Sex

THERE'S A SLIGHT BREEZE blowing in through the cab window, cooling off some of the sweat I've been working up. It ain't the only thing blowing. I reach up and stretch, locking my fingers together, and pull my knees wider apart. They can only go so far with my jeans down around my ankles. I look down at the back of Eddy's head, watching it twist back and forth as I fuck his mouth with long, slow strokes. "Hell, Eddy," I laugh. "I do believe you're getting bald."

Eddy stops his sucking and looks up, still holding my cock in his hand. He gives me one of his easy, good ol' boy smiles. "You should be careful what you say to me while your dick's in my mouth," he growls.

I grin. "Sorry. Didn't mean to break your stride." I scratch my beard and settle back into the truck's seat. "Go ahead. Don't let me stop you."

Eddy's blue eyes gleam. I swear, somewhere back in Eddy's family tree some great-granddaddy must have fucked a wolf, 'cause I can see the family resemblance now. He slowly runs his tongue up the length of my dickmeat, sucking gently on the head, tonguing my cum slit. It always excites the hell out of me watching my dickmeat pump the face of a man as handsome as Eddy. Without any warning, he plunges down, swallowing all eight and a half inches. I feel the softness of Eddy's beard press down against my low-hangers. Up and down his mouth goes, his tongue wrapping around my dick, squeezing it, caressing it. Sweet Jesus, can that boy suck cock! It's one of his most endearing qualities. I look up at the cab's roof, letting the sensations

147

sweep over me, and start giving out some mighty groans to show Eddy my appreciation.

Eddy's sucking on my balls now, first the left one, then the right, rolling each one around in his mouth, while he strokes my fuckstick slowly. He's humping his fist with the same, even tempo, and I reach down to give him a helping hand. His dickmeat is slick with spit and precum and slides in and out of my hand as easy as butter on a hot skillet.

My other hand rubs and strokes across Eddy's chest, feeling those pumped-up hard pecs and the soft fur that covers them. I grab his left nipple between thumb and forefinger and squeeze hard. Eddy, his mouth full of my balls, grunts his approval, and I slap the back of his head. "Didn't your mama never teach you not to talk with your mouth full?" I grin. Eddy laughs and I pull his face up to mine, shoving my tongue deep into his mouth.

Eddy rolls over on top of me, and his muscular arms wrap around me in a powerful bear hug. I feel his hard flesh pressed tight against mine, the sweaty skin sliding back and forth across my chest, his thick dick dry humping my belly. I breathe in the strong man-smell of Eddy's sweat; we've both just gotten off an eight hour shift of logging redwoods and we reek. I work a finger into Eddy's tight bunghole with excruciating slowness, up to the third knuckle. My finger is encased in warm velvet. I wiggle it, pushing against the prostate, and Eddy goes fucking crazy, thrashing around in the cab, squirming against me, groaning loud enough to wake the dead. This boy needs a serious fucking.

Still kissing Eddy, I pull my finger out of his ass and grope in the glove compartment for a condom. I roll one down my shaft, Eddy shifts his hips up, and we resume playing dueling tongues as I slowly impale him. I fuck Eddy with short, quick thrusts, and he pumps his hips to meet me, matching me stroke for stroke. My hand's wrapped around Eddy's thick shaft, jerking him off like there's hell to pay.

Fucking in the front seat of a truck cab ain't the most comfortable way to get off. Eddy's head is bent down to keep from bumping the roof, and the stick shift keeps hitting me in the leg. But neither of us is complaining. I settle into a steady rhythm of plowing ass, Eddy's face just inches away from mine. I look deep into those wild blue eyes, and he stares back at me, his eyes narrowed in concentration, his lips pulled back into a soundless snarl. A low, half-whimper comes out of his mouth, and then another. I spit in my hand and continue stroking his dickmeat. The whimper turns into a long, trailing groan. I stroke faster now, and he groans again, loud. I squeeze his nipple and that does the trick. Eddy arches his back, and his body begins shuddering as he shoots his load. The first squirt gets me right in the face, just below my left eye. The next two hit me on the chin. Eddy's bellowing like a damn bull-moose, and the squirts just keep on a-coming. I'm soaked with the stuff before he's done.

I shove my dick once more hard up its entire length into Eddy's ass and that does the trick for me. I groan loudly, and Eddy plants his mouth roughly on top of mine. He tongues me damn well down to my throat as my jizz shoots into the condom up his ass. There's a lot of thrashing about, a lot of crashing into ashtrays and door handles, until finally, things quiet down. Eddy softly licks his cum off my face as I lay back, eyes closed, feeling the late afternoon breeze blow in through the window. I can hear the leaves outside rustling, and, farther off in the distance, the buzz of the chain saws of the afternoon shift.

After a few minutes, Eddy pushes himself up. "I gotta take a leak," he says, and climbs out of the cab. I watch him lazily, admiring his fine, tight ass, as he stands on the road edge buck naked and pisses down the hillside.

Protein Shake

I PEELED THE SINGLET FROM MY BODY, a red singlet now crimson with sweat. Pumped up to perfection, I took a moment to admire my hard work in the full glare of the studio lights. The mirrored walls in the gym reflected back firm pecs, bulging biceps, and a washboard stomach. I allowed myself a satisfied grin. Pushing those last few sets had paid off. Another week and then the big competition. I'd been working up to this one for months but tonight there was no anxiety. Tonight I was brimming with confidence as I gathered up my gear and headed off to the changing room.

I'd expected to find it empty. It was late and, as usual, I made the most of late closing hours. But tonight, as I opened the door, I was met by the glorious sight of naked, hairy buttocks. Jeff, the owner and chief trainer, looked back over his shoulder.

"Pretty heavy workout tonight, Tom?"

"Yeah, I guess you could say that," I replied, as I started to strip alongside him.

Fresh from the shower, Jeff stood with his back to me, towelling himself dry. I stole a look at him, admiring his stocky muscularity. He must have been around fifty, but was in prime condition. Years of body building had given him a really well proportioned torso, big shoulders and arms, massive pecs, a broad, well-defined back, and great legs. As I was looking and admiring this hairy vision, he suddenly turned around to say something and caught me looking at him.

"Not bad for an old man, eh?" he said, smiling.

"No, sir, not bad at all," I said appreciatively. He really was a fine specimen, I thought as I headed off to the showers.

I was busily soaping myself up when I felt a tap on my shoulder. It was Jeff, standing there bare bollocked and holding out a can of Bud.

"Thirsty?" he asked, looking me straight in the eye.

After the initial shock wore off, I nodded.

"Me too," he winked impishly, looking me up and down. "Looks as if all that work is paying off nicely," he said, as he ran a hand over my back and the ridge of my shoulder. "Great muscle definition."

"Thanks," I said appreciatively, slugging on my can. "My muscles sure feel tender."

"That so? Need a back rub?"

His big, tough hands didn't wait for a reply. They spread over my back and began to grind into my flesh. I was surprised as his palms curved around my buttocks. I quivered with excitement but made no move. He reached around to stroke my tits before turning me round to face him. My prick was up and throbbing.

"This need a massage too?" he asked, as he knelt down to take the head between his full lips.

I could feel his rough tongue pressing up against the length of my dick as it inched towards the back of his throat.

Instantly, a surge like electricity jolted me. From deep down inside, somewhere between my asshole and my balls, a rush of pent-up excitement leapt up and out, escaping from my lips in a low moan. My entire body, in a state of shock, focussed solely on getting the spunk out of my balls and into the soft, wet hole before me. The surge grew more insistent and I began to pant—my hips thrusting and my hands grabbing onto Jeff's head, plunging my cock into his mouth with an urgency tempered only by the sweet tormenting ache that wanted this moment to last forever. Then came the first sizeable tremor; my head arched back and I let out a howl of mixed pleasure and anguish as my prick began to pulse.

The first shot was like a wave of release, replaced almost immediately by a second flood of tension and pressure and then came the second shot, accompanied by more howls and whimpers. Shot followed shot and I lost count as the tension dissolved into Jeff's eager mouth. Long after the last drop of sperm had left my body, he continued sucking until the shock waves subsided. Finally, I looked down at him, and he, smiling, drew me down until I was kneeling opposite. His lips were smeared with cum and he brushed them against mine. The taste of my own spunk mingled with his saliva. I opened wide, licking my tongue over his mouth as he let a thread of jism pass from his into mine.

Raising himself up to tower over me, he pumped his cock in his fist while I reached up to pinch his tits.

"Yeah, Tommy," he purred, "fuckin' twist those fuckers, pinch them, man."

Grabbing his stiff nipples between thumb and forefinger, I pinched harder.

"Harder, Tom, yeah that's it, fuckin' twist 'em," he growled. "Yeah, baby, I'm fuckin' gonna shoot this load right into your mouth, man, right in there with your own spunk. Gonna give you a double dose. Fuck, yeah."

His fist got even tighter, squeezing the shaft of his big, fat cock, the head throbbing purple in front of my face.

"Just open wide, baby, open wide, here it comes."

And with that, Jeff let out a hoarse whoop as strings of hot white creamy spunk spurted from his quivering prick and filled my mouth up with the salty male essence.

"Better than beer, Tom. Pure protein. Yeah. Straight after training is the best time of all. You need a real protein shake, and that's just what you got right there. Drink up and enjoy!"

I rolled my tongue around my mouth, mixing up the twin tastes of Jeff's cum with my own, then with a big gulp I swallowed the whole lot back. My muscles well and truly fed.

T H E A   H I L L M A N

Close to Coming

THERE ARE CERTAIN THINGS I NEVER DO. *I never call my mother. I never brush my teeth—I don't have to; I never get bad breath. I never cook meals for my boyfriend. I never say "I love you." If the book is set in the country, I'm a farm boy whose only chores are romps in the hay and overnight camping trips with my buddies. If the author makes me a student, I never do homework, but I study my dates very closely. And if I'm a cop, it's the strangest thing; all the speeders I pull over are men. I've been called every name in the book, from Steve to Buck to Frank to Bradley. And I've been nameless. I've been fucked in cars, bathrooms, bushes, penthouses, under bridges, behind blackboards, in back rooms—and then been a virgin again by the next story. I've been through it all, again and again, the same story written a million different ways. And the thing is, no matter how similar the story is, it works, it gets me off. . . .*

"Easy, easy, man," I said. I spit on my hand, greased his shaft with my saliva. He was going crazy under me, wiggling like a trout, flashing his muscled belly, his bulging thighs straining against my weight. All the time trying to keep control, hearing his groans, one hand working his rod, the other tumbling his balls, I couldn't hold myself back any longer. "Turn over," I growled. Grabbing the lube, making it real wet and no longer being gentle, I forgot myself, pounding and thrusting myself into him, his screams echoing like the distant sirens outside. When I finally came back, I felt kinda sorry for doing him so hard and wanted to say something. I realized I didn't even know his name.

The air at the Dick Dock was balmy, ripe with the aromas of baby oil, leather, and manswear.

It had been a long time since I'd even wanted to give it away. I'd even started wondering if I was capable of true passion, that crazy-hard you get when it's there, more than just a fuck for fun or for money.

I held his head as I pounded my cock into his hot mouth, filling it, making him take it all down his throat 'til he choked, saliva and pre-cum escaping his lips, wetting his chin.

It was a typical Saturday night in the Manhattan meat-packing district. The leather boys, posers and lifers, stalked, chapped, and chained, the fuckers and the fuckees, descending the dark steps to the Vault, where one discreet glance and returned look would separate the men from the boys.

I'd never done anything besides jerking off with the guys behind the bleachers.

It was late, and no one in the bar looked good besides me and the bartender.

It was late summer after my senior year in high school. Something about the sharp bite of fall in the air made me think about football and the guys.

"I'm going to teach you what real men do together," he said as he ripped open my fly. He reached under the waistband of my Jockeys to grab my already stiffening cock. "You're ready to learn, aren't you, stud?" he asked as he bent his head.

It was 2:30 a.m. The park was almost empty. Just a few hustlers and an occasional queen staggering home, still looking for action after last call.

I'd never done anything besides playing doctor with the kid next door when I was little.

"No, wait," he cried, but his ass opened to me, the bud red and wet, and I knew I had to be deeper inside it, my prong probing his guts, feeling that tight ring squeezing me, shooting my load in that tight, firm ass.

They were the greenest bunch of players I'd seen in a long time, wore their leather like starched shirts.

The blows rained down relentlessly, hotter and harder than any fuck I'd ever had. He was pushing me, I tell you, higher than I'd ever been, and I kept begging for it. "More, you bastard. Give it to me."

I sucked on those great, heavy-hung balls like a baby sucking its mother's tit, the smells of sweat, stale piss, and the taste of his meat almost pushing me over the edge.

And while fucking is great, I usually never see the guy again. I mean, sometimes the writer wraps everything up neatly and we spend the rest of our lives together, but even still, I never fall in love. I never get to just hold a guy. And I've asked the writers why it has to be this way: a little development, a little narrative build-up, then climax, then the end. What about going on an actual date? What about a character that spends hours just kissing the stud he brings home from the bar? And the writers tell me, that's what sells: balling, sex; a muscle-bound character into lots of fucking. What about fucking plus? If I wrote myself into being, this is what I'd do:

I wanted him like I'd never wanted another man. In fact, I wanted something I'd never wanted before; I wanted to kiss him.

As we rolled, the sand found its way between our fingers, buried itself in our pubes and the crevices between our asscheeks. It stuck to our sweaty backs and salted our kisses.

He wasn't in a hurry to fuck like the last one. He started by stroking my face, running his fingers down my cheek to my lips, which he kissed, ever so softly.

We both had cases of five o'clock shadow. I rubbed my stubble against his, loving the feel of his strong, angular face, then turned so my lips could caress away the evidence of a long, hard day.

I started by peeling off his socks. He'd left them on, along with his underwear, but I meant to fuck every last piece of him. I took his baby toe into my mouth, sucking it like it was the sweetest, most decadent morsel I'd ever tasted.

And he walked me to my door, thumb stroking the side of my hand. The light over the door illuminated him, making him appear to shine. He looked so beautiful, a lump rose in my throat. "You look so beautiful," he said. And then he kissed me.

Clear Objectives

HE SAT DOWN OPPOSITE ME on the morning commuter train. He looked about ten years older than me, close to forty, and was wearing a tailored grey suit and a starched white shirt. I studied the way he folded his jacket, the way he pursed his lips as he read the *Wall Street Journal*, the way he absently stroked his clean-shaven jaw.

He must have been an athlete in college, for he was powerfully built. I could tell he tried to keep in shape. The knowledge that he was twenty pounds over his ideal weight, though, appealed to me. His thinning blond hair was graying on the sides and I could see the thick golden fuzz on his forearms when he reached forward and the cuff of the dress shirt pulled up. I imagined blond fur covering his chest and arms and legs as well. I leaned back, closed my eyes, and imagined my tongue darkening and flattening that hair, searching for his nipples.

He could have been my boss. I opened my eyes and looked at his left hand which gripped the carefully folded newspaper. The sight of the plain gold band on his second finger gave me an erection which burned against my thigh. I shifted my legs and the ribs of my corduroy pants stroked me just as his hand might.

He looked over at me, then his gaze darted away. When he focused on the paper again, I studied his profile—his authoritarian nose, his executive jaw. As I stared I became more anxious that we should meet, that I should kiss his chest and take his dick into my mouth, but it was up to me to manage it. It was up to me to bring him to the point where desire got the better of caution. I closed my eyes and started to formulate a strategy.

■ ■ ■

One evening after work, late, I loiter in the parking lot of his building. He can see me from his office and comes down to let me in, slips me past the security guard, and pushes me down labyrinthine corridors. He isn't wearing his suit coat now. His tie is loose and his shirt sleeves rolled up almost to his elbows. The hair on his forearms is thick and soft, as I suspected.

I feel him next to me, tall and powerful, and smell his mix of sweat and starch and cologne. When we reach a closed door, he hesitates, then presses against me, leaning forward to unlock it. His chest touches my back. I move just enough to push my ass into his crotch and his breathing grows faster, flavoured with the smell of secret cigarettes. His grip on my arm loosens and I feel his hands move down my sides, grasping me around my hips. They are narrower than his hips. This realization, the tactile fact of it, makes him hard. I reach behind, brush my fingers along the bulge of his dick and shiver as he pushes into me.

"Go on," he whispers.

The storage room is small and dim and stacked with boxes. He closes the door, standing near me as our eyes adjust. I pull away, let the stillness linger, then move into action. First I remove his tie, then open his shirt one button at a time, revealing his chest which is covered by thick, curly hair. I move closer, kiss both of his nipples, sucking them, then work my tongue down his body as the buttons come undone. When I reach his stomach, I'm crouching. The last button gives way. I drop to my knees and look up. His eyes are wild, expectant, but his smile is paternal. He knows what's next.

On my knees, I unzip his pants. He grasps my head with tenderness, holds it with both hands, caressing me. I can feel the hair on his forearms brushing my cheeks. His dick strains at his underwear, bulging out of the opening in his pants. Gently, I pry open the fly and his dick springs out, entering my waiting mouth with a pop. I can feel his shock of pleasure as he jerks a bit, then pushes into me, testing how far he can go. When he realizes I can take all of him, he moans, grabs my head less tenderly, and shoves all the way in. His movements grow faster. I run my hands up and down his chest, grabbing clumps of hair, releasing them, stroking his nipples. I look up. His eyes are closed now, his head thrown back, and I know he's fully mine.

His pleasure doesn't last long but his orgasm is explosive and shuddering. In this fantasy, I swallow it all. I drain him—won't let him pull away. The force of his ejaculation and the pungent taste of his sperm triggers a silent release in me, but I don't come. His body stops jerking and eventually I let him go, watch him stagger back and lean on the dusty boxes to recuperate. He looks a bit ludicrous with his shirt still open and his dick hanging out of his dress pants, drooling. I offer him my hand.

"We should go," I say. "There's a train to catch."

■ ■ ■

The conductor called out my stop. I opened my eyes and looked over at the crisp, unrumpled object of my reverie. Our gaze met and he gave me a barely perceptible nod.

This wasn't his stop but that didn't matter at all. I gathered my things and moved toward the front of the car. I felt him watching, silently appraising me as I strategized. With a smile, I glanced back at him. Tomorrow I'll get his business card. Tomorrow, he'll be mine.

High and Tight

PAUL'S MY BARBER. His clippers hum and glide over the back of my neck. The cramped barbershop is busy this morning. All three chairs are occupied and a few more men sit and wait, flipping through newspapers or just watching what's going on. The clippers are a tease, just a little ticklish, but not quite satisfying, and my dick hardens as Paul trims the hair just over my right ear.

There's a mirror on the wall behind Paul's chair, so I can see the back of my head, and watch the clipper blade turn my short crop of hair into stubble. This is a weekly ritual because my hair grows so fast. Once a week I leave the shop with the top of my head perfectly angular, a wedge of thick brown hair that quickly fades around my ears and above my neck.

It's gotten shorter over the years. Paul keeps pushing it a little closer and I keep wanting more off every time. I've joked that we'll hit my limit one day, but as yet, it's nowhere in sight.

The first time I got my hair cut in a flattop Paul didn't do it. It was my trendy stylist whose thirty-dollar haircuts had been getting progressively shorter as I hungered for something different. One day he said, "How about a flattop?" and there it was. It was fun getting my hair cut by him; along with the cut came espresso and chat about the latest goings-on in South Beach. But it didn't make my dick hard.

I found Paul's shop when it was time to get my flattop trimmed. Everything about it was exactly right, from the old-fashioned striped pole outside to the weathered chairs and combs soaking in disinfectant solution. The first time he ran the clippers over my neck I knew I was on to something.

That night, a beefy man with a furry chest and a full, luxurious beard ran his hand over my newly trimmed scalp. Before long, I found myself sucking his heavy shaved balls. I realized that a new flattop rubbing over a spit-soaked ball sac would feel really good. Moments later, my new pal confirmed that.

Paul puts down his clippers and begins trimming the top of my hair with scissors. Little bits of hair fall down past my face and shoulders, onto the clean white apron. Paul's probably in his fifties, bald, with a trim moustache and beard, and pale blue eyes. He's quiet and unassuming, but still a classic daddy. He looks at my head and concentrates, trims a little more off the front, goes back to the side again, and gradually lowers it all 'til you can just see my scalp beneath the short hair in the centre. I'm dying to stroke my dick which strains rock-hard in my jockey shorts, but that will have to wait. Instead, I concentrate on the snip-snip sound of Paul's scissors.

One Friday night when I was in Los Angeles, a stranger in a bar said, "Nice haircut!" as he passed by and disappeared into the crowd. I grinned, and a week later reported back to Paul that his work was getting rave reviews on the west coast. Whenever I sit in his chair, all of these adventures are in my mind—the men who've admired the cut in bars, the guys who've seen it and cruised me on the street, the uninhibited guys who've just reached over and rubbed it in sex clubs. I don't report everything back, but I'm always thinking about it there in his chair.

I don't usually tell people much about getting my hair cut. It's probably dangerous to let everyone know that if they rub the top of my head just right, I will probably do anything they want. Even Paul doesn't know this, though it must be clear to him that I like this. We all have our buttons, and mine are the stubble just over the nape of my neck and the short even hair on my scalp.

One of these days, while Paul is evening out the sides, or putting the Krew Komb wax on just above my hairline, I'm going to shift in the chair, and my dick is going to slide against the worn cotton of my underwear just right. Perhaps through the cotton I'll feel the zipper biting into the sensitive skin of my cockhead, or maybe just then Paul's hand will brush across the back of my neck where his clippers just were. But one day, all of these things will happen just right, and I'll shoot a load in my jeans right there in the chair.

Paul may have figured out how thoroughly he's got me. Maybe he knows that one quiet morning, when I'm the only customer in the shop, all he has to do is turn and lock the door and I'll be his as long as he wants. Maybe he knows that he can make me come without ever touching my cock, that I owe a thousand little adventures to him and am ready to pay him back whenever he calls in the debt. Maybe he's figured this out. But Paul's my barber. He's a professional. He just cuts my hair, then sends me out onto the street.

Tonight I'll probably go out and drink beer in a smoke-filled bar. It might be a night for adventure with some new buddy, or perhaps one I already know. Either way, I'll be thinking about it next week when Paul says, "The usual?" and his clippers call my cock to attention beneath the white apron in the crowded barber shop.

JEFF   RICHARDSON

Anything
for Her

IN A PAST LIFE, I WAS A WHORE. A male whore—slut-boy, really—but in a religious context. It was a privileged position. I lived in a temple devoted to the Goddess. There were huge rooms delineated by Doric columns and I remember draperies billowing in the breeze and moonlight ceremonies followed by feasting that continued well past dawn.

The Goddess was paradoxical, as is the wont of major deities. She was, above all, the Protectress of Fertility, and yet, during the Julepps—those days solely devoted to Her worship, ten per year—She demanded that no man lay with woman. During those days women had to seclude themselves and when the seed of man was spent, it could only be spent upon the loins of another.

The problem was, the men were mainly heterosexual and, left to their own devices, wasted the Julepps playing sports together or, more likely, sitting beneath trees *talking* about sporting games that *others* had played. They did not see the day's absence of women as a chance to get it on, but rather, as a welcome respite from sexual activity altogether. The Goddess was not pleased.

She decreed that all men must congregate upon her holy days at the temple where sacred sex rituals would take place involving each and every man with at least one other. But the men were awkward, unskilled, their fumblings offended Her, and so at last She saw the need for specialized sex workers—a priestly fucking clan, who could bring some finesse to these manoeuvres.

I was not born into this clan but my natural proclivities in the area revealed themselves early. I won't bore you with the details of how I proved myself to the necessary authorities. Let's just say that the age of admittance to the Julepps Manly Whoredom is not one that can be written about, legally, in this country today. Accepted I was, and trained, and still retaining some modesty I can tell you that I was good at my craft.

The frustration, of course, had to do with the timing of sexual encounters. As I've mentioned, there were only ten Julepps per year and, once training was complete, priests were not allowed to practice with each other. Their minds were to remain focused on the Goddess and on fulfilling Her through servicing the men on the next blessed day. There were twenty-seven Manly Whores—twenty-seven being the Goddess's power number—and some 5,500 men in the community. You do the math. We had from noontime until the cresting of the moon to complete our task. Most were simple blowjobs, though how "simple" can fellatio be when one's jaw aches absolutely from overuse? I love to suck—I'm the first to admit it—but there were times with some slow-comers I simply wanted to scream, "Get on with it!"

Some men required anal penetration: they of us or we of them. It was all highly ritualized. Who did what depended on their star sign, the casting of the Goddess Stones, the Wise One's Wishing and, most often what we would call today, their *hunkiness*. Yes, it's true. We priests got to pick and choose—though of course the men never knew this. With all the chanting in an ancient priestly language, the incense, the stylized gestures, they thought the Goddess Herself was directing who got fucked and who didn't. Then again, perhaps She was, and we were simply the agents fulfilling Her true wishes.

The day would go so fast and suddenly it was over. We would lie in hot baths for three days after, our bodies unable to move, and although we ate highly spiced foods, our taste buds still registered cum, cum, and more cum. Rested, restored at last, on the fourth day was the Binding: the high priest would place butt-plugs up our asses, and lock chastity belts around our genitals, and thus secured we would wait for, *pine for*, the next holy Julepps.

I have no way of proving that past lives actually existed. Julepps could be a variation of mint juleps, my favourite steamy-summer slutty drink. I could be projecting onto the past all experiences I've desired but yet elude me in this life. Nevertheless. If there was a Goddess, wouldn't She want me to have a memory just like this one?

Ten days of the year, in this life, now, I call the office and tell them I'm sick. It bothers me to lie, but after all, Christians gets Christmas. Why shouldn't I get Julepps? I go down to the baths and—well, you get the picture. Of course it's a little different now, there's less need to hurry. But even though we're no longer dealing with some 5,500 to be serviced, between noontime and the cresting of the moon, I do my utmost to please the Goddess.

DANIEL COLLINS

Blessed Be

WE WERE FINALLY DRESSED. The four of us left the cabin a shambles, discarded tulle and rejected glamour scattered everywhere. We scampered along the soggy path, giggling beneath dripping evergreens. I was glad I had chosen to wear the practical green rubber elf shoes with red dingle balls. My feet stayed dry while all around me spike heels sank into the moist Oregon terra firma. The pantyhose was also a great idea, warming against the nippy late winter mountain air and delightfully salacious as my swishing thighs created silky friction under my flimsy orange and blue diaphanous faerie dress. The blond-streaked, waist-length Fabio wig also helped keep me dry and warm. My cabin mate Chris had decided to go butch after all, wearing leather chaps, cap, and vest with lavender silk panties. Lenny, as Courtney Love—before the suicide when her make-up was so-o-o easy—wore three baby doll tops tied together with fluorescent condoms. Our mentor, Plum Blossom, wearing what Pocahantas would have worn if John Waters had made it instead of Disney—a shocking pink bikini with lime green fringe and matching wrist and ankle cuffs—led the group into the large hall of the main lodge. About one hundred and fifty assembled faeries, in an amazing array of fae costumery, hissed their collective approval as we made our way over to the fireplace—the best focal point—according to Plum Blossom.

It was one of the best "No Talent" nights ever. Darlene, the ambassador's wife, doing his six-foot six-inch love-goddess-M.C. routine kept the parade of wackiness rolling. Crowd favourites were a new faerie singing a Callas aria while hula-hooping and especially Luna Moon-beam who did Tina Turner's "Proud Mary" with two male, open-mouthed blow-up sex dolls attached to a broom handle across his shoulders. Together they cleverly resembled a trio of lip-synching drag queens in matching tinsel shimmy dresses and wigs, their six hands joined to another broom handle doing hand-jive routines. I laughed so hard my cheeks hurt. The room just screamed.

Afterwards a roaring fire was built in the walk-in fireplace and the lights turned low. Drums arrived and men started to dance, myself and my cabin mates included. We were soon distracted. It got warm right away and immediately shucked dresses, sarongs, kilts, sequinned long Johns, silky scarves, sparkly veils, and especially pants came flying off the dance floor. Underwear became hats. Clusters of mostly naked men danced en masse or lounged on pillows in groups of three, five, and six. Still wearing the blond streaked Fabio wig, I shyly and somewhat reluctantly removed the blue and orange faerie dress and was just about to slip out of the pantyhose when a husky voice lisped, "Ooo! Guthetleth pantyhothe. Leave them on."

I turned, smiling, to the source of a voice like that and saw a tall, red-bearded, balding faerie, naked except for black fishnet crotchless pantyhose under a black with white polka dot leather loincloth, black with white polka dot gloves to the elbow, and a tiny black and white straw hat with white polka dots on a full veil.

Catching my eye and perhaps hearing the zing in my heart he said with a big smile, "I love the feel of a leg in nylon," and caressed my willing thigh. "I'm Thweet Pee. Care to danth?"

"I'm Takky Wynotte until my faerie name appears," I replied, noting that my nylon-restrained cock, trapped down one leg of the pantyhose, was beginning to feel more squashed.

We danced until the fire in the hearth was down to a flesh enhanc-ing orange glow. My pantyhose was also crotchless by that time and the Fabio wig long gone. Sweet Pee's hat and loincloth had both gone with the wig. Danced out, we swooned onto the cushions and gazed around the room in wonder at the scene. Someone had thoughtfully scattered condoms around and at least fifty naked and latex festooned faeries were involved in many and inventive forms of sexual expres-sion all around the darker edges of the large hall. Single "watchers" sat or stood about masturbating until they chose a group to join or were invited over. The air was thick with sweat, sperm, and sexual exuberance tinged with a lower note of mountain air and wood smoke. Sweet Pee directed me to "rub his bumps" by which he meant slowly caressing the little nubs of flesh that protruded between the cross threads of his fishnets with my silky nylon legs. I especially loved it when he rubbed his bumps over my belly-squashed boner, trapped again and visibly straining under the nude no-pantyhose. Sweet Pee took me on a personal guided tour of the many changing hues of his redhead's body hair which sprang up from his ample expanse of pink-nippled, creamy skin in fiery clumps. My favourite hairs were the tongues of flame which ringed his rosy anus.

"An asshole has never looked this hot," I told him as we moved into sixty-nine position, his end lit up by the flickering embers.

Incense wafted from the altars. The drums were stilled. Tender murmurs and lustful laughter bubbled up over the sounds of a flute playing in the lobby as two post-coital faeries slow-danced naked in the middle of the much blessed hall.

We slept in his cabin after a soak together in the rock-lined hot springs meadow pool. Sweet Pee had been a faerie for years and told me as we cuddled in the early morning light waiting for the breakfast bell, that he'd never seen everyone getting it on in a group that large before. "It mutht have been the Body Electric workthop that Martheau led thith afternoon," he pondered, smiling at the memory. "I mean, in the old dayth, at the bathth, thometimeth collective thingth would happen but not with thith many men. And that felt only temporarily fulfilling, while thomehow thith felt thoul-enriching."

"Soul enrichment," I murmured, snuggling into Sweet Pee's warm expanse, "Maybe that's what makes a faerie radical."

"Pothibly," answered Sweet Pee, perusing the drag-littered cabin, "Can I wear your orange and blue faerie dreth to breakfatht?"

I knew we were going to be pals when I noticed Sweet Pee's penis transform while trying on my silky frock. He let me wear his fishnets which were still warm when I put them on. We never made it to breakfast.

DANIEL CURZON

Body and Soul: A Fable

ONE DAY MR. SOUL, a lean yet muscled young man, was sitting in his bed with a thin blanket pulled up to his neck as if he were asleep. But he wasn't, not really. A young, dark-haired man of some twenty-five years, though very handsome, he often worried about "things"—gay things, other things, especially in the morning.

Mr. Body, as he was known to Mr. Soul, was lying between Mr. Soul's legs. Mr. Body was quite extensive as penises go—almost in the realm of the mythical, some might think—high, wide, and rambunctious. The last time Mr. Soul had measured Mr. Body (in his teens, this was), he had counted at least half an inch beyond the end of the twelve-inch ruler he'd been using.

"Ah, another day!" Mr. Soul said, yawning and at last waking up completely.

"Ah, another day!" said Mr. Body, also yawning, noisily, rising to the occasion and making a big mound in the bedcovers between Mr. Soul's legs.

"Oh, not again!" Mr. Soul said, pushing Mr. Body away.

"Don't start putting me down already," Mr. Body protested.

"It's only six a.m."

"Don't give me any lectures, okay?"

"Can't you get lost for a few days!" Mr. Soul sat up in his bed.

"I didn't bother you all day yesterday," Mr. Body said.

BODY AND SOUL: A FABLE

"And what a relief that was."

Mr. Body rose up a bit—which was more than a bit. "Just give me what I want, and I'll shut up."

"No!"

Mr. Body stood his ground. "We're going out, whether you want to or not."

Mr. Soul drew up his legs. "No, I'm going to stay in and read."

"Listen, Mister, we're going out for a treat, and that's all there is to it." Mr. Body now rose to his full height and made the bedcovers look like a tent.

"Who do you think you are, giving me orders?" Mr. Soul said.

"If it weren't for me, you'd never go *nowhere!*" Mr. Body said, his grammar not quite as extensive as he was.

Mr. Soul half-yawned and snuggled against his pillow. "Yeah, I'd stay here and just think and dream and . . ."

"You'd be a vegetable in two weeks."

Mr. Soul sat up. "Because of you, I'm nothing but an animal!"

Mr. Body made himself wave back and forth under that very thin blanket. "Sticks and stones may break my bones," he said in a sing-song, "but names'll never hurt me!"

Young Mr. Soul stared down at the moving Mr. Body. "I used to be happy until you started bugging me!" he said.

"That's absolute horseshit! I've given you the happiest times in your whole puny life! Just give me what I *want*, and I'll go back to sleep." He stuck up—a command.

Mr. Soul began pushing the other down. "No! It's dirty!

"You just slept for eight hours. Was that dirty?"

"That was different."

"The hell it was! It's okay to sleep for eight hours or to eat three meals a day, but when I ask for five little minutes you deny me!"

"It's immature," Mr. Soul answered, rather haughtily.

"So it'll keep you youthful! Come on."

"Why don't you go find somebody else to bother?"

"'Cause I'm stuck with you, that's why." Mr. Body waved back and forth.

"What if somebody came in now and saw you like this!"

"Who cares! They're no different from you, simp!"

"They're not walking around with this big old thing sticking out all the time."

"I give you a good time, don't I?" Mr. Body asked, in a very coaxing way.

"Well. . . ."

"Do I or don't I give you a good time, hmm?"

"But you're always nagging me!"

"Damn it, you keep me cramped inside your shorts most of the time!"

"If I give you an inch, you take a mile."

"I thought we were partners. Almost lovers."

"Not after that awful drip you had last month."

"A little head cold! For that I should be put in isolation?"

"I'm sorry, we're *through*, and that's all there is to it!"

"Okay, so I got us into a little trouble." Mr. Body stuck up for all he was worth. "So *beat* me."

"No!"

"Go ahead, beat me!"

"You'd just like that."

"Well, how about rubbing me on the chair then?" Mr. Body pointed to the chair beside the bed.

"I don't want to." Mr. Soul folded his arms.

"Come on, just a little bit." He started sing-songing again: "*Back and forth* on the chair, okay?" He was moving like an oversized metronome.

"It will make a stain on the wood," Mr. Soul complained.

"Naw, it'll put a nice polish on it!"

Mr. Soul crossed his legs. "No, I'm working on my self-control."

"If God didn't want me to spout off, why'd He put me here?"

"As temptation."

"He put me here because He knew what a lousy world He'd created and He wanted you to have at least a *few* good times!" Mr. Body said.

"But to please you I'll have to get up, get dressed, go out and find somebody who's looking for the same thing, and then we'll—"

"Naw, you don't, pal. We can handle it—*ourselves*."

"But that'll grow hair on my palms!"

"Then you won't need no gloves this winter."

"I could go blind!"

"I got this friend over in the school for the blind. He tells me the blind guys there start to see *better* if they do it!"

"It's no use. I'm swearing off—forever. I'm through with low-lifes like you." Mr. Soul turned his head away, glaring at the wall.

"I'm sorry I'm not the high-society type." Mr. Body began what sounded like sobbing sounds. "Go ahead, abandon an old buddy. Go ahead!"

Mr. Soul looked back at him. "Don't be like that now."

But Mr. Body was inconsolable. "Go ahead, leave me after all I've done for you!" He slumped down, out of sight.

"Oh, come on, don't be hurt."

"Go out with your high-falutin' friends, if that's what you want."

"Don't be mad."

"What do you expect me to do, jump for joy?"

"From now on I just want to be spiritual, that's all."

"You're dumping me for some new-age, artsy-craftsy creeps and I'm supposed to accept it?"

Mr. Soul waited for more words, but nothing came. He leaned closer. "Don't be mad at me, okay . . . ? Please."

"Well, I *am* mad at you!" Mr. Body said, sulking.

"Come on, that makes me feel bad."

"Well, it don't make me feel so hot neither!" Mr. Body's voice was almost muffled.

"Say you're not mad at me, okay?"

Mr. Body was reluctant and silent.

"Please! Say you're not mad. Huh?"

Mr. Body barely moved. "Well . . . maybe." He suddenly shot up to an amazing height and aimed himself toward Mr. Soul's chest. "Shake on it?"

Before he could think, Mr. Soul said, "Sure!" He grabbed Mr. Body and began to shake.

"Thanks," Mr. Body said as Mr. Soul continued to hold him. "Feels *good*, don't it?" he said slyly.

"I'm not sure . . ." Mr. Soul replied, but his face was betraying his true feelings.

"Come on, just a little shake or two more," said the clever Mr. Body.

Reluctantly Mr. Soul began to stroke Mr. Body. First a little bit, then faster and faster.

"That's right! Way to *go!*" said Mr. Body wildly.

Now Mr. Soul began to use both hands to stroke Mr. Body, who began to writhe, growing louder and louder, more ecstatic. "Way to go! Way to go! Way to go! Way to go! Way to go! Way to go, you mother-fucking *motherfucker!*" Mr. Body jerked about frantically, then ended up coughing—no, more like spitting. Indeed he was quite noisy, and there were several phases to his . . . fit. Then he fell over, limp. There was one final little cough.

"Thanks, pal. I needed that," Mr. Body said, sighing. Then he sang forth: "Hey, see you *tomorrow!*" crying out with what can only be described as utter glee.

Realizing he had been duped, Mr. Soul shook his head, then wiped his slimy hand on the top of the blanket, giving a final little shake with both hands—but not entirely displeased, if truth be told.

LAWRENCE   SCHIMEL

A Blend of Food and Desire

I SPRUNG A BONER when Erica asked me to pass the blender. The memory of that night Robert and I first had sex with a blender is hardwired into my libido.

Robert had visited his grandmother, and she'd given him a Macy's credit slip that she'd been keeping. It was about to expire, so he had to use it that afternoon. Robert lost no time in dashing off to The Cellar and came home with a blender—which he wanted to try out immediately.

Now I love watching Robert cook. The spectacle of anyone preparing food, especially when they are cooking just for me, turns me on. Robert was so obviously excited with his new toy, which in turn got me excited. I stood behind him and rubbed my crotch against his ass as he read the instructions.

My cock is one of few things that can distract Robert from cooking. I've got to be careful, though. I've distracted him once too often when the stove was on, and dinner was burned as a result.

But Robert hadn't even got his new machine plugged in, so I felt it was safe. He turned around to face me, and we began to kiss. He unbuttoned my shirt, and slid down my chest to nuzzle at my right nipple, flicking the silver ring that pierces it. His hands dropped to fondle my crotch and unzip my jeans. He crouched down before me, pressing his mouth against my cock, breathing moist, hot air through the cotton of my briefs. He tugged my underwear down my thighs and my cock sprung free. Robert rubbed his face against it, licking my balls, then slowly worked his way along the underside of the shaft.

173

I braced my arms against the countertop as his lips locked around my dick and slid down along the shaft. Slowly I thrust my hips back and forth, pushing deeper into his mouth.

I was staring at the blender parts scattered across the countertop as he sucked me off—the whirling blades that looked how my innards felt as his tongue and lips worked their magic on my cock.

Then suddenly, my cock popped free as Robert stood up. I thought he just wanted some reciprocation for a while, but instead he turned around and went back to work on the blender, as if I wasn't even there.

I was insulted.

I stepped out of my jeans and underwear, dumping them in a heap behind him. Normally I was careful not to mess up the kitchen, which was Robert's domain, but I was pissed off. I pulled my shirt off and tossed it on top of the dish rack.

"I'm going to go watch some porn and jerk off," I said, sounding petulant, even to my own ears.

"I'm not through with you yet," Robert said, still busy with his new toy.

"It sure looks like you are."

"You'll see," he said. "Here." He reached atop the fridge for the fruit bowl and handed me a banana.

"This is supposed to keep me entertained while you play with your new toy?" I asked.

Robert turned and faced me. "You're such a bitch today." He was smiling. "Just peel the damned thing and trust me."

I stroked my dick, still slick with his saliva, and glared at his back. I was being a bitch, I knew, but I hated being ignored. I peeled the banana and fumed in silence. I took a bite, a last rebellious action, and with my mouth full of banana said, "Here."

"Thank you," Robert said, as he stuffed the banana in through the top of the machine, and then plugged in the blender. "Ready?" he asked, closing the lid.

I stood behind him again, forgiving him, wanting to share in his excitement, wondering what was to come next. "Sure," I said. "Can't you tell I'm ready?" I rubbed my hard cock against his ass as I looked over his shoulder.

Robert smiled and flicked the machine on. In seconds the banana was whacked into a purée by the sharp steel blades.

Big deal, I thought. I grabbed Robert's hips and ground my crotch against him. "*That* was more fun than this?" I asked.

"You have so little imagination," Robert chided. He lifted the top half of the blender from its base and held it before him. "Sometimes I wonder how I could have married you," he said, switching places, so that I was pressed up against the counter. "But then I remember." He knelt down before me, still holding the blender. He poured the banana purée all over my dick and abs and thighs.

"Oh," I said, letting the vowel shift from one of surprise as the viscous gel touched my skin, into one of pleasure as Robert eased the blender down on the floor and began licking the warm, sticky liquid from my skin. "Mmmm," I purred, as he licked the inside of my thigh.

"You should taste it down here," Robert grinned. "Mmmm indeed."

I laughed. Later I did taste it on him. We went through most of the fruit bowl that night, pureeing items alone and in combinations—kiwi and apple; strawberry and pear—and then eating the drippy pulp from each other's bodies.

And ever since, the sound of a blender, sometimes the mere thought of it, gets me hard.

I must've stepped funnily as I crossed the room with the blender in my hands, trying to shift my cock within my jeans, which suddenly felt far too tight. Erica noticed, and looked down.

"Men!" she exclaimed. "Can't you pay attention, the company'll be coming in fifteen minutes. And there's no time for you to come before they do, so go set the table and calm down."

I laughed, and said, "It's a long story."

"You'll tell me another time, then. Use the table cloth that's in the top drawer."

I went into the dining room to set the table, trying to ignore the whirring sound of the blender which was keeping my dick rock hard.

Breathless

I SAW THE AMERICAN VERSION first, the one with Richard Gere, which I later discovered wasn't as good as the French, but it suited me fine at the time. Richard Gere kept taking his clothes off and at fifteen, that was more important to me than New Wave cinema or existentialism. I would lie awake at night with my hands roaming my body, trying to pretend they were someone else's, dreaming of rescue, escape. Like this:

I skid down the night-dampened lawn toward the curb, where a stolen car, a red convertible, sits idling and I jump in easily, fluid, nothing in my hands or my pockets because *I need nothing* but the wind in my face and this man by my side and the darkness around us, and he puts his foot down hard on the gas and we veer off into the night, dark suburban streets disappearing behind us like a dream fading, sparks flying off of our cigarettes into the backdraft so that anyone on the road behind us thinks they're following a comet or a rocket, something travelling fast in one direction.

When dawn starts to bleach the sky from mauve to pink, we pull over and stop at a motel at the side of the road with a huge sign advertising XXX MOVIES and KING-SIZED WATERBEDS, and while he goes in to get the key I sit and wait in the car with my nerves humming like piano wires after the mallet strikes, and after forever or longer he comes out of the office, that loose-hipped, rolling walk, and he opens the passenger side door and says, come on, come with me, and we go up the concrete steps to the second storey of the motel where he slips the key into the lock and turns it hard as if he can't wait to get inside and I follow him in and the door has barely shut before he is easing me back on the bed.

He pulls his t-shirt up over his head and tosses it into a corner, and I straighten up from the position I am sprawled in to get a better look, my mouth going dry as his hands move to the fly of his jeans, and he undoes the buttons slowly which undoes me quickly and the thicket of dark hair comes into view as he begins to push his pants down his hips and his cock springs up and I can measure the time between his heartbeats by the way his shaft pulses, and I crawl the length of the bed until I am kneeling at the end of it, inches away from him, and I duck my head down and take him into my mouth, tasting salt and sharp and sweet.

Days of driving, living on gas station coffee, cigarettes, each other.

Los Angeles surrounds us like a strand of flawed jewels, a degraded dream. We are hidden away in another motel, and there is another car, a black one this time, and I have not asked where it came from or where the last one went, because this is the way things work in his world and I am in that world now.

I am mesmerized by the bullets of water stripping me of the layer of smog, cigarette smoke, sweat, cum, and the last three days swim in my eyes like a mirage, we've spent them in the hotel room and haven't gotten dressed once and I focus on the memory of watching his firm compact butt as he strolled to the door to pay the pizza delivery guy who was visibly taken aback by this hungry naked stranger bearing a handful of crumpled bills, and while I savour this image he comes into the shower behind me and runs his hands up my back over my shoulders and down my chest slowly, presses himself against me and I can feel him getting hard against my ass rubbing against me and he takes my dick in his hand and begins to slide it up and down in his fist and behind me he works one of his fingers into me, opening me slowly and the sensation is sending me, sending me and bringing me back again.

We feed each other rum and food from cardboard containers, living like animals, coming out only at night. We have almost forgotten how to speak.

We are in a lot behind a deserted warehouse at dusk and he is teaching me how to hold and fire a gun just in case, he says, and I don't think I want to know in case what, so I say it's a bad idea to be walking around firing guns as if this were the wild west and he says,

THIS *IS* THE WILD WEST and the way his voice sounds when he says *wild* convinces me and I soon find I am aroused by the way the metal draws heat out of my hand, the way it bucks against the soft pad of my palm when I touch it the right way but suddenly I hear the sound of an engine, knowing how unlikely it is that someone would make their way through this web of alleys and abandoned buildings by chance, and the fear slides up my flesh making it seem too tight to contain my quaking nerves and as the front end of the black and white car comes around the corner we turn and run and I am fast, faster than he is and I keep going heedless, I hear gunfire, one shot, two, and I can't look behind me as I keep running through the labyrinth of scarred brick walls and finally I am at a dead end frenzied and flushed and I hear heavy footfalls behind me, someone grabs my shoulder and I spin around quickly and he pulls me into his arms and we're both drenched in sweat, trembling, breathless.

M I C H A E L   C O N R A D

He Talks

I'M CLOSE. Dave moves me into place, pulling my ass in until my balls press his. He pushes me on my back and leans in so he can grab up both our dicks in one hand, then begins slow, rhythmic pumping. He asks me if I'm ready for it, and covers my mouth with his foot. With his free hand he pulls down my balls so I can't come. And as I work his toes with my tongue, he strokes our dicks and talks:

"Think of the army. All those men in close quarters. Picture it, Brian: some hot, humid island. Picture those young, butch studs putting on their big, heavy black boots in the morning, sweating 'em up all day, then trooping back into their barracks at shower time and everybody peeling off that sweaty foot-gear. Can't you just smell the group-stink of all those sweaty, butch, young-guy feet? Can't you see them, laughing and talking and totally oblivious to the electricity of every single thud of a combat boot on the barracks floor? Brian, just smell the sopping socks they peel off, inside out. Then maybe they just dump their socks on the floor so that their buddies pick up the wrong pair when they're cleaning up for inspection and wear 'em the next day, mixing their own soldier sweat with some other guy's in that sweaty green cotton."

He replaces his left foot on my face with his right. He pumps our two cocks in his hand more gently. Pre-cum slithers out of both our puckering dick holes and gets pressed, crackling with stickiness, between the cock heads. He can tell by my fat, tight balls how close I am. He continues slowly:

"Picture them all playfighting in their underwear, wrestling in twos on the bunks. Their dicks are grinding into one another. Each guy's sweaty feet is leaving smelly sweat trails along the other guy's calves and shins as they go at it. These guys are so used to living with men and so used to their own and each other's stink they can't tell the difference anymore.

"So maybe, since they take guy-smells so much in their stride, there'll be a practical joke, where they're all laughing at how bad their feet stink after a day in the army, and they pick on this one guy, this one really good looking guy. They wrestle him down. Then they line up and put their feet on his face, one man at a time, and force their big, long toes into his gagging mouth. And fuck, they stink. Then they get a handful of the raunchiest socks and stuff them in his mouth. He thinks he'll pass out from the smell and taste. And then they pick up the socks of this beefy hairy guy who sweats so much an actual stream of stinky sweat can be wrung out of 'em. One of the soldiers squeezes the socks above the victim's face, and the foot-sweat just streams and streams through his hard, dirty fingers. And there it is, that warm G.I.-sweat pouring over the pinned-down soldier's eyes, over his cheeks, his lips, and down into that wet, rancid ball of soldier-sock jutting out of the poor guy's stuffed mouth."

I'm squirming now, I need to come so bad. Same time as the soldier got it from his buddies, Dave rammed his toes into my mouth, forcing himself in until I thought my jaw would snap. But he won't let me come. He keeps pulling my balls down.

"Then they're all trooping off to the shower. They're all frisky and clumsy and not too bright, and they're in such a crowd they keep stepping on each other's toes and heels, leaving wet smears on top of already steaming feet and ankles. Picture us in the middle of that crowd marching off to the shower, Brian. You and me and the other foot-stink soldiers. We can almost slide on that barracks floor with its fresh, swampy coating of soldier foot-slime. You and me, Brian. We slog off in a stink-cloud with the other jar heads to soap down our cocks and cracks and let all the soapy water and boot-camp foot-stink flow down that lucky drain for another day."

With that, he squeezes his fist so tight it hurts, and pumps our dicks like crazy. He forces his heel so far in my mouth I'm sure it'll hit my throat—sure his ankle bone'll knock in my teeth. I explode, just come and come—my balls bouncing like a punching bag against his. And I keep coming. I almost panic, I'm coming so long, my body heaving and bobbing as I watch the cum fountain endlessly above our two dicks pressed together and flood our pubes, our navels, in white. His cock pumped so hard against mine I thought I was still shooting—that I was going to keep on forever. No sign of where I ended and he began.

Both of us fall back. We each reach out with one hand to cup the other's dick and suck each other's big toe like babies.

L. D.   L I T T L E

Undersides

HE FOLLOWS ME INTO AN ALLEYWAY, down a filthy crack in the façade of civilization. The alley opens into a cramped, dirty lane where the backsides of buildings crowd together to form a dim brick canyon, dotted high up with small, greasy windows. The stench of rotting garbage rises up through the smell of piss and rusting iron stairways. Just sucking in the air makes me hard. Knowing he is behind me, all gruff sweat and attitude, sets my heart racing.

When I turn and grab him, he lets out a low growl from the back of his throat. I yank at his belt, spin him around, forcing him spread-eagled up against the wall and frisk him. He has a jagged little scar, the shape of a cartoon lightning bolt, on his jaw, just to the left of his chin. I flatten his face tight to the wall, hold it there with my cheek as my hands tear at the denim between us—struggling to liberate impatient, hard cocks. The chalky smell of the brick floods my nostrils. He swallows hard. Then my cock is at his hole, my fists full of his ass. I slide my fingers down his crack. A garbage can clangs and rolls over, echoing through the alley, releasing a new wave of rot into the air. I ooze pre-cum.

"Now, boy. . . ." My voice, all gravel and dirt, makes me even hotter. I split his ass cheeks open, force my thumb up against his puckering hole then jab my dick into him. I ram him hard.

"Fuck me," he croaks. "Jesus, man, fuck me."

I oblige him. Hot and fast, I fuck his ass. Deeper and deeper until I lose myself in my throbbing cock—become my cock. Spasms of pleasure rip through me. He squirms and moans. He may have come, I don't care. His squirming blasts me to the edge of my orbit. My eyes roll upwards and my balls pull up tight. I hold my breath, shoving deeper, grasping for one more thrust. One more. One more. Then hold on, suspended in a vacuum of ecstasy.

I snap, shooting my hot flame of cum deep into him. Gasping, I collapse against him, his hard body sandwiched between me and the wall. I clutch at his naked thighs, his cock and flat abdomen, finding the wet, sticky puddle of his cum to draw my fingers through. The juiciness of it sets a new wave of hunger plunging through me. I bite his ear and draw my teeth along the rough stubble on his jaw.

I slide down his body until I'm kneeling, my face in his ass, enveloped in his scent. A soft dampness soaks my knee where someone has pissed. My fist closes around his rod, again half hard. A switch flips over in me, changes my track, from *fuck* to *get fucked*. I want that cock. My throat opens for him, beckoning, begging. He swivels his body and it's in my mouth. Smooth as steel, wide enough to make my jaws ache. My prick stiffens as I work him. Several delicious strokes and he's hard as a hammer.

Then suddenly he shoves me backwards. I try to scramble to my feet but he takes me off balance and grabs me around my waist. In half a second he has me bent over, braced against a step on the iron staircase and his swollen prick is up against my asshole. A stab rips through me as he sinks his cock deep inside me. I cry out. From one of the windows above someone curses and slams a sash down. He grips my hips in a vice, thrusting into me, his pace accelerating. The steps clatter and rattle with each thrust of his pelvis. I am being fucked by a train. A run-away train. Completely out of control. Hot steamy panting fills my ears as his piston fuck-rod fills my ass, fills all the emptiness I've ever felt. Spasms explode through me with each pumping of his iron tool. Then my cock jerks and shoots streams of white cum onto the rails beneath me. Again. Again and again.

He comes with a bone-shaking groan. Gradually he releases his grip, the tension collapsing in on itself. He drops me onto the steps where I lie half crouched, bare-assed and gasping, listening to him stuff himself into his jeans. Through the stairs I watch him disappear back up the alley, his jean jacket hanging straight from his shoulders, his ass tight.

I ride the bus home. I feel powerful, dangerous, on a razor's edge. The back alley smell swarms around me, almost buzzing. My eyes shine hard and I smirk. "I suck cock." I stare down a purse-lipped old man in a grey cardigan. "I just had a dick up my arse." I saunter down the bus aisle past a woman laden with groceries and a whiny little kid. "I fucked a guy up against a brick wall." I bristle with cockiness. "Kiss. My. Ass." I am *alive*.

Kevin isn't there when I get home. I expect him any minute, though. I rush through a quick shower, wash my hair, bury my dirty clothes deep in the laundry hamper. I put a couple of chops in the microwave to thaw, smooth a fresh tablecloth onto the table, set out china, silverware, crystal. When I hear his key in the lock I am preparing the vegetables, scraping carrots, posed in the kind of domestic tableau that is crucial for my mental stability but murder on my sex life. He appears, gleaming fresh from the locker room at the club, all soap and Old Spice and crisp, tidy cotton.

"Honey, I'm ho-ome," he calls in a whispering sing-song and crosses the kitchen where he gives me a friendly pat on the bum. I smile and place a chaste kiss on the little zig-zag scar by his freshly shaved chin.

T H O M A S   S.   R O C H E

.357

HE LOCKED HIS ARM ACROSS MY THROAT. I saw he had a gun in his hand. He pushed the revolver flat up against my face, holding it tight. My scream stopped low in my throat when I heard him growl, "Say a word and I'll kill you."

"Just don't hurt me," I whispered.

"We'll see," he sneered. "Get undressed."

He kept the gun close to my face, letting me know he'd kill me if he had to. Up against him, I struggled out of my shirt, my jeans, my undershorts. I stood up against him naked, feeling the rough fabric of his jeans, his cock bulging through them against my ass.

"Please," I said. "Just don't hurt me."

"Like I said," he growled, "we'll see." With a fluid movement of one hand, he got the handcuffs out. He put the muzzle of the gun up against the back of my head while he slapped the handcuffs on, tight. I squirmed a bit and he ground the revolver up against my flesh, into the soft spot at the top of my neck. Then he put a gag into my mouth, buckled and locked it tight around my head. He took hold of the cuffs and yanked them hard, so my arms were extended painfully. He started lifting them.

"On your fuckin' knees," he growled. "Legs spread. Wide!"

I struggled onto my knees, my heart pounding. He stroked my face with the barrel of the gun, letting me see it. It was a .357 magnum revolver, black. I noticed that the front sight had been filed off.

He came around behind me. I felt the gun tracing a path of ice down my back to my ass. He played with my ass with the barrel of the gun, nudging apart the ass-cheeks. I whimpered in terror.

"Shut the fuck up!"

I struggled to remain still while he nuzzled my asshole with the gun.

"Way I figure it, asshole, you're dying for the ultimate ass-fuck. I hear you're a real ass-slut, that's why I broke in here. You wanna be fucked up the ass but good, like you never been fucked before! Well I'm gonna give it to you. Hear me? Tonight you're getting the ultimate buttfuck! *Hear me, asshole?!?*"

I nodded slowly, tears running down my face.

He popped open the jar of lube from the nightstand. My eyes went wide as I realized that he was really going to do it. My head spun, but every time I tried to squirm or move, he yanked harder on my wrists and pain shot through my shoulders and back. Then I felt the greased tip of the .357 sliding between my cheeks.

He pushed me forward, hard, ramming me into the floor.

"Apart! *Wider!*" He slapped my ass with the butt of the gun.

I wriggled my legs slightly further apart, my ass lifted uncomfortably in the air. He held on to my wrists as he wedged the barrel of the revolver into the shallow notch of my asshole.

"That's the way you like it," he growled. I felt the gun pushing open my tight ass. Felt the cold steel between my cheeks. Felt the greased metal cock working its way inside me as he jiggled it back and forth, getting it up into the sphincter. Then he pushed it home, as deep as it would go.

He let out an evil laugh, like this was the best thing in the world, fucking me with this gun, humiliating me this way, playing with my life like it was nothing.

He started sliding it in and out, real slow, letting me feel every inch. Stroking it all the way in and twisting it just a little, so I could feel the butt against my thighs. Letting me know that it was a gun.

"Feel good, punk?"

He let go of my wrists and reached down to feel my hard prick. He took hold of it and started jerking me off.

"Feels real good, I guess. What a fucking sicko."

His warm hand around my cock felt good. Blood pounded in my head as I felt the thick metal organ of the gun working its way in and out of me.

"Come on. Come on, give it up, pal. I'm gonna let you go when you come. Soon as you spurt I'm gonna pull the trigger. Won't that feel nice, now. I'm gonna come inside you. Come on, let it out. Come all over my hand, faggot. Do it. Do it!"

I let out a muffled yelp of terror and pleasure as my orgasm exploded deep inside my ass and cock. I felt my cum spurting out, hitting my belly, spraying all over me. Felt the raging pleasure set my whole body on fire. Felt the ecstasy. Then, with a dull thud, I felt him pull the trigger.

A shudder went through me. I felt like I was falling end over end. A bright light flared all around me and I thought I could smell smoke and shit and blood.

I began to quiver, slumping forward onto the wet sheets. I felt my bladder letting go, squirting warm urine over my thighs.

I lay there, unable to move. Gently, he began working the gun out of my ass, inch by inch. My ass-muscles were wide open, my cheeks smeared with lube and other things. I felt him unfastening the cuffs and then undoing the gag, laying me out on my belly.

"Now it's my turn," he said softly, reaching down to open his pants.

I felt him climbing on top of me, working his thick cockhead into the open cleft of my ass while his arms curved around me. He held the lube-smeared .357 up against my face. He positioned his cock and then he pushed it home, giving me the whole shaft, fucking me in long, rough thrusts. When he came his groans were violent.

He pulled out of me, tied off the condom, tossed it into the trash. He rolled me onto my back, careful not to hurt my arms, which were bruised and very sore. He looked down at me, stroking my sweat-soaked hair.

"Master," I whispered.

He turned me on my side. Using the towels spread across the futon, he cleaned up my ass and legs and laid me back down. Then he went into the kitchen to make some tea.

While he was gone, I considered the gun on the nightstand. It wasn't even a real gun—the cylinders had been filled in. The scene had been perfectly safe, down to the condom, down to the water-based lube, down to the safeword. Four short grunts in a pre-established rhythm. But the danger, the terror, the agony as the imaginary bullet tore through my guts—it had all been real. He had followed my request exactly, down to the moment when he pulled the trigger.

I faded in and out of reality. He brought back the tea, let it sit for a few minutes while he rubbed my chest. He sipped some tea, helped me sit up, helped me to sip some tea, then kissed me with chamomile lips.

M. V.   S   M   I   T   H

The Glass-Licker

TONY STRADDLED HIS SEAT at the small kitchen table. Although it was early afternoon, Owen, in the chair opposite, still wore his bathrobe.

"Let me get this straight," Tony said. "I've just come here to dump you, and you *still* want to fuck?"

"Yes," said Owen. He played nervously with the thin chain around his neck. "I want you," he said.

Tony shivered. He knew he had a problem: how to convince a man you're not good together when *you're* perfect, and he's the scar on the beautiful face of your relationship? Tony was a hunk. Today he wore blue shorts with a racy white stripe across the front, bumping at his bulge like letters across Dolly Parton's t-shirt. Flattering. He filled his pants, filled his shirt, filled his size twelve-and-a-half shoes. Owen, on the other hand, was less than god-like.

"I want you," Owen repeated.

"Sure," Tony sighed. "It's no wonder. Only I have no interest in screwing you, Owen."

"But why not? What have I done?" Owen's lip trembled, his eyes began to fill.

Tony looked away. "You're always hanging around my neck. And asking too much. You push."

"I'm sorry," Owen mumbled. "I'll try harder."

"Good," said Tony.

Owen cleared his throat. "So when will I see you next?"

Tony slapped his forehead with a meaty palm. "Never? No. That sounds too soon."

"I'll buy you more things. I'll put you in that movie," pleaded Owen.

"Even that's not good enough anymore." Tony stood, heading for the door.

Owen jumped from his seat and made a grab to hold him back. "Don't!" he cried.

Grabbing his thin wrists, Tony peeled him off and threw him to the floor. "Okay," he said. "Have it your way. You want to fuck, Owen? I'll fuck you."

Tony pulled his t-shirt off. A bead of sweat, caught in the trail of chest hair between his pecs, trickled loose and rolled down his chest.

From the floor, Owen gulped.

Tony then pulled his shorts down, slipping both feet out. His cock hung lazy between his legs. When he sat back down on the wooden chair, his balls rested on the seat like velvet eggs. His cock snaked between them, predatory.

"What are you waiting for?" he jeered. "Take your robe off. Let's see your little dick, Owen."

Shameless, Owen stood. He undid the tie at his waist and dropped the terry cloth robe off his shoulders. His stubby dick thumped against his stomach, already dripping like a loose faucet.

"Come here, then," Tony challenged, waggling his cock. Owen stepped forward.

Making a fist in the hair behind Owen's head, Tony pushed him forward, bending him at the waist. Instinctively, Owen's mouth opened and he gulped Tony's sausage down his throat. Tony pulled him back by the scruff of his neck, and pushed down harder. Pulled him back and pushed. Back and pushed, like an eight-inch spring, like a pulley. Tony watched his large arm flex as he forced Owen's head back and forth. He gave his bulging arm a lick.

"Ooo," he sighed, pouting out his lips. "You lazy fuck. Suck me, man. Suck harder. I won't get nothing out of it if you don't work at it, boy."

Owen's mouth clamped down, his cheeks squeezed in, so the suction tightened around Tony's meaty stick. His dick shifted from rubbery to hard.

"You're too pushy," he said through his teeth, thrusting his hips on each word. "Pushy." Tony pulled him off his cock. "Get it?" he asked.

Closing his eyes, Owen nodded slowly. "Kiss me," he sniffled.

"Fuck," Tony said in disgust. He pushed Owen to the long window off the kitchen. Pressed against the glass, he was in full view of the apartment complex opposite. Three old queens sat on their balcony in straw hats, drinking highballs at a plastic patio set.

Owen's stubby cock jumped against the glass like a caged rabbit.

The queen without sunglasses pointed towards the window.

"Oh, cripes," Owen cried. Tony worked his ass with a thick finger.

The other two fags pulled off their sunglasses to watch.

Tony pushed Owen's legs further apart. He squeezed his dick hard and butted it against Owen's fuzzy hole. He spit on his dick, and pushed steadily 'til it wedged inside Owen's ass.

Owen gasped.

"You like that? You like people seeing us together? Are you proud people know I fuck you? That I picked *you?*"

Tony slid his long cock up Owen's ass, and down again. Up he drove it, farther the next time, pushing Owen's body against the window. Owen's ass squeezed around his dick like a wet throat. His hole moved like a mouth.

"Lick glass, buddy. Let's see your tongue clean the window."

As Owen stuck his pointy tongue out, Tony squished his face into the pane.

Outside, the fags gulped their drinks, incredulous.

Tony bucked against Owen. "I'm going to come up your ass, Peewee." He fucked harder. His balls rolled up tight and slapped against Owen's thighs. Owen's cock drooled over the glass 'til Tony's cock swelled and pumped, shooting up his hole.

"Fuck," Tony barked, sweating and jerking with the orgasm.

Owen's cock spit twice on the glass, then spit once more as Tony pulled his long cock out of his ass. His eyes closed, Owen remained leaning where he was, exhausted.

Tony stepped to his clothes and put them on. "See you," he said. He walked to the door and hesitated.

Owen's heart jumped.

"You might want to bow," Tony said.

Owen opened an eye. The three queens raised their glasses in a toast. With a shriek, Owen jumped out of view.

The door slammed shut. Tony strode down the hall knowing it would have to be nighttime before Owen would dare clean the window, and all that was left of his love.

Take That!

IT WAS OVER BRUNCH, not long after we'd started dating, that he told me about it—that, while living in London, he'd realized what he'd truly wanted and actually found it: a punk whore to tie him up, verbally abuse and painfully punish him for being the yuppie he was. Robert's ultimate thrill was to be at the mercy of his inferiors—something like the sick thrill bigots get when having sex with a member of a race they abhor, or the excitement of the hypocrite homophobe while taking guilty pleasure.

For Robert, though, it was a matter of class. His excitement was enhanced by the fact that at least some of the sadistic abuse he was paying for was genuine. The master felt true contempt for the slave.

I lay my fork down, slightly sickened at the revelation, then quickly reminded myself that whatever Rob's shortcomings, he got his yuppie body to the gym on a regular basis.

Robert next regaled me with an explanation of the verbal commands he and the British dominant had employed. The code was set up like traffic lights: green, yellow, and red. Proceed, prepare to stop, and stop.

After brunch I took Robert home and we had sex. I decided to take his earlier comments as a hint and employed a pair of handcuffs. Robert's excitement level was heightened, to say the least. I had a great time too, but I felt terribly undersupplied. I longed for a fully equipped dungeon. Then I remembered the ad of a guy I knew who had a dungeon for hire. I got an idea.

I made all the arrangements, then phoned and told Robert I had a surprise. As soon as he got in the car I blindfolded him, then drove him to the address I'd been given. I soon had Robert hooded, spread-eagled, and vulnerable on every side.

Of course I wasn't used to it. I'd never flogged anyone before. At first, I didn't hit Rob hard enough. Rodger, the dungeon master, actually rolled his eyes at my clumsy attempts, but then he began to instruct me, silently guiding my hand. Soon I was delivering blows at just the right intensity, well within Rob's pleasure zone, but beneath his pain threshold. Then, I roughly fucked his hot reddened ass, all the while verbally abusing him. He loved every minute of it.

Hours later I finally untied him. He staggered off to the shower, but I stayed to talk to Rodger. He asked if I would consider helping him sometime with "group scenes." I said yes. He wrote down my number, then Rob emerged from the washroom, still high on whatever chemical the body in pain generates. I didn't mention Rodger's offer to Rob.

For the next few months I pursued my relationship with Robert. I should have known it wasn't going to work out. He was anal retentive, a control freak, and worked nine to five. I, on the other hand, was a bohemian night-crawler. To further complicate matters, he enrolled in a business course which took place on Tuesday, the one evening we had free in common. Our sex life deteriorated, but Robert kept calling and taking calls. We met for lunch several times. With dawning horror I realized Rob was trying to make me into a "friend." This is, of course, the accepted guppy method of dumping someone. I felt humiliated. Then I became angry, my anger fuelled by my conviction that Rob's reason for dumping me was not so much our schedules, but Rob's feeling that he could and should do better. I finally asked him if it was over for us. It was.

That night I got a call from Rodger. He said he had a regular coming over and this night the customer wanted to be dominated by more than one man. Could I make it? I headed downtown.

Rodger led me down to the dungeon where the client was waiting, strung up and blindfolded. On the way, he explained that this customer came over every Tuesday night and paid to be degraded for being a guppy. I walked around the client. Even in the dim light I could see that it was indeed Robert. Rodger had forgotten that we had first come as a couple to his dungeon. I guess Robert had not mentioned me on any of those Tuesday nights. I wondered if Robert went to the dungeon after the business class or if the class ever existed at all.

Rodger put a paddle in my hand. Suddenly I felt strangely excited. I began to beat Robert's chest and thighs. He responded well, but then he said "Yellow," so I eased off a little. Rodger gestured for me to have at it and left the room to have a smoke.

I was just getting started. I selected an extra large butt plug and forced it up Robert's ass. As the widest point passed his hole, he started with the "yellow" shit. I took a hood, yanked it over his head, and pushed the plug home.

Then I began to speak the words he had once paid a London punk to utter. I spoke them in earnest. I called him Guppy Scum, Preppie Faggot, Privileged Pansy. His dick jumped to attention. I picked up a large crop and started whipping him. Welts bloomed red on his guppy gym-buffed body.

My whip-wielding arm seemed to take on a life of its own. I was in a near trance when he began speaking again.

"I love you," he said.

I faltered.

"I love you," he repeated, almost whimpering.

It reminded me of the "I love you" a child will cry out through tears to mitigate a parental spanking, but I resumed my work with the whip.

Suddenly the word that Robert screamed through the hood was "Red." It came as the first blood was spilled. Also red. For some reason this struck me as funny and I continued to whip the now blood-spattered client. I watched a rivulet of blood snake across his shoulder blade and down his spine, and finally disappear between his quivering, sweat-slick ass cheeks. I continued to beat Robert until Rodger returned and, panic-stricken, overpowered me.

J I M   M c D O N O U G H

Waiting for the
Ball to Drop

"I CAN'T STAY LONG," said Paul as soon as he crossed the threshold. "I left work a little early. We have about twenty minutes. Tony will be waiting for me at home. There's a bunch of people coming over for New Year's."

He stood in my front hallway, his coat damp from the drizzle, the dim light from the outside hallway forming a halo around his mass of brown curls.

"Are you at least going to take off your coat?" I asked.

Paul stepped closer, his brown eyes darting back and forth. He was nervous. He was always nervous. I wrapped my arms around his neck and pressed my lips against his. I kicked the door shut, not wanting the neighbours to see me kissing another man, kissing another man who had a boyfriend waiting for him at home.

"Are you going out tonight?" he asked.

I shook my head. "No, I'm staying here. I don't feel like dealing with all the crowds."

"What am I going to do with you?" he asked.

You could invite me to come by your house, I thought, but quickly dismissed the idea. The other man at the happy couple's party—what a way to start the New Year.

Every time Paul came over, I told myself it would be the last time, but then he would call or stop by unexpectedly and I couldn't say no. I couldn't resist his smile, those dimples, his laugh, his kiss, his sex.

Paul pulled me closer. The kiss was urgent, almost frantic. We were on the clock. We had to work fast. I opened my mouth and he pushed his tongue inside. I tried to peel off his damp coat and get him comfortable as we kissed, hoping I was going to get more than a quick blowjob in my front hallway.

Paul reached up inside my shirt and pinched my nipples. I let out a groan. He knew by now that I liked this. After a few hard pinches, I would be ready for anything. I reached down and grabbed at his crotch. His cock was already hard.

When I tried to pull off my shirt, Paul insisted we go into the bedroom. I glanced at my watch—fifteen more minutes.

As soon as I lay on the bed, he was hovering over me, smiling. He grabbed my crotch. My cock was hard, too. It had been hard since he called saying he wanted to come over.

Paul bit on one of my nipples, reached downward, and unfastened my belt buckle. He slipped his hand inside my shorts and pulled out my cock. Ten more minutes.

Paul kept biting my tits as he began to stroke my cock. He kept stroking faster and faster, tightening his grip on my shaft as he pumped away. My body tensed as I got closer to coming. I glanced at my watch. I couldn't help myself. Five more minutes.

I arched my back when it got to be too much. Globs of pearly white cum shot out of my cock, landing all over my belly and coating Paul's hand with sticky goo.

Paul smiled and kissed me again. I reached out to unfasten his belt buckle.

Paul shook his head. "Don't have time. Tony is waiting for me."

I lay back down on the bed, pissed for having let it happen again. I could have jacked off and saved myself all the fucking complications.

Paul bent down to kiss me again. I turned my head, still pissed, and his lips brushed across my cheek. "Tomorrow when I take my bike ride. I'll have more time. I promise."

He disappeared into the bathroom to wash my cum, the evidence, off his hands. When he was done, he walked back into my bedroom, stroked his hand across my cheek, and then kissed me again.

"Happy New Year, Rob."

"Yeah, Happy New Year."

He laced his damp fingers with mine.

"Gotta run. I'll call you." He squeezed my hand tight and then let go.

Two hours after he left, I was still lying in bed, the lights dimmed, my pants hanging around my ankles, his taste still lingering on my mouth. The scent of his cologne hung in the air and on my sheets. My cum, dry on my belly.

Lying there, I wondered what Paul's boyfriend Tony looked like. Was he handsome? Did he have blue eyes like mine? Did he even suspect? I never pressed Paul for details, not sure how he would react, but I was curious. I often thought about riding by their house, hoping to catch a glimpse of him, but then I didn't want Paul seeing me. He thought I was content with our little arrangement.

The TV was on in the living room. The countdown to the New Year had begun. I wanted to get up and shut it off, but I didn't. I lay there just staring up at the ceiling, watching the ceiling fan spin.

Were they doing it right now? No, they were probably getting ready to kiss at the stroke of midnight, all warm and happy, sipping champagne with their friends just a few blocks from my apartment.

I rolled over and clung tightly to my pillow, inhaling Paul's scent and realizing that it was all I really had of him. All I would probably ever have.

The crowd in Times Square roared in the background. The ball had dropped.

The Stripping Room

WHEN YOU CAME IN to take over the number one spot from your father, a lot of the guys in the shop—in the stripping room—grumbled about it. "Just fell out of his old man's lap," they said. "Doesn't know a thing about film stripping."

They didn't like having a boss younger than themselves. You were about thirty, but most of the boys were in their mid-forties.

As for me, well, you know, I'm just old Charlie the janitor. I've seen so many guys come and go—even people at the top. Your old man was good to me, kept me on when he didn't have to. But by the time you arrived, I was about ready to take my retirement, and way past caring.

Mario was about the same age as the other guys, but he seemed younger. The others called him "The Kid." Either that or "The Italian Stallion." Not very original, but that was them. They admired the fact that he'd never settled down like they all had. Figured he'd had every girl in Montreal North. If someone had told them that Mario had a massive crush on some guy, they'd have been dumbfounded. If they'd known it was you, they'd probably have strung poor Mario up by his balls. What ended up happening to him wasn't much better.

But as unknown as Mario's real self was to everyone else, I could read him like an open book. He was always under somebody's spell—a girl or a guy. I'd seen it before. Only with guys, he was quiet about it—really quiet. How I'd know he'd fallen for someone is that he'd take to wearing this pair of tight old jeans. Always the same ones—faded and molded around his legs and ass in such a way that all the shapes, even the head of his dick, were real visible. He didn't do much work, but spent a lot of time thinking about or even watching the object of his fancies, because it usually ended up being some new guy on the floor. It sounds kind of creepy, but it wasn't. He would never hassle anyone. In fact, I'm pretty sure he never acted on his feelings. The guys he was hot for, for the most part, never even sussed anything. On the outside, he was calm, almost noble. He reminded me of one of those Roman statues—looking out at the world for years and years, always strong and solid, never expecting anything in return. Only occasionally, if you really watched for it, would you see his chest heave in deep breaths as if he'd just finished unloading a truck or something.

When it came to you, since you so rarely showed up on our floor, he would, instead, always be turning and looking up the stairs, maybe hoping for just a glimpse of your heel as you passed by on the landing above. If you did grace us with your presence—usually to bitch to Jean-Guy, the production manager—Mario would kind of circle in behind you, coming in quite close, but never uttering a word. At first, I couldn't believe you didn't figure things out, you with your McGill degree. But, after all, I guess you did.

Then the big event happened. I overheard you in the hallway that Friday afternoon, asking him to come in on the Sunday to reorganize the storage area. You casually mentioned that you'd be coming in yourself and would be available to help out if needed.

What happened that day, I've pieced together and run through my mind many times. First, there were the clothes, the ones I later found on the floor—Mario's Montréal Alouettes t-shirt, the one he wore all the time despite the hole just above the left breast, and those jeans of his, or what was left after you'd finished with them. It was obvious he'd worked like a bloody slave that day. Most of those dusty old boxes—the ones that weigh a ton—had been piled up neatly in a row, almost reaching the ceiling. It must've been doubly hard for him to concentrate on working, knowing you and he were alone in the building. He must've really wanted to impress you.

I can picture you coming quietly down the cement stairs, Mario, at first, not hearing you, and then turning and standing there, startled and breathless, a hulking buck caught in headlights. You asked him to show you what he'd been doing, and he turned, scratching his head with one hand and gesturing with the other to the newly cleared-out area, hardly able to speak.

Then you came up very close behind him. You put out a hand and almost touched his big hard ass. Mario turned and could do nothing but smile down on you. Yeah. He was quite a bit bigger than you, wasn't he? What a contrast the two of you were: Mario, so clearly made of flesh and blood, bone, sinew and muscle, while you, you seemed as if your tight little body contained other things—maybe ground-up metal shavings, rods and gears, thick diesel fuel for blood—nothing human that could be hurt. I bet you never guessed I thought like this, but I've been watching your type for all my life—the type I've always worked for, the ones who take advantage of the muscle and heart of others.

So there you were, Mario so close to you, offering his whole big body to you. But you didn't smile back or even look into his face; you just concentrated on his growing bulge, expanding the faded pocket of his jeans. Then, as if doing a quality control inspection, you undid the button and pulled down the zipper. I bet Mario had decided not to wear underwear that day. With a little prodding, his cock sprang out, a big muscle throwing off drops of pre-cum. Some even splattered your forehead. You grabbed hold of that big piece of meat, and like a severe mother with a child who's done something wrong, led him across the room to the large cutting table. Here, you took the man's knife, clicked off the used blade to get a nice fresh one, and began to remove Mario's jeans, cutting them off in strips. I've got to hand it to you, it must've taken a lot of control to just cut through the denim and not the skin. Mario must've kept real still for you.

You handled the gaffer tape well, too. After having pushed Mario back onto the table, you secured his thick, heavy ankles to the corners. You did the same with his wrists, so that the whole of his body seemed to lead into that centre where his cock lay heavy and pulsing, reaching up his abdomen. Through it all, Mario said nothing, but simply looked up at you, helpless and trusting.

Then, using the opaquing paint and brush, you wrote a word on Mario's balls. He didn't lift his head to see what you were doing. He assumed this tickling was something that would lead to much more. His cock throbbed. But that was all. In a moment you were gone, leaving him there. I would have thought that big, strong Mario could have broken those tape binds. But something else held him there. To remove them would be to put an end to this whole thing. And you knew it too, you bastard. You knew he would just lay there waiting, through the afternoon, evening and night, twisting and sighing, then swearing to himself.

Finally, as the first light of dawn came in through the warehouse glass, he fell asleep. In a dream, you came back. You touched his big, barrel chest, then ran your fingers down to his waist and below, following the long scratch marks made by the knife. These lines had become quite red overnight, and in the morning light seemed to glow, illuminating the curves of his great, muscular thighs. You let your hand rest there on that warm spot on the inside of his leg, just below his balls. Your fingers felt dry and a little cold, which surprised him. He winced a little in his dream, but a smile spread across his face, so glad you'd returned. His cock stirred and lifted itself once again, and began to produce more clear liquid that made the whole big head glisten. Then, you lightly kissed it, the wetness gluing itself to your lips as if it were an attempt to keep them there. Slowly, you went down on him, your tongue exploring the surface of the hard shaft, pulling him in until the big, heavy head touched the back of your throat. You nearly gagged, and pulled back, then repeated the action over and over. Mario's head tightened and convulsed underneath you, his naked skin chafing against your clothes. Then, with one deep gasp, the first sound he'd made, he shot out a hot liquid blast.

When he finally opened his eyes, he found me hunched over him, wiping my chin with the tails of my old workshirt. I cleaned off the word you wrote on his balls: Charlie—his name. Because you knew I'd be the first to find him Monday morning, Mario was your gift to me, my retirement present. I undid his wrists and ankles, and handed him his clothes. I'd like to tell you he took me in his big arms, held me tight and thanked me. But no, he just kind of pushed me aside, wrapped what was left of his jeans around him like a pleated skirt, and stumbled up the stairs.

As you know, neither Mario nor I ever came back to work in the stripping room.

DOUGLAS G. FERGUSON

Phil

PHIL AN' ME BEEN EYEING EACH OTHER all year, but he was with that Derrick squirt with the plain features and reddish hair. But when it ended I was the first in line, the first on his list. *Phil wants me. I want Phil.* Phil with the lean muscular body, Phil in the wife-beater shirt, Phil with the tattoos on his arms, Phil with the shaved head and brooding good looks, Phil, Phil, Phil! So he takes me home from the club, both of us sweating, both of us on "E," both of us waiting for this moment for far too long, and he's hot and sweaty and radiating heat like a register, and I rub my crotch against him like a cat, and he grabs my ass with both his hands, *his large rough hands* grabbing my ass, *my small sweet ass,* and I wrap my legs around his waist as he stabs my mouth with his beer-flavoured tongue, and carries me to his bed, and I roll off his shirt, rub my hands along his hard chest, and in seconds we're totally naked, and my dick's so hard I'm scared I'm gonna blow, and he hovers above me, my neck between his knees, and his large dick starts fucking my mouth and its skin is soft and velvety like a rodent and I can barely breathe but don't care 'cause it feels so good, smells so good, tastes so good I'm scared I'll bite it off, *eat it for breakfast,* and his body looks so incredible, so fucking hot above me, Phil with the washboard stomach. Phil with the hard chest and tattoos. Then he slips his wet dick outta my mouth and flips me on my back without saying a word, and I grab hold of the railing and he grabs my hands and starts ramming me *hard,* not *in* me, but *between* me, between my sweet cheeks, his hard velvety rodent searching frantically for my burrow. And I suck and nibble his salty forearm, and gasp and shoot without even touching myself, and I feel him quiver, hear him groan, feel his warm cum *spray my spine* . . . and when it's over, he goes to the kitchen to get us water. And I hear him checking his messages, and it's his ex *Derrick*, and Derrick's weeping on the machine, saying he misses Phil, saying he's lonely, and fifteen minutes later, Phil still hasn't returned with the water. So I creep through the hall and peer into the living room and Phil's sittin' there *naked* on the floor with his back against a cushy chair, and the phone machine's beside him, and he's smokin' a cigarette in the dark, and I know he's thinkin' about him. And I know that he's probably forgotten all about me, or wishing I'd go home; that I'm shit-in-his-eyes. That he resents me as much as I suddenly resent him. So I slip on my clothes and write my number on a book of matches, leaving it on the night-stand. And I tell him to call me, and he says, "Sure thing." But I know he won't.

Aromas Etched

THE AURA OF EX-BOYFRIENDS fades, but not in gentle, measured steps. First you put out the fires: extinguish expectations, eliminate hopes, and neutralize desires. Time does heal, and memories begin to erode. Four months later you're not able to remember what you saw in him. He's not the same, you're not the same as when you met. You've changed. Partnering and parting have turned you into different men.

But don't think you can forget how it felt that afternoon he took your hand and slipped it underneath the waistband of his shorts and lay on top of it. A public park, in the middle of July. Warm sun, cool grass. Families were eating chicken salad from picnic baskets less than twenty yards away.

His cotton underwear was moist, his pubic hair was slick with perspiration. He hardened in your palm, and grew onto your wrist and forearm. Your fingers cupped his hairless balls.

Your face was turned away, as if by not looking at him you could insure that no one else would be able to see what was going on. You were lying on your stomach too, your erection flattened against the ground. When you turned his way he looked straight into your eyes and silently confirmed he knew exactly what he was doing.

He fucked your hand. It was the hottest thing you've ever experienced, before or since. Despite the people around you, who even now were talking about daycare centres. Or was it because of the people around you, who even now had no idea that he'd begun to leak pre-cum onto the tendons of your wrist, that the sweat of your palm was mingling with the sweat from his groin? Couldn't they see his butt flex and rise as it ground against your hand?

The earth echoed your heartbeats and quickened breathing. You didn't wonder any longer just how far he'd go. Your neighbours now were talking about electric breadmaking machines, but you smelled only sex, rising on the summer breeze.

You half-expected him to shout when he came, but he didn't. You were looking at each other now. You would have liked to kiss. One last rise of his buttocks. He closed his eyes and exploded into your hand.

Seagulls cackled overhead. A child with a dog walked by only ten feet away. You thought for sure the dog would come over, trying to sniff out that sweet stench, but it didn't.

You gently rolled his balls with cum-smeared fingers, and made him squirm. "Are you ready?" he asked, and you assumed he meant if you were ready to come. But when you nodded, you felt another, warmer, wetter flood engulf your hand. He was pissing in his shorts! He was pissing on your hand. You came immediately, with a force that soaked through your own shorts and into the blanket beneath.

You both lay there perfectly still for several more minutes. You thought he might have fallen asleep. You wondered how the two of you would be able to walk the hundred yards to the car on a brilliant Sunday afternoon with cum- and urine-soaked shorts.

But it was easy. You stood up, pointed at each other, laughed, and walked back to the parking lot. Slowly. And in the front seat of his car you kissed.

Since then you have forgotten exactly how the inside of his mouth felt to your tongue. You've forgotten which brand of toothpaste he used. But when you start to wonder if those months you spent together might have been imagined, you bring the fingers of your right hand to your nose and you can smell him still.

J A M E S   M E R R E T T

Suckers

ALVARO STANDS AMONG THE AVOCADO TREES washing his lean, athletic body. Dipping a plastic cup into a bucket, he ladles steaming hot water over his silky black hair and cinnamon-hued shoulders. Then he picks up the bar of soap I've brought from New York and rubs the lather all over his chest.

Behind me in the dirt-floor kitchen, Doña Olga stirs a pot of boiling plantains as Alvaro's little sisters gather around her begging for mamones; she calls to me in the lilting Nicaraguan Spanish which my ears are just beginning to adjust to.

"I'm coming!" I call back, still loitering at the window so I can watch Alvaro bathe. His biceps pulse like little snails of muscle as he soaps up his taut belly; then he picks up the bucket, shuts his eyes, and empties the rest of the water over his head, rinsing the suds from his glistening torso, soaking the cotton briefs which are supposed to protect his modesty, but which are now clinging sheer as oilskin to his furled sex.

Doña Olga calls again. She fills the little girls' cupped hands with mamones and leaves some for me on the kitchen table next to the bag of beans I'm supposed to clean.

And then, with squeals of delight, Alvaro's little sisters crack open the green mamones and pop the spongy yellow fruit in their mouths as their big brother dabs droplets of water like gelid sunshine from his chest, cinches the white towel around his waist, and lets the wet cotton briefs slide down—depositing them on the upturned nose of Toby, his little white dog. "That's for staring," he says.

"Oh, wow!" I smile as I taste mamones for the first time. "All day suckers!"

In the living room picking twigs and pebbles from among the beans, sucking on tart mamones, I wonder if Alvaro knows how magically beautiful he really is; how altogether splendid he looks stretching near-naked in the morning sunshine. And just then he pads in nuzzling Toby's snow white softness, like a splash of whipped cream against the cinnamon skin. The towel clings precariously to Alvaro's slim waist, until the dog breaks free, snags the end of it and pulls it away like a magician snapping a tablecloth, leaving all the pretty settings in place. Alvaro doesn't seem to mind having his privacy stripped away in front of another man. He stares back at me as if completely unaware that his nakedness is capable of turning a living room into a shrine, then puts his hands on his hips, as if to say, have a good long look, and what's all the fuss about? Then he sits down on the sofa and drags on faded blue jeans as I put the clean beans into a pot.

"*Los mamones*—delicious," I tell Doña Olga as she covers the beans with water and leaves them on the windowsill to soak.

"Suckers," Alvaro says, savouring the English word he has just learned from one of his little sisters. We are on the rooftop, lazing about in what the natives call "a furious heat." "Tomorrow, if you like, we can go swimming," he says. When I remind him that I don't have a bathing suit, he replies, "neither do I." It all seems so tempting, and yet dare I take the risk in this little red-roofed Catholic town?

But Alvaro seems to have decided for me. He presses his slim brown fingers against my pale gringo skin. "You look like peeled yucca," he teases. "You need some colour." Casting about for something to do, I have brought along my coloured marking pens, but there is no paper at hand, so Alvaro suggests we colour each other. I hadn't known you could draw on skin with magic markers, and yet Alvaro demonstrates by nimbly sketching a magic marker tattoo of an anchor on my chest. He draws the rope and keeps on drawing to the ticklish part of my belly just above my belt.

"How low can you go?" I ask. He jokingly says he'll draw it all the way to my asshole if I want him to, then he pushes me away and says, only kidding. Next he draws—to my utter surprise—a spurting cock on my shoulder—replete with raindrops of cum. "You better erase that before your mother sees," I say, but he keeps on drawing them.

I push him down and draw the only thing I can draw—a pig with a curly tail—on his chest. Some ink accidentally gets on one of his nipples, so I lick my thumb and slowly rub it away in velvety circles; continuing even when the ink's erased. He smiles. We lie back on the roof and drink rum from the same bottle and soak up sun with nothing in the world to do until dinnertime.

Every once in a while he points a finger at Toby and says: "Sucker."

As the only men in this house, we share a room—twin beds separated by about a metre of floor space. That night, when I return from washing up, Alvaro is already in his bed—naked under his white sheet; propped up on one arm, he watches me read my Sherlock Holmes. Every time the quoits of his bed squeak I look up from my book to see if he's getting out of bed. I'm sunburned, drowsy, still a little drunk, and my head keeps falling on the page. Finally he tells me he's turning out the light. I protest—I've just come to the climax, where the hound is bearing down on Baskerville, but it's no use, I'll have to wait 'til tomorrow. I save my place and toss the book onto the floor just as the light goes out. "*Buenas noches*," I say, but the words just hang there in the darkness, and then there's the jangling of bed quoits—and he's telling me to move over and make room. His skin is velvety, like the flesh of a perfectly ripe avocado—even in the furious heat. He puts his lips softly against my ear and whispers, "I hear you like mamones."

207

Belgium

MY STOMACH GRUMBLED and I pulled my coat tighter. The train rolled on and I stared at the gun-metal sea on the other side of the window. There's something sinister about the coast of Belgium in January, I thought. The baby two or three compartments down started crying again and a conductor with brown teeth and a tobacco-stained moustache came in and demanded my ticket.

He talked excitedly in Flemish, pointing to my ticket to Amsterdam. I didn't understand, though I began to suspect. Eventually he mustered enough English to make me see.

"Bad train," he said, shaking his head.

"You," he continued, pointing the opposite way to our direction, "go back Brussels. Change."

I was never very good with directions and timetables. I looked over at the soldier sitting opposite and smiled goofily. He held my eyes briefly then looked away. The conductor left. So, miraculously, did the fat man who'd been drinking beer in the seat beside me. I was alone in the compartment with the soldier, whom I'd been admiring since leaving Brussels. Indeed, he was the reason I'd chosen the seat. He hadn't shaved for a couple of days and I looked again at the patchy, dark stubble.

"Do you speak English?" I asked, deciding it was a good time to strike up a conversation.

He frowned slightly and shook his head. Then he shifted in his seat and looked back out the window. His uniform was scruffy and his boots were dirty. His hair was tousled and greasy, but his skin glowed and he had big lips.

The afternoon light was fading. A nameless town's streetlights came on, quite magically, as the train rattled past the main square. I looked over at my soldier again and cleared my throat.

"*Parlez-vous français?*" I asked.

He shook his head and turned away again. A tired-looking woman appeared at the door and inquired politely in Flemish whether there was a free seat. I didn't understand what she said, of course, but I knew what she meant. After a brief interchange with the soldier she went away. When his eyes met mine, I breathed in sharply. He quickly turned to look out the window again.

My heart thumped. He'd lied and looked like he felt guilty. Certainly a little nervous. But when I looked again his face was a mask. I know that trick, I thought, suddenly confident. I smiled and shifted in my seat. The bells of a level crossing clanged, masking my second throat-clearing. So I cleared my throat again.

"*Sprechen-sie Deutsch?*" I asked, not that I spoke much myself.

Now he stretched in his seat, quite luxuriously, and gave a brief apologetic gasp when one of his boots brushed against my leg. He smiled the tiniest little smile and shook his head. Then he looked out the window again. My eyes were drawn to his crotch. I shifted around a little more in my seat and continued to stare at him, but he continued to stare out the window.

I looked at his leg and realized it was not far from mine. With a little plausible shifting, I figured I could accidentally brush up against it. As I began the manoeuvre, the fat man came back with another beer and began chattering away in Flemish. My soldier looked annoyed and answered in either grunts or shrugs. When his jacket fell open I noticed then that he wasn't, in fact, all that skinny. He seemed coiled and threatening, like an attractive but dangerous animal. A panther or something.

The fat man, clearly annoyed, guzzled the rest of his small can of beer, shifted around in his seat and then fell asleep, breathing heavily. I resumed my manoeuvre. As my leg made contact with the soldier's I felt a jolt of pleasure at its warmth. He looked down, tutted, and quickly moved his leg.

I felt like an idiot. I think I even blushed. Then the brakes squealed, the bright lights of a station flooded in and the conductor returned and told me in broken English to change trains. The fat man woke up and began complaining. I gathered my things and left.

What did I think was going to happen, anyway? Wrong train. Wrong country! I was walking angrily along the platform to the stairs to cross over to the other side when I heard someone whistle. I looked back and saw the soldier standing by the entrance to the men's toilet. He jerked his head and went inside.

I smiled and followed.

Florence and the Crisco Kid

I WOKE TO THE SOUND OF SCOOTERS racing below my window. Opening the tall wooden shutters, I found the city of Florence asleep under the stars. It was my last night in Italy. Pulling fresh clothes from my backpack, I got dressed to go out.

The streets were cool and quiet, abandoned by the daytime hordes of summer tourists. Crossing a deserted neighbourhood of crumbling porticos and moonlit piazzas, I circled the great Cathedral and entered a narrow street of rough granite walls and locked metal grates.

The Crisco Bar was easy to miss. It had no windows or lights, and the black steel door was locked. Hearing the faint beat of techno music, I decided to knock. The doorman peered through the eyeslot. He let me in, and the cashier gave me a little white card to record my bar tab. The minimum was fifteen thousand lira, but if I lost my card, the penalty would be sixty thousand lira. I stuck it in my pocket and went inside.

The bar was long and narrow, lit overhead by blue neon signs.

Nodding at the bartender, I said: *"Birra per favore."* He opened my bottle with a flourish, and replied: "Here ya go, honey." Taking my bar tab he stamped it: fifteen thousand lira.

I settled into a corner to survey the room. The men were all white, at least ten years older than me. They didn't dress like the trendy fags back home, but more like someone's uncle at a summer barbecue.

A middle-aged guy with salt-and-pepper hair smiled hello.

"Are you from China?" he asked.

"No. Canada."

"Ah. You speak Chinese? *Ni hao ma?*"

I shook my head. "English."

He shrugged and laughed. He told me about his recent trip to China, and said that the Chinese were the friendliest people in the world. I smiled politely, but was losing interest fast.

When he stopped, I told him my name.

"My English name is Paul," he replied.

"Paolo?"

He shook his head. "Paul."

I nodded. He offered me a cigarette, but I didn't smoke. When he went to buy a drink, I decided to check out the next room.

It was painted all black, lit by a single red light bulb. Men stood against the wall or sat on the edge of an empty stage. They were silent, mesmerized by the porno video, all runny flesh tones and murky groans. The thick, musky odour was making me tense. I finished my drink and plunged through the far doorway.

The next room was dark, hot and sweaty. Around the corner, I found tangled silhouettes coupling in the darkness, arms gripping backs humping shadows kneeling down. Settling against the wall, I stopped to listen to the stifled groans and muffled sighs. I waited for my eyes to adjust to the darkness, but could only see dim shadows drifting by.

One stopped in front of me. A hand reached out, resting lightly on my chest. I touched it, and a body melted onto mine, lips smearing across my neck. Tentatively, I put my arms around his shoulders, before drawing him close.

He took my hand and led me further into the maze. In a dead-end corridor, we began necking again. He opened my zipper and dropped to his knees. I steadied myself against the wall and another man started to stroke my butt. My partner brushed the hand away and stood up to kiss me. His shorts were down low, his cock digging into my groin. I reached around to grab his hairy butt, hiking his body up close. Even then, I couldn't make out his face in the darkness.

Turning to face the wall, he guided my hard-on up his ass. A hot surge of pleasure pulsed through my cock, unshielded by latex. A guilty worry whispered across my mind, but the danger seemed too far away. My body contracted, forcing my cock deep inside him. Each pull's suction sent a burst of rapture into my groin, drawing each thrust deeper in. His neck arched back onto my shoulder, and he whispered Italian into my ear. *"Gusta mi,"* he said. *"Gusta mi."* I stroked his cock, and he shuddered as his cum hit the wall.

. Kissing me goodbye, he stumbled away. A minute later, I walked out too. In the crowded front room, I couldn't recognize his face, and didn't really want to. Instead, I found Paul getting ready to leave. I was also ready to go, so I suggested we walk together. With a shrug, he agreed.

I reached for my bar tab, but it wasn't there. With a mounting sense of panic, I checked every pocket. It was lost. I had to find it, or pay a fine of sixty thousand lira.

Retracing my steps, I ended up back in the dark room. It was even more crowded than before. Fumbling my way past necking couples, I returned to the spot where we'd fucked. Unfortunately, another couple was already there, in a passionate embrace. I paced around them, hoping they might move on. But they were stubborn, and held their ground.

Finally, I crouched down to search for my bar tab. It was too dark to see, so I ran my fingertips over the cement floor. I only found the grit stuck in dry sticky spots. It was hopeless. I thought about getting a match, but these guys might get upset if I lit a flame around their ankles. Racking my brain, I tried to figure out what to do next.

Suddenly I had an idea. Aiming my wrist at the ground, I pushed the night light button on my watch. In the faint glow, I saw my bar tab, trapped under the heel of some cowboy lover. I moved his foot with a discreet shove, and collected my ticket.

Paul was still waiting for me at the front door. We paid our tabs, and stepped out into the cool Florentine night.

My Kingdom for a Bed

MOTHER AND I WERE WATCHING the Sunday night Hindi movie when the phone rang. The villain had strapped the hero's mother to a pillar in his mountain hide-out.

"Oh ho," said my mother, barely able to contain her annoyance at whoever was calling at such a critical moment.

I picked up the receiver. Mother leaned forward, ostensibly to listen to the dialogue better, but really to try and hear what I was saying on the phone.

"Hullo," I said.

"Hi," said the voice at the other end.

Oh my God. It was Arun. We had met just two months ago at the neighbourhood park. He came and sat down on the bench I was sitting on. Neither of us had a place of our own—the eternal problem for all of us in India. We rubbed each other through our trousers 'til an approaching heterosexual couple forced us to spring apart. We had met a few times since then. One rainy evening we had even managed to bring each other to climax behind a tree. What we wanted more than anything was to do it on a bed, but that was impossible. If mother was not at home, my brother was. If brother was not at home, then the maid was. And even if no one was home, our neighbour's living room looked right into my bedroom.

"Hi," I replied guardedly, looking at mother.

"What are you doing?"

"Watching TV."

"Can you come over now?"

"Right now? But it's past eight."

"I know—but my mother has gone to the airport and the maid is away at her sister's. We'll have the house all to ourselves."

"But, but," I spluttered, "what will I say?"

"I don't know. Make up some excuse. Good God, Anil, this is what we've been waiting and waiting for."

I glanced over at mother. She had given up all pretence of watching TV and was looking at me quizzically, trying to figure out who it was from my one-sided conversation.

"But," I hissed into the phone, "you should have called earlier. I jerked off this afternoon."

"Oh God." He sounded exasperated. "I didn't know. Anyway if you are not coming, tell me. I'm going to call this other guy. I can't waste this chance."

"I'll be right over."

"Bye." He hung up. I stood still holding the phone to my ear pretending to be listening as I tried to figure out a good excuse.

"Okay," I said. "I'll be right over. Do you have the calculus book though?" I put down the receiver, took a deep breath, and turned to my mother. "Calculus homework," I said without looking at her. "I'd forgotten about it. Have to run to Sumit's."

"Now?"

"I'll never be able to finish it on my own."

"But—"

I ran and splashed on my father's aftershave and brushed my hair. I needed to shave and I'd have liked to take a shower, but there was no time. As I hurtled down the stairs, I heard my mother's voice: "Be careful. What time are you coming back?" But I was out of the door by then.

It was winter and the smog cloaked everything in a sulfurous haze. I sat in the bus watching the city go by. The people muffled in monkey caps and scarves, the swerving taxis, the rickshaw-pullers, the cyclists darting through the traffic like suicidal sparrows, the young men chatting on street corners. I wondered what we would do in the freedom of the bed. Would Arun try to fuck me? Did I want to be fucked?

By the time I reached his house I had worked myself into a state of nervous collapse. My heart was thudding. My palms were sweating. My tongue was made out of cotton wool.

He lived at the end of a quiet narrow lane. I took a deep breath, ran my fingers through my hair, then rang the doorbell. I heard a window open. He stuck his head out and yelled, "Coming." Then he clattered down the stairs and opened the door. He stood framed in the hall light, grinning, his black wavy hair tumbling over his face. He was wearing his old grubby Holiday Nepal t-shirt and pajamas. He hadn't bothered to dress up for the occasion.

I stood there grinning nervously. He waved me in and turned and ran up the stairs. I took my shoes off at the top of the stairs, followed him into his bedroom—and gasped. He had turned his messy little room, with its scattered books and torn posters, into a little fantasy land. He had covered his bedside lamp with red tissue paper so that the room was filled with a thick red light, the colour of sealing wax. He had the bedcover off and the light spilled onto the white sheets turning them a shadowy red. I stood there open-mouthed looking around as he grinned at my astonishment.

"Go on," he said. "Sit down."

I sat down gingerly on the edge of the bed. He went over to the stereo and fumbled with his cassettes. Then the soft tinkle of the piano wafted through the red air.

"*Beethoven Favourites*," he grinned, "That's the only classical music I have. My aunt gave it to me." He returned to the side of the bed. "Are you ready?"

I closed my eyes and nodded. I felt like I was at gym class and any minute I'd hear the referee going, "On your marks, get set, go." But instead of the crack of the gun I felt his arms around me and the rasp of his chin on my face, the touch of his lips smelling faintly of toothpaste and cigarettes on my closed eyelids and then his tongue nuzzling my lips. I opened my mouth and let his tongue in. He was kissing me passionately, now rubbing his crotch into mine. I felt his hands fumble with my zipper. He bit my neck and nuzzled my ear. So this is what it was like to have sex in a bed. You didn't have to constantly look over your shoulder, you could close your eyes, you could—

He pulled my pants down and undid his pajamas. I felt him hard and hot against me just like in the books. I reached down and took him in my hand.

"Ohhh," he moaned. "Suck me, Anil." I tentatively touched the tip of his penis with my tongue. He groaned and thrust his penis in my face. It was at that moment a car stopped in front of his house. As if from far way, I heard a door shut. And then a woman's voice carrying through the still night air: "Arun, Arun."

Arun sprang away from me and ran to the window.

"Ma?" he cried, incredulous.

"The car broke down. I had to take a cab back. Can you call Pratima and tell her I couldn't go to the airport? Maybe she can pick your father up."

The next couple of minutes were a whirl as Arun tore off the red tissue, jumped into his clothes and threw my pants at me. I hopped around the room trying to find my socks and calculus book. As I ran down the stairs to the door I could still hear Beethoven, the notes bravely trying to reclaim romance from the air.

When I got home my mother's face was grim.

"Sumit called. He didn't know anything about any calculus homework."

Athens/Chad/
Thanksgiving, 1996

THAT'S NOT WHAT *I* call straight," Chad says in the English pub of the dowager hotel.

"Well," you say over the remnants of dessert, "maybe straight men in Greece like getting fucked."

"Or maybe," Chad says, "the word is meaningless."

■ ■ ■

Chad stands on the balcony. He's wearing red jeans and a white t-shirt with a logo from the ship he works on. The Acropolis glows behind him, lit up under a crescent moon. His black skin gleams in the light of a single lamp.

"It's spectacular, isn't it?" you say.

"I guess," he says.

"You don't think it's magnificent?"

"I think if you came from slave people, you wouldn't have such a high regard for the Greeks, pagans or not."

You hear traffic but see only Chad's soft and troubled eyes.

"Am I your first black man?" he asks, "or are you the kind of white boy who only sleeps with black men?"

"Neither," you finally say, enormously sad. You put the palm of your right hand on his chest. Your hand looks brown against the white cotton of the shirt.

He reaches down to his waist, pulls the shirt off his chiseled dancer's body, and puts your hand back on his chest. Your hand is alabaster now.

■ ■ ■

His lips, when they touch yours, are soft, warm, open. When you kiss him back, he sighs, and his body sinks into yours. You cross into the country where thought is outlawed. You forget all the differences between people—just as you did when you first saw him dance.

■ ■ ■

You brush his eyelids with your lips, or perhaps with your breath alone. You kiss one eyebrow hair into your mouth. You draw the tip of your tongue across the place on his forehead where wrinkles will grow. You rub your beard along his cheek, his neck, his neck, his neck. You are dreaming now of breath and neck, of lips, of tongue, your tongue, your teeth. You are leaving a mark on him, dark and purple, the mark of your having been men together making love on a Thanksgiving Thursday.

■ ■ ■

Your mouth works down his body. You lap his nipples up to full attention, drawing your beard past the complex knot of his navel. You rest your chin on the trimmed patch of black crotch hair. It smells of soap and desire. You take his cock in the fist of your throat. He undulates like the wild Aegean, roiling all the way here from Istanbul.

You pull up onto your knees and kneel before him, pushing upward on his thighs, licking his balls, and the place where the balls hang from the thighs. You draw your wettest tongue along the shaft of his cock to its head. You slip your mouth over the top of his dick and pull down on his skin as you swallow him whole.

"Oh, God," he says. You feel his body rustling the bed linens and wonder which God, or gods, he means.

You push back on his thighs and put your tongue on the dark pucker of his asshole. When he can't take the pleasure of it any longer, he shifts you onto your back and throws his legs across your chest, kneeling over you, your cock instantly in his mouth and his asshole inches from your own.

You push your thumbs into the nubs where the thighs and buttocks meet and spread the cheeks with your hands. He shifts back toward you and you start to circle the hole with your tongue. Concentric

219

inward movements. Then you put your tongue on his asshole while he sucks your cock, and you push the tip of it into him as far as it will go, wetting it as much as you can, pulling the cheeks further and further apart and widening the opening of him. Your bodies are beginning to flow with sweat in the warm Mediterranean November.

You pull him around, attack his mouth with your mouth.

"What do you want?" you ask.

He does not answer. He looks into your eyes.

"You want to fuck me?" you ask.

"No, baby," he says, "I want you to fuck me."

■ ■ ■

Straddling your hips, he slides one long finger down into your asshole and pulls up on your scrotum with his nails. And then he puts you in, and then he starts to rock.

You are thinking and feeling nothing, nothing but your cock up the ass of this beautiful boy/man, the sweet hot pain of your nipples gripped between his fingers. You smell the sweat of him and his cologne, taste the salt of his palms, hear the breath of him coming faster between the groans while he rocks faster and you arch your back and push into him, his cock in your hands, his rippled torso dripping seat, until he starts to whimper like a child, until he snaps his head back and pulls your hand off his cock and he grabs it and pulls the skin of it down to his balls and then shoots straight up in the air and then again, both hot spurts of white cum hitting your body simultaneously, then another and another on your chest, neck, face, hair. You hear it hit the pillow behind you.

And you pull out of him, pull the rubber off your dick by the tip, tossing it across the room as it snaps, and you pull until you cum, the hot fluid splashing your chest and stomach, splashing his shoulders, waist, hips. And you let out an animal groan of your own and shudder so hard it's almost a spasm, and this surprises him, and he puts his hand over your heart as you turn to him and kiss him again.

■ ■ ■

You wrap him into yourself, pull the cool white sheets around his dark satin skin. The Acropolis is dark now, too. Soon a rosy dawn will creep over the hills of Athens and find you, asleep together—and giving thanks.

Contributors

Tommi Avicolli Mecca is an Italian/American performer, writer, activist, and events co-ordinator at A Different Light in San Francisco. He is still trying to publish his first novel about three generations of an Italian/American family (it has two queers, and no mafia).

Damien Barlow lives in Melbourne, Australia. His work has appeared in *Picador New Writing 4*, and *Queer View Mirror 1* and *2*. He is currently working on a novel tentatively titled *The Sodomitical Whore* and planning a *coup d'etat* of Australia's current crypto-fascist, racist/misogynist/homophobic government.

Alan Bell's personal essays have appeared in *Sister and Brother: Lesbians and Gay Men Write About Their Lives Together*, and *Friends and Lovers: Gay Men Write About the Families They Create*.

Randall Bolin is a writer and quilt artist living in San Francisco. His published work has appeared in *Evergreen Chronicles* and *Advocate Men*.

Allen Borcherding is a radiation therapist, neophyte gardener and cold-weather writer living with a perpetually shedding rabbit. His work has also appeared in *Queer View Mirror 1* and *2*.

Perry Brass has published nine books including *Sex-charge*, a book of poetry, and *Mirage*, the first of a trilogy of gay science fiction novels (followed by *Circles* and *Albert or the Book of Man*), both nominated for Lambda Literary Awards. His latest book is *The Lover of My Soul*, a collection of spiritual and erotic poetry, and his next book will be *How to Survive Your Own Gay Life*, a primer on adult relationships for gay men.

John Briggs is a native of Connecticut, and a Massachusetts resident for more than twenty years. He moved to Vancouver in 1993, where he continues to write, sculpt, and walk a great deal. His poetry and fiction have appeared in many Canadian and American periodicals.

CONTRIBUTORS

Justin Chin is a writer and performance artist. He is the author of *Bite Hard* (Manic D Press).

Lawrence W. Cloake was born in Ireland and spent his formative years in Wales. He returned to Ireland and moved to Dublin after graduating from secondary boarding school. He came out at the age of twenty, and at twenty-one met his other half, with whom he still lives in monogamous bliss.

Robert Chomiak received his BA in Dramatic Arts at the University of Lethbridge and completed two years of film studies at Simon Fraser University. He has written several short stories and plays. Currently he is in pre-production for a film he co-wrote entitled "Fido."

Daniel Collins is, or has been, an actor, activist, advocate, care giver, (caretaker, clerk), clown, (cook, dancer), director, (dishwasher), gardener, journalist, (mime), organizer, (paperboy), photographer, publicist, swimmer, (teacher, treeplanter, tutor, waiter), volunteer, and writer. His award-winning photography has been internationally exhibited and has graced the pages and covers of several magazines, journals, and books.

Michael Conrad is a Toronto author of erotic fiction. He was recently published in *Canadian Male* #6.

jem coones, Toronto—23 GWM 6' 180# br/gr gdlkg well endwd Fr A/P Gr P likes wrestlg—sks lrg gdlkg top 30+ bdy hair a must! all photos get replies. jem is one third of the zine *OrchidMouth*, and this is his second published story.

Daniel Curzon walked the minefields when gay writing was not only not *commercial* but not possible, except in clandestine and coded ways, and read by few. His 1971 novel, *Something You Do in the Dark* (G. P. Putnam), gave a picture of a world where gays were so terrorized by unthinking bias that they could not even speak out to defend themselves, afraid of rejection by society, family, and friends. *Something You Do in the Dark* is now out of print.

David Dakar's fiction has been published in anthologies and magazines in Canada, the U.S., and Australia. He lives in Vancouver.

J.R.G. de Marco lives in Philadelphia. He has edited *New Gay Life* and has written for *The Advocate, New York Native,* and *Philadelphia Gay News.* His work appears in *Black Men, White Men, We Are Everywhere,* and *Gay Life,* among others. He is working on a novel and a non-fiction book.

Dennis Denisoff is the author of the novel *Dog Years* (Arsenal Pulp) and the collection of poetry *Tender Agencies* (Arsenal Pulp). He has also written a monograph on the poet Erin Mouré, entitled *Erin Mouré and Her Work* (ECW), and edited a collection of gay fiction, *Queeries* (Arsenal Pulp). He is the co-editor of *Perennial Decay: New Essays on the Politics and Poetics of Decadence* (Pennsylvania University Press) and has just finished editing George Du Maurier's novel *Trilby* (1894) for the Classics Series of Oxford University Press.

Shaun de Waal was born and lives in South Africa. At present he is the arts and books editor of the national South African newspaper *Mail & Guardian*. In 1996 he published a collection of short stories, *These Things Happen*.

Viet Dinh, a graduate from the Johns Hopkins University in Baltimore, Maryland, is not at all paranoid about sex. He currently lives in the world capital of conspiracy theories and manipulative media, Washington, D.C. But who are you anyway and why do you want to know? What's *your* agenda, huh?

Lew Dwight has published in *Advocate Men, Freshmen, Advocate Classifieds*, and in the anthologies *Nature in the Raw, Up All Hours*, and *Friction*, all from Alyson Publications.

Douglas G. Ferguson was born in Yorkton, Saskatchewan, in 1971, and currently resides in Calgary. He has won the Mount Royal Award for his play *Coffee with Christ and Titania*, and has had work appear in several journals. He has just finished writing his first novel.

Reg Flowers is the author of several produced plays. He is included in *Wanderlust, Southern Comfort* (both BadBoy), and *Queer View Mirror 2* (Arsenal Pulp). His series Ozland appears monthly in *VICE Magazine*. He won a 1995 LA Ovation Award for "Belize" in *Angels in America*. He is a graduate of University of the Arts and Yale. He lives in NYC with his partner, Chris.

Michael Thomas Ford is the author of more than twenty-five books, including the Lambda Literary Award and Firecracker Alternative Book Award-nominated *The World Out There: Becoming Part of the Lesbian and Gay Community* (The New Press) and *Alec Baldwin Doesn't Love Me and Other Trials of My Queer Life* (Alyson).

Kenneth G. is twenty-four and lives in London. His writing career has so far been short and sweet! His *Quickies* story was inspired by a man who lives near him.

David Garnes is a frequent contributor to a variety of reference works and anthologies, including *A Loving Testimony: Remembering Loved Ones Lost to AIDS; Gay & Lesbian Biography; Connecticut Poets on AIDS*; and *Liberating Minds: The Stories and Professional Lives of Gay, Lesbian, and Bisexual Librarians and Their Advocates*.

David Greig is a Toronto writer and artist whose work has appeared in *RFD; Waves: An Anthology of Canadian Poetry, The Day We Met, Lines: Anthology*, and other publications.

CONTRIBUTORS

Wes Hartley is a Vancouver poet, playwright, storyteller, and a queerelder out since 1966. He has just finished his thirteenth book, *Appleseeds*, a long poem tracing the life journey and labours of the pioneer American folk hero Johnny Appleseed. Wes intends to learn how to write screenplays for the movie moguls.

Matthew R.K. Haynes lives with his lover of four years, Rhett Tanner, and their two cats, Xochitl and Keoki. He had a short story published in *Queer View Mirror*, recently published a chapbook, *16 november 1996*, and is currently trying to publish his first novel.

Thea Hillman, a San Francisco poet and fictionographer, is currently undergoing psychoanalysis to cure a severe case of fag envy. Her writing can be found in the magazines *Ragshock* and *Black Sheets* and the anthologies *Noirotica, First Person Sexual,* and the upcoming *Between Our Lips*.

Reed Hortie is a queer Vancouver playwright and comedian. His musical comedy, *B Average*, toured to New York as part of the cultural festival of the 1994 Gay Games. His most recent play, *Queer Foetus*, premiered at the 1998 Vancouver Fringe Festival. Reed will perform stand-up comedy at the 1998 Gay Games where he will also compete as a bodybuilder.

Jeff Kirby—artist, performance artist, activist, and educator—is author of *Cock & Soul* and *Drunk On Cock* and appears in the anthologies *Queeries, Stallions and Other Studs,* and *Queer View Mirror*. He is currently at work on his latest chapbook, *Joe,* and his first novel *Head Cleaner.*

Kevin Knox lives in Vancouver. This is his first published story. His parents are proud of him, but he probably won't let them read it.

Robert Labelle is a graduate of Concordia University's Masters program in creative writing. His work has been seen in *Queer View Mirror 2* as well as Montreal's new writing magazines, *Fish Piss* and *Sugar Diet*. He lives in Montreal.

Michael Lassell's latest collection of poetry is *A Flame for the Touch That Matters* (Painted Leaf Press, 1998). His previous books include the Lammy-winning *Decade Dance* and *The Hard Way*. He is the editor of *The Name of Love, Eros in Boystown,* and (with Lawrence Schimel) *Two Hearts Desire.*

Tom Lever was born in Dublin, Ireland and has travelled extensively throughout Europe and the world. He currently lives and works in Germany where he's happily married to a hot, hunky English Bear.

L.D. Little lives in rural Nova Scotia. She writes occasionally about sex, usually about men, always about struggling for balance. Her short stories have appeared in a variety of journals and anthologies. She is working on her first novel.

Michael MacLennan is a playwright and screenwriter who divides his time between Vancouver and Toronto. His play *Grace* won the 1996 Canadian National Playwriting Competition. An earlier play, *Beat the Sunset*, won numerous awards across the country.

Harry Matthews is a freelance writer and tour guide in New York. He's been an advertising copywriter, administrator of an educational exchange program, and a leader of gay history walking tours. The Cincinnati native is the author of the *Condo/Co-op Owners' Survival Manual* and a collector of urban folklore.

Tom McDonald is an artist and writer living in his native Brooklyn. His fiction has been published in *Queer View Mirror 1* and *2*. His artwork was most recently shown at the Diversity 5 show at La MaMa Gallery in the East Village.

Jim McDonough has published about fifty erotic stories in over a dozen gay porn magazines in the past few years. His work is also featured in *Queer View Mirror 2*. He is still working on his first novel *Reckless Abandon*.

Alan McGinty is a secretary at a medical school in London. He has been editor of the newsletter of the *Terrence Higgins Trust*, the U.K.'s leading AIDS charity, and was a contributor to the *Body Politic* magazine in Toronto. He is currently working on a play.

James Merrett's work has appeared in *The Nation*, *The New York Times*, *The Village Voice*, *The Advocate*, *The Guide*, *Frontiers*, and numerous other publications. He was a contributor to *Flesh and the Word 2* and *4* and the Lambda-Award winning anthology, *Sister and Brother*. Jim is a New York-based journalist who left his heart in Toronto. This story is from a work in progress.

David Mueller is a ten-year veteran of San Francisco. His journalistic experience includes a stint as the San Francisco correspondent to *My Comrade* magazine and his work in the field of social criticism has appeared in *Tantrum*.

Chad Owens is a freelance writer whose daily struggles include keeping his head straight jumping from one short story to the next in the magazine market, wry amusement over the fact that delivering newspapers often pays better, and dismay over his mate's latest obsession, "Beanie Babies."

Douglas Parish won the Deep South Writer's Conference Award for his play *An Ode to Auden at an Hour Till Midnight*. His one-act play *The Bomb Bumbled Or I Feel Most Sorry Today* was produced at New York's off-off-Broadway Dramarena Theatre. He lives in Morehead, Kentucky.

Edward Power lives and writes near Waterford City in southern Ireland. He has written a novella, *The Sepia Zone*, which has a gay, Anglo-Irish setting, and is working on a second. His fiction has appeared in *Queer View Mirror 2* and elsewhere.

CONTRIBUTORS

Gary Probe's work has appeared in *Queer View Mirror 2, Acta Victoriana, The Church-Wellesley Review, A Queer Sense of Humour,* on CBC Radio and in a variety of fine newspapers and magazines. He lives in the east end of Vancouver with his partner Larry, cat Claude, and dog Angus.

Andy Quan is an Asian-Canadian, singing, songwriting queer currently living in London and working in HIV prevention. His poetry and short fiction has been published in anthologies and literary magazines in Canada, the U.S., and the U.K. He is currently hunting for publishers for his short fiction and poetry manuscripts.

Jeff Richardson is a Toronto writer, writing teacher, and creativity consultant. He has recently produced a creative writing course on audio-tape, entitled *Your Imaginative Mind: A Writers' Workshop.* He lives with Robin, his beloved partner of sixteen years, and their three feline Nemeses: Teaser, Jenny, and Nanki-poo.

Thomas S. Roche's short stories have appeared in numerous erotic magazines. He is currently at work on a collection of short stories and a novel. He lives in San Francisco.

Charles L. Ross is art director and senior editor of *Veranda* magazine. He was art director of *Architectural Digest* from 1979 to 1985. His writing has appeared in *Christopher Street, The Advocate,* and *GQ*; his novel, *Inside,* about life at an interior design magazine, will be published by Alyson Publications in 1998.

Sandip Roy grew up in India. He writes software by day and edits *Trikone Magazine* by night. In between all that he has had his work published in *Men on Men 6, Queer View Mirror, Contours of the Heart, My First Time,* and other anthologies and magazines.

Joey Sayer has written for several magazines, including *QC Magazine, Clue!, AGLP, Modern Pink, Perceptions,* and *The Leader.* His monthly column, "Thank You and Good Afternoon," ran in some of these titles for over five years. He is currently working on a number of prose and comic book projects.

Lawrence Schimel is the author or editor of more than twenty-five books, including *The Drag Queen of Elfland, The Mammoth Book of Gay Erotica, Two Hearts Desire* (with Michael Lassell), *Switch Hitters* (with Carol Queen), *Things Invisible to See, Food for Life,* and others. He lives in New York City.

Simon Sheppard is an unrepentant smutwriter whose work has appeared in magazines such as *Drummer* and *Powerplay,* and in numerous anthologies, including *Best American Erotica 1997, Best Gay Erotica 1997, Strategic Sex, Noirotica 2: Pulp Friction,* and *Eros Ex Machina.* He has size 12 feet. "Sneakers" was previously published online in *Fishnet* (www.fishnetmag.com).

CONTRIBUTORS

Seth Clark Silberman is the editor of *Generation Q* (1996), a Lambda Awards finalist. He is finishing a Ph.D. at the University of Maryland where he teaches African Diasporan and gay literature and film. He also teaches literature, psychoanalysis, and film at the Maryland College of Art and Design.

M.V. Smith sprang from the small city of Cornwall, Ontario, and grew up to publish a short story in the anthology *Stag Line*, stories by Canadian men. He's not very interesting, and simple to a fault.

Sam Sommer lives in New York City. He is an actor, writer, and director. His writing most recently appeared in *Queer View Mirror 2*, an anthology of short, short gay and lesbian fiction. This past August, *'Til Death Us Do Part*, three one-act plays, previewed off-off Broadway at the 42nd Street Collective Theatre.

horehound stillpoint's work can be found in *beyond definition, Queer View Mirror 2, Butch Boys,* and *Sex Spoken Here*. Chapbooks include *Dovetail, The Inside Dirt,* and *Some Holy Googolplex*.

Jonathan Strong teaches at Tufts University and is the author of eight books, most recently *The Old World, Offspring,* and *An Untold Tale*, all published by Zoland Books. His novel *Secret Words* won a grant from the National Endowment for the Arts. He lives in Somerville, Massachusetts.

Matt Bernstein Sycamore first came out in the public bathrooms of Washington, D.C. His writing has appeared in *Flesh and the Word 4, Queer View Mirror 1* and *2*, and other publications. He is currently working on an anthology of writing by male sex workers, and a short story collection.

Jim Tushinski's short fiction has appeared in the anthology *The Gay Nineties: Contemporary Gay Male Fiction* and in *The James White Review, Pen and Sword, Prism International,* and the *San Francisco Sentinel*. He is currently finishing a novel.

Paul Veitch's articles and stories have appeared in a wide range of Australian publications. Apolitical, queer, a novelist, and obsessive reader, he lives and works in a small city in Victoria, Australia. In his spare time, he sleeps.

Bob Vickery's stories over the years have appeared in numerous gay erotic magazines, and he is currently a regular contributor to *Advocate Men*. He has two anthologies of stories out: *Skin Deep* (Masquerade Publications) and *Cock Tales* (Leyland Publications), and has stories in other anthologies, including *The Best American Erotica, 1997* and *Queer Dharma*. In his off time, he bakes muffins for a Zen Buddhist monastery in northern California.

Barry Webster is a Toronto-based writer, musician, and teacher. He has published both fiction and non-fiction in various magazines and newspapers including *Event, Dandelion, The Toronto Star,* and *The Washington Post.* He was recently awarded a Toronto Arts Council grant to complete a collection of short stories.

John Whiteside lives in Washington, D.C. By day he's a marketing manager in the Virginia suburbs; by night, he writes, among other things. His work has appeared in *Bay Windows, Queer View Mirror 2,* and the *Encyclopedia of AIDS.*

Michael Wynne was born in the west of Ireland in 1971. In 1997 he won a prize in the inaugural Irish Queer Writers' Award. His work regularly appears in Ireland's *Gay Community News,* and he has contributed to the anthologies *Quare Fellas* and *Queer View Mirror 2.*

Paul Yee is a writer who lives in Toronto. He was previously published in *Queer View Mirror.*

Wayne Yung is a writer and video artist whose work has often dealt with issues of race, culture, and identity. Born in Edmonton in the Year of the Pig, he is now based in Vancouver.

ABOUT THE EDITOR

James C. Johnstone's writing has been published in the Lambda Literary Award-winning anthology *Sister & Brother: Lesbians & Gay Men Write About Their Lives Together* (Joan Nestle & John Preston, eds.), *Flashpoints: Gay Male Sexual Writing* (Michael Bronski, ed.), *Prairie Fire, Icon Magazine,* and *The Buzz.*

He is co-editor, with Karen X. Tulchinsky, of *Queer View Mirror: Lesbian and Gay Short Short Fiction,* and *Queer View Mirror 2.*

A Japanese-language interpreter, translator, and tour guide by trade, James enjoys spending any free time he can get out in his garden with his daughter smelling the roses.